"From the first page, Bryan Burnell launches you into a thrilling adventure that will electrify your imagination. *Saving Yukon* is an intense, magical journey involving the search for self and acceptance. A spectacular debut!"

——Dennis K. Crosby, award-winning author of *Death's Legacy*

"Compelling and provocative. Carlos Castaneda meets John Muir. A VERY satisfying read!"

——J.A. Maloney, author of *Breakfast Ball: A Brad Stephens Novel*

"The Alaskan wilderness, a young man's cryptic sixth sense, and a dangerous journey of self-discovery, *Saving Yukon* is the thrilling, page-turning debut novel from Bryan Burnell that will leave you spellbound."

——Tony Angellotti, film and television publicist, The Angellotti Company

SAVING YUKON

BRYAN BURNELL

Helping talented writers publish exceptional books

This is a work of fiction. Most characters, organizations, and events portrayed in this novel are either products of the author's imagination or are used fictitiously, and any resemblance to actual persons, living or dead, businesses, companies, events, or locales is entirely coincidental.

*To the Lost
and
to those with exceptional fortitude
and to that which guides them*

CONTENTS

ONE
A CESSATION OF EXISTENCE
THE ATTACK, PART I, 1984

There was zero chance of survival for the four of us. Although I did not know the two criminals, for a split second I felt a sense of remorse for them. My thoughts were on the survival of my friend, Gabriella, since she certainly did not deserve this treatment. But then again, no one did. My wish to die first was not granted. I watched in horror as the first man shrieked the moment before his head was ripped off his shoulders. Without blinking, I watched the dead man's head fly along, bounce once, and careen down the steep hill like a runaway ball. I remained mesmerized as the second, younger man began to crawl away with the knife still in his leg. He too was mowed down in a flash of dismembered arms and legs flying through the forest air.

I began to dry heave, gasping for air as the head of the second man landed near me with a thud. His shocked eyes remained wide open, staring directly at me.

The furious beast turned on my friend and swatted her through the air with a half swing. Gabriella flew over the edge of the hill, and I screamed, "*No!*" The terrifying beast stopped, ignored his task, gave me an evil eye, and then rumbled toward me. The rope around my neck that kept me bound to the tree tightened as I struggled to free myself. My arms were useless, tied behind my back. There was no escaping this attack.

The sinking-gut sensation came quickly. I had not felt that amount of dread since the sudden loss of my five-year-old daughter, Rose, years ago. As I was seated on the ground, I crossed my legs, closed my eyes, and prepared for death. Everything switched to slow motion, and untimely thoughts of Gabriella sifted through my mind. I hoped she could survive. I've heard that preparing for a sudden death is eerily calming in some bizarre way since the body's central nervous system locks down in shock. The ground shook beneath the pounding of the beast's massive paws for what seemed like an eternity. His ferocious growl was deafening. I took a deep breath, and darkness enveloped me. Death was my only cure.

Dying is easy; it's living that is difficult.

TWO
THE EARLY YEARS
1960S & '70S

At an earlier age, I did things that the masses could not. I wasn't weird or strange or dangerous in any way, just different, and all my friends still liked me. None of them realized the full potential of my peculiarity. I, of course, never let on. One time, at Sierra Ranch Beach in San Diego, I predicted some sort of disaster at the spot on the sand where all six of us had our towels. Without alarming anyone, I convinced everyone to move their towels closer to the lifeguard stand since it was next to the water. One minute later a cement truck came crashing through the beach fence landing directly on top of our previous spot. In simple terms I could often predict, with scary accuracy, the results of events yet to come. I could solve a puzzle or a mystery rather easily. Whodunnit novels were boring because I always got the ending long before it came. Call it ESP, or telepathy, or even clairvoyance. Call it what you wish. I had it. Others didn't.

My parents taught me poker at age ten, and I could pick out a bluff most of the time. I say "most of the time" because I was about 80 percent accurate. Later, experts informed me that this was a staggering percentage of success. I applied my gift to almost all my daily activities, and it just became a game. I could come up with a close estimate of the final score at my high school football games at Sierra Blanca. *And* who would do the scoring. I played on the soccer team.

For the most part, I could predict the questions asked on our final exams. At about age thirteen, I decided to keep this artistry to myself because I was apprehensive of negative comments from adults and maybe from my friends. Folks might begin to suspect something strange about me. I enjoyed the game by myself. But from time to time, I played poker with all my friends, and I always won. Eventually, this group started to suspect me of cheating, so I drifted away from that game. I received warm praise from my parents. Being Italian, they assured me of their Code of Silence on the subject. My mom called it intense intuition, or something akin to that. I called it *cool hipness*.

At about this time, I became aware of a gnawing feeling that I got concerning my skills. It was as if some kind of higher forces were guiding my powers. My intuition suggested that perhaps it came from above, somewhere high in the sky or universe, especially while I was in nature or at least outdoors. Frequently, I would venture into the natural preserve behind our house and walk until I found a boulder to sit on and to contemplate while gazing at the sky, searching for what made my skills and senses click. I always came up empty trying to solve the puzzle, but I stayed vigilant for the discovery of this guiding force, the one that seemed to fertilize my clairvoyance and intuition.

As a teenager, I used this skill to help me predict which

girl would actually have me. And of course, I chose Judy, whose nickname became Sweet Judy Blue Eyes, or for me, just Sweet. In those eye-opening days, we all ran with nicknames. If someone didn't have one, they were considered out of it. Since I was mostly Italian, my label affectionately became Da Dago, or just Dago for short. Sometimes Stinking Dago. Adults considered this derogatory, which it was, but among all my misfit friends, it was a badge of honor. I gloriously embraced it—Matteo Dago Ferrari. How could I go wrong with that? It made my buddies laugh and the girls giggle. My friends and I formed our own special club called the Gargoyle Squad, made up of girls and boys. There were many incredible nicknames, such as Edgy, Booby, Dirt Mouth, Jaime, Itch, CarCar, Foamfoot, Pussycat, Header, Beanhole, Lob, and many more.

No one ran by their normal names in those days. Our own world. A sign of our rapidly changing time in an Age of Vietnam, sexual awareness, herpes, and the rightful revolution of women and minorities. Everyone was trying, with confusion, to find their unassigned places in life. The Gargoyle Squad led our little revolution, and thus, an evolution.

All the guys galloped around holding their dicks trying to find a warm, juicy place to put them. The girls tried as well but were less obvious. We had fun chasing booze, blow, and each other, in no particular order.

Sweet Judy and I dated for many years. Even though we were young, we adored each other. I did inform her of my peculiar skills, and she accepted my words with love and respect. She could not wait to watch me in action. At the time, we did not realize how similar we were. We loved the same food, the same drinks, the same music, and the same outdoor activities. We spoke our own crazy dialect that the others could not understand. We were sexually congruous with a few off-the-wall habits, such as eating pizza while making love. Now that's a little greasy and odd, but it's harmless.

Judy was a beautifully shaped athletic woman. At five foot eight inches, she fit perfectly under my arm as we strolled along. Judy was one of the few women who played beach volleyball with me and the boys. With long flowing sandy blonde hair and large blue eyes, which often morphed into other colors upon emotional request, she seemed like a goddess of the sand. Her sense of humor matched her beauty.

In the mid-to-late '60s, we often ventured up the coast to the lovely seaside city of Santa Barbara where we attended concerts at the Earl Warren Showgrounds and saw great bands, such as Janis Joplin with Big Brother and the Holding Company, Jimmy Hendrix, and Iron Butterfly singing the long version of *In-A-Gadda-Da-Vida*, and many other bands. We even saw The Doors perform at Santa Barbara City College. All these wonderful artists stopped here on their way to San Francisco.

We grew to love the city. Our favorite short trip to Santa Barbara included a two-day affordable stay at the West Beach Inn along Cabrillo Boulevard across from West Beach. We packed food and water at the hotel, took the bus to Montecito, and made our way to Miramar Beach. During low tide, we ventured out on a long sandy excursion north. We would travel all the beaches like Butterfly, East, West, Leadbetter, Shoreline, Hendry's, Hope Ranch, and others. Eventually we landed on Goleta Beach near U.C. Santa Barbara. After finding the nearest bus stop, we caught a ride back to West Beach and our hotel. Following a hasty clean up, we made our way to the breakwater at the harbor for a quick drink while hanging out. It was here that we both realized the full impact of Santa Barbara. It was one of the rare places in the world where saltwater meets a bustling city that rises into a picturesque riviera which then launches straight into magnificent mountains; all viewed from multiple locations along the beaches. And to top it off, the weather was almost perfect. One could wear shorts and a T-shirt for eleven months of the year! Our final stop was the iconic Joe's Café for a fabulous Cadillac Margarita and their world-famous Omaha open-faced Tri-tip sandwich.

The next day, we drove all along the forested Camino Cielo at the top of the Santa Barbara mountains and eventually found our way to Paradise Road via San Marcos Pass. After a few miles, we parked, hiked across the Santa Ynez River and ended up at the pools of Red Rock. From the highest rocks, we looked down on the serene, spiritual waters. Gathering our courage we each jumped, sans clothing, into the refreshing pools below. All stress evaporated with each successive plunge. A good day! Upon returning to San Diego, I described the whole area to my parents, encouraging them to move there.

Eventually we both attended college. Me at UC Berkeley, and Sweet at UCLA. We managed to stay together through thick and thin, and we both encountered other brief relationships, but in the end, we stayed together, and our genuine love grew.

After two years at UC Berkeley, I grew weary of ordinary college classes, mostly because of my skill. The predictions of daily life became too easy. I signed up for a lecturing class since I found speaking to a group to be entertaining, and it brought smiles to those who were listening. I learned to craft humor with intellect. It helped me with day-to-day life and made my clairvoyance and intuition flourish.

I read various books on meandering topics, such as color aesthetics, basket weaving, and the art of kiln construction. Everything else in classes made me yawn. My saving grace was playing soccer at a high level on the collegiate team at UC Berkeley. It was on this illustrious team that I met my first minority, a handsome jet-black man from Uganda named Mukasa. He and I played mid-field halfback positions which required playing defensive as well as aggressive offensive support for our front forwards. We became quite a pair, and our teammates affectionately labeled us Ebony and Ivory. We continued to win through the season, as I often predicted we would.

Before the games, I sat cross-legged on the floor with my hands comfortably in my lap, eyes closed. My mind focused on the subject that required my prediction. I discovered if I held some sort of object associated with my intended subject matter, then my percentage of success rose. I used it so frequently that my cohorts on the soccer team at Berkeley thought I was really into meditation or yoga or something similar. I accurately predicted that our team would go all the way to the championship, and that Ebony would lead us to victory by scoring two goals! I scored one as well which I had failed to predict.

Other than soccer, I was immensely bored. Then one night, as I lay in my dorm room, I experienced the loneliest sound in the entire world. Through the thin walls, I listened to other people making love. That did it. I missed the effervescent Judy even more. It became time to head home. I said farewell to Ebony, and we agreed to stay in touch whatever course our lives took. He headed back to

Uganda. I came home at the age of twenty and was unsure of my next step in life, except that Sweet and I were together. She came home after her third year. I guess we were college flunkies, but higher education isn't for everyone. We decided to leave San Diego, and soon we moved into a small, quaint apartment in Santa Barbara. Sweet Judy got a job as an assistant manager at the Chart House. Her incredible customer service skills matched her beauty and resulted in her elevation to manager within a few short months.

Judy managed all aspects of the restaurant and the bar. She had over twenty-five employees to guide, and she meshed with their personalities with relative ease. I would have failed miserably managing such a large group. Judy had desire, strength, and courage like no one else I had ever met. Nothing was too much for her to handle. Atta girl, Sweet!

I experimented with various careers, and nature continued to be a motivating force for me, resulting in my drifting back to the forest and gardens.

Judy and I married in a small ceremony with just a few folks, and shortly after, Judy got pregnant. What a great time for us!

When Rose was born nine months later, we realized the insignificance of our own selfish lives, and Rose became the rightful focus. My parents gave Judy and me many breaks by babysitting so that we could continue our dedication to each other. Judy's parents lived in Oregon, so they flew down from time to time to help. I also managed to sneak in an occasional poker game with other friends aside from the Gargoyle group which Judy wholeheartedly encouraged.

Between the ages of two and four, Judy and I noticed

how Rose was extremely advanced in some ways. The biggest amazement became her love of words and books and her scribbling of many different shapes, most of which were uninterpretable. She learned to understand parts of a book, like the cover title, and she muttered parts of the story accurately. She even developed a vocabulary and would try to read some of my books. One day, I found her sitting in front of my bookcase playing with some rather complicated books that I was forced to read in college, such as *Crime and Punishment* by Fyodor Dostoevsky, and *Moby Dick* by Herman Melville.

She made me read some of each, and she remained focused. I would hand age-appropriate books to her, and while she enjoyed the pictures, she spent little time on them and was more in tune with all the letters and words in my books. It was amazing, and we gladly accepted her advancement.

I would take Rose into the forest where we would sit on my favorite boulder. I would do some spiritual work while Rose would sit and scribble with a pencil and her notebook. I quietly observed her listening and watching certain things moving in the woods, such as a black bird. She would repeat something that resembled "black bird" and then scribble a black object in her notebook. She also wrote some letters, without any formal training from Judy or me. She was writing using just her ears and eyes. It didn't take long for her to master the alphabet. She was way ahead of all her friends. Her virtue left me with the desire to be graceful and excellent on my path forward, knowing that I wished only to help her and Judy in any way. Rose directly led my life to take shape. I wondered if she possessed some of my skills, and I grew excited to revisit that subject with her when she grew a bit older.

At the time, I did not understand how precious this love for Rose was. Judy and I loved each other with full dedication, but little did we know that this love and affection for our daughter was far different, yet undiscernible to some. It was this love that made us all vulnerable. While our love for a helpless, innocent child gave us empowering courage, it also left us exposed. This vulnerability would become brutally apparent in the future.

My Uncle Tony, who also lived in Santa Babara, called me, and my life changed. Everything began to take a sharp turn along a new path, and while exciting, some of this trail was treacherous.

THREE
UNCLE TONY

Walking into my uncle's house, I was greeted, "Matteo, how the heck are you, my incredible nephew?"

"Hi, Uncle Tony, long time. I'm pretty good. Got married and all that, you know?"

My uncle was a strapping Italian man with a thick Burt Reynold's mustache, broad shoulders, and a husky voice. He stayed in excellent shape by playing lots of badminton, ping pong, and Bocci Ball. He was kind of odd, but in many ways just like all of us.

"You didn't invite me to the wedding," Tony said with a smirk on his furry face.

"Sorry, Uncle, we invited hardly anyone. We just felt it better to get it done and get moving in life. And as you are aware, we have that bouncing baby girl, Rose. She always wants to see you, Uncle." I felt bad that we had not invited my uncle, but he would get over it.

Without warning, I had that sinking feeling. This happened when I began to realize something was coming, and I would quickly try to predict. Like that time in high school when Lisa Merritt told me she was going on a very short trip to Mammoth on her aunt's beautiful new six-seater plane. My gut sank, and I told her she shouldn't go. I had that inexorable feeling. I never saw Lisa again. The next afternoon Lisa and everyone aboard the plane crashed in the Alabama Hills above Lone Pine.

I had been right again.

"So, I understand from my brother that you are jumping around from job to job. That true?"

I wondered what Tony was up to. "Well, a little bit, I suppose. What's up?" I asked, staring at him.

"I have a proposition for you that would use your special ability."

I jumped up. "Tony, how did you know about my skill? Did my parents tell you?"

"Well, yes." Tony grinned. "But it just came out as we were chatting about my job. You know what I do. You have always asked me about it."

My uncle was right. I had always inquired about his assignments. They were somewhat intriguing. Like the time he and his associates had to help solve the horrific scene of severed hands being delivered to retirement homes, or the one about disappearing young men who would randomly show up, naked in a daze after being missing for exactly thirty days. While interesting and far more compelling than the normal nine-to-five job, I still found it somewhat unnerving.

"Look, Uncle, I have no desire to be a detective in your Special Cases Division. That's not for the faint of heart, and you know me. I'm anti-Vietnam War, a hippie from UC Berkeley, and my hair used to flow down my back. Judy and I aren't aggressive folks, Uncle."

"Matteo, just hear me out."

"Okay, let me have it." I slumped into his recliner chair.

"We deal with many cases each year. Some we solve quickly, others not. But we keep trying, and we don't close a case for years unless it's solved. And you know you find it interesting."

"I don't want to be a cop."

"Trust me, we don't want you to be a cop."

"Well, then what?"

As Tony wandered around the room, he lit a Pall Mall and then blew out a smoke ring. "We just want you — I mean, your talent. Whatever you want to call it, pal." My uncle squinted and stared at me.

"Not sure how my *skill* equates to being a detective in your department." I reached out to the pack he presented to me and pulled out a cigarette.

"You won't and can't be a detective. I want to subcontract you so you can help me solve these horrific crimes. Your gift, your ability. Lately, we don't have a good success rate, and Captain James Burns is breathing down my neck."

"How do I get involved if I'm not a detective? Do I receive compensation? What the hell are you saying?"

"Just relax. Me and my partner Harold got it figured out. We bring you in when we are struggling with a crime, and let you do your deal. We would pay you as a consultant and the pay would be great. Trust me."

"What if the crime is not solved?"

"You get paid anyway. What do you have to lose? It's a no-brainer. Try it for a while, Matteo. You'll enjoy it, I know, and it will keep you out of trouble," Uncle said with a grin.

"I don't get in trouble." I snuffed out the cigarette and

said I would think about it, then I walked out. As I strolled, I realized something extraordinary: I don't even smoke!

Although Sweet and I spoke at length regarding Uncle Tony's proposal, we decided that it did not fit our profile in life. I informed Tony of the news, to which he replied, "Okay, fine, Matteo. Just keep it in mind and think about the service you would be doing to help the good folks in society."

"Thanks, Uncle. Will do!"

It was at this time that I made the graceless, kneejerk decision to apply my skills to making money, applying them to a card game I had perfected years ago: Texas hold 'em.

FOUR
CALL OF THE CARDS

Sweet was not in favor of my gambling scheme, but eventually she encouraged me to follow my dreams. Rose playfully helped me pack my bags, adding some of her stuffed animals to keep me company. Judy thought I should not dress too sharply as this might attract attention to me as "one of those players." So, she laid out jeans and T-shirts and one collared shirt.

I laughed, "You two are little help! I'm not going to dress like a bum and show up with a stuffed animal at the poker table."

Judy and I hugged and kissed, and Rose climbed all over me, babbling something incoherent to me but sensible to her. They wished me well.

On my first venture to Las Vegas, I inaugurated my career with several kinds of gambling. I launched into good cash but became apathetic toward all the games except for Texas hold'em. This one piqued my senses because I could dissect and categorize each player and could count cards with ease. I always remained calm and unreadable while my special powers worked relentlessly, allowing my brain to absorb all the moves and innuendos of my opponents. Before long, my success rate grew to epic proportions. My haul of easy money began to flow, and even Sweet was amazed because she had never witnessed my powers in full gear.

Both of us wished the same thing. To provide a safe haven for Rose and two more future kids. Our lives had changed, and it made me wish to do the right thing: Provide.

Sweet and I were able to put a downpayment on a small house in the hills of Santa Barbara. My parents had already moved there when I went to Berkeley. Our existence seemed mindlessly fluid. Then things began to tangle.

On my third trip to Vegas, I kissed Sweet Judy goodbye and headed off on another money-making trip. While on the Pear Blossom Highway, my mind wandered and conjured eerie thoughts in a frightening way. I skidded off to the side of the freeway, parked, and tried to predict what this all meant. Closing my eyes and embracing the moment resulted in no clear solution. I sensed some sort of guidance enveloping me, but shortly I ignored the emotion. After my mind and body calmed, I continued down the lonely road.

What had happened? Should I turn back or just continue on this journey? Something was telling me something, but no solution came, so onward I went.

Once in Vegas, I went to the poker tables and got involved. In a few short hours, I amassed close to $7,000. Not a bad day's work! The next day was even more fruitful with a haul of approximately $11,000. I usually called this off after two good days but decided to embrace a third day of fun and sport and money grabbing. The day went as predicted with a gathering of $4,500. It was late, so I wandered out into the pleasant Vegas evening for a casual walk, and then all hell broke loose.

FIVE
SIN CITY BLUES

thin, black cloth bag slipped over my head, and something struck my face and stomach. I stumbled onto my knees gasping for air and was dragged into a vehicle.

"Don't say a word," a deep voice uttered in my ear.

After a few moments of gathering my breath, a sense of fear shot through my aching body as the unknown had invaded my soul. I decided to say something, but wisely concluded that speaking would break their rules. Soon I was in a well-lit room tied to a chair, and the hood was removed. While blinking to adjust my sight, I noticed that the room was surprisingly nice, like that of an influential CEO or manager. Three men stared at me; two were big and the other, a much smaller man who sat at an ornate desk. My heart sank with fear and confusion. I almost wet my pants as my nose dripped blood. The man behind the desk continued to examine my California driver's license with a wad of money sitting directly in front of him. I assumed the stack of money was related to my winnings.

The man spoke with a subtle Italian accent. "Hey, Eddie, this is an Italian boy, Matteo Ferrari. Maybe he is related to the Ferrari car company. Or possibly another family is trying to edge into our world."

"Well, we will need to find out. Lots of good clients are complaining about you and your tactics. Tell me how you are doing this, Matteo. It would be in your best interest to be factual and honest, okay?"

When I was younger, my dad always taught me to reply with "sir" when in a tough predicament, as this appeared to be.

"Yes, sir."

"What method of cheating are you using to justify your constant winning? Counting cards, stealing cards? Working with a group of players?"

"No, sir. I have no method other than my senses." That did not sound convincing — even to me.

All of them laughed and Freddy said, "Looks like we have a comedian, fellas! Maybe he can fill in for Steve Martin when he can't make it to work!"

They all chuckled, and then suddenly stopped and stared at me.

"Look Matteo, ah, this is your real name?" Freddy asked.

"Yes, sir."

"My boss wants us to get info from you one way or the other, and then get *rid* of you. Eddie here thinks it would be best to rip off your fingernails one at a time, break your kneecaps, strangle you a few times with his bare hands, stuff you in a barrel and dump you in Lake Mead. That sound okay to you?"

"No, sir," I muttered slumping even further into the chair.

"Okay, good. We are on the same page. Then let's start over, and don't use some bullshit about your senses, alrighty?"

I paused and then said, "My arms really hurt, and I'm about to pee all over your office. May I use your bathroom, and then I can tell you my story?"

"No, tell us now."

My dad also taught me to speak the absolute truth in these bad situations. Folks will identify with this, and maybe the fire can be squelched. It took a while, but I managed to detail my early years with precision, and when I finished up, they were yawning.

Freddy chuckled and said, "Your buddies actually called you a Dago? That was your nickname?"

"Yes, sir."

"And you were fine with that?"

"Yes, sir."

They all laughed.

"I would have shot them in the forehead," Freddy said with a smirk. He cleared his throat, lit a cigar, and then continued. "Wait till the boss hears about this. He's not going to believe it. He will say to dump you in Mead."

Fearfully, I said, "I'm being completely serious. I do possess a troubling ability to read situations and people, and to predict many future events. I can read the emotions and personalities of those I choose. It's best if I hold some personal item of the person I'm analyzing. Works better that way."

Freddy laughed and blurted out, "So maybe you hold my dick, and then you can read me!"

"Uhmm, not required in your case, Freddy. I see you as a practical man who analyzes the situation well," I lied. "And who makes the correct and decent approach most of the time." I was using my limited college lecturing education to the best of my ability.

Eddie laughed.

Freddy stared at Eddie. "What's so fucking funny, Eddie?"

"Oh, just the part about being decent!" Eddie wiped the tears from his eyes and returned to his serious face.

It seemed odd to me that the third man had yet to speak.

Freddy continued, "Look, you little Dago, this is so farfetched that we will chat and then decide what to do. But you can plan on swimming with the trout and the bass in Mead."

Granting my wish to pee, they led me to the bathroom, chained me to the toilet, and locked me in. I slid down onto the floor and pondered. Closing my eyes, I tried to predict my immediate future, and at first, I felt only dread. Shortly, a wave of clear white and bright light washed over me while my body relaxed. *They will not kill me.*

The door opened violently, and they threw me back into my seat facing not Freddy, but the third man, who had yet to utter a sound. He was large, about six foot five, and an imposing 250lbs.

At last, he spoke, in a stronger Italian accent. "My name is Bruno, and I am da boss. And by da way, Freddy is not decent unless I tell him to be. Your story is so preposterous that I almost believe it. You will have a few choices, but not really. Tink about it for a few seconds before you decide. The wrong answer, and you will have to learn ta swim with cement shoes, capisce?"

"Yes, sir." I prepared to analyze Bruno's various options.

"One, you say nothin' more and die slowly. Two, you

hand me more wild stories and die even slower. Three, you become Freddy and Eddie's bitch and die a miserable demeaning death. Four, since you are Italian and not with another family, you come ta work for me and use your alleged skill and weed out all da fucking cheats and card sharks in our respectable establishment. Five, we let you go, and you go home unharmed."

Thinking briefly, I said "Um, I'll take fiv—Wait, ah, four. I'll take four!"

"You don't like da udda numbers, Matteo?"

They all laughed.

"No, sir, but I did consider five, but that seemed too obvious."

They conferred for a brief, few moments, and Bruno said, "Okay, you will stay in our joint in a room that will lock from da outside, and in da morning you will start. If you can't do what you have promised, den we will be forced to chop you into little pieces, got it?"

"Yes, sir, and one question, if I may?"

Bruno sighed and waved his hand in approval.

"I will need to call my wife and tell her something, yes? Otherwise, she may put out a missing persons alert."

"You may call Judy."

"How did you know her name?" I asked.

"Ya told us in your long-winded bullshit story, idiot."

"Oh, correct. Sorry, sir."

"Tell Judy ya had a wonderful job offer from dis great casino, one ya could not refuse, and it requires your attendance right away, and it will last two ta four weeks."

"I'll try, but she may find this questionable."

"Not our problem, Matteo."

"Also, Bruno, I assume that I can't keep my winnings?"

"No, but if you perform as advertised, den I will double it. Now beat it."

The boys led me on a long walk through the winding hallways in the casino hotel. Why did these places always have gaudy, horribly ugly carpet that made your head spin? Upon arriving, Eddie said they would bring me food, and a "nice lady" for my enjoyment.

"You mean a prostitute?"

"Of course, what else?"

"I'll just take the food, but I'd like to substitute the lady for a big glass of bourbon."

Eddie chuckled. "We can bring you a nice boy, if you prefer!" He slapped me on the back.

I sighed and groaned. "Thanks, but no."

"What kind of bourbon do you prefer?" Freddy asked.

"Maker's Mark Reserve, if you can."

As the door bolted behind me, I leaned against it and rubbed my forehead to ease the pain and stress from a brush with death. What had I done? What a pickle!

Sweet would be skeptical of my assigned explanation, but what choice did I have? I held my head and tried to predict some sort of game plan, but I found myself drifting back in time to how my intuitive sense would always seem to guide me properly. Like the time I worked as a cleanup man at the local favorite bar and restaurant called 1129.

My shift started at 6:30 a.m. and on this day, I believe it was a Sunday, I moved all the bar stools aside and began to sweep. I always found odd things like packs of rubbers, cheap earrings, and a variety of drugs, all of which I chucked into the trash. But on this day, I found a tightly rolled bunch of dollars. Peeling off the rubber band, I discovered thirty-one $100 bills! All crisp, with a grand total of $3,100. I smiled since this was far more than I would make in months of part-time work at minimum wage. I hastily wound up the cash and stuffed it in my pocket. Marvelous for one day of work.

At about 10:00 a.m., I had just finished scrubbing the bar surface when a disheveled man walked in.

"Sorry, sir, the bar isn't open. Will be in an hour," I explained.

"I know this is crazy and wishful thinking," he moaned. "But I was in here late last night, and I lost a rolled-up wad of money."

I sighed. "How much was it?"

"About $3,000."

I chuckled, hesitated, and then retrieved the roll from my pocket, returning it to him. He was in shock and thanked me profusely.

Another time, while attempting to work out at the local gym with the best intentions of developing my curls for the girls, I came upon a large diamond ring lying on the weight-room floor at my club. Looking around, I saw no women that it could belong to, so I stuffed it in my pocket. I contemplated turning it over to the front desk but reconsidered because most likely one of the front desk clerks would, conveniently for her, abscond with it. After having it appraised for the shocking amount of ten to twelve thousand dollars, I posted on the club member board that I had found a piece of jewelry and left my phone number. In a couple days a frantic woman called and described the ring in exact detail. I returned it to her.

As I sat gloomily in the Vegas room, I thought back to my parents' instruction that I always do the right thing. Why had I not? I even had a clear sign in the desert warning me of impending negativity. Obviously, I had failed to take heed. I lay on the bed and gathered the courage to call Sweet.

"Hi, Judy, how goes it? I have some good news for you!"

"Fine, but you were supposed to be home yesterday," she nervously complained.

"Judy, I've had a wonderful job opportunity here at the casino in the poker department. It requires my immediate attendance for approximately three to four weeks."

"What? What sort of job?"

"I'll know more tomorrow when they lay out all the details in earnest. Something to do with management. As the boss said, it's something that I can't refuse."

"How long do you need to be gone? Do I need to move? You know I detest Vegas."

Following some rigorous banter, Judy acquiesced and sullenly agreed that if the pay was extraordinary, then it would help us to achieve some lofty goals, and she would wait and shoot out to visit me from time to time.

"Thanks, Sweet. We won't regret this opportunity," I said without realizing the end game.

All tranquil for the time being.

Over the next few weeks, I diligently examined potentially risky card sharks from the time they entered the casino to their exit. I asked the waitresses and pit bosses to provide me items my suspects had handled, such as glassware, cigarette butts, and other items. Focusing physically and mentally on these objects proved wearying to me, and I asked my boss if I could take these items out into nature instead of staying in the illusion called Vegas. I was escorted, of course, to a pleasant desert location among the cactus and even among a few large trees. There my mind fired up, and I did get results that I favorably reported to the boss. He quickly took charge of it, and within a few short days, Bruno happily informed me of an 87 percent success rate.

"So, Bruno, what do you do with the guilty parties?"

Taking the cigar out of his mouth, Bruno stared at me, and then chuckled, "You ask too many questions, Matteo. All I can say is ya did a great job!" He slapped me on the back as he walked away.

My heart sank with the realization that some of the suspects I fingered may have suffered dire consequences. What a mess, but my survival took precedent. Examining the true underground misery of Vegas made me realize what a snake pit of degradation it was.

Ironically, Vegas bloomed around 1905 as the result of a wonderful act of nature, a life-sustaining bubbling of water at an artesian spring about three miles west of Vegas. This spring had attracted an assortment of Native Americans for thousands of years long before railroads and pioneers and even European settlers arrived. And then, of course, gambling entrepreneurs created this quagmire, a world-class tourist destination. The beautiful lifeblood of nature, a natural spring, laid the foundation for creating the concrete and steel jungle that now lay beneath my feet. Folks come and go from this Sin City with hopes and dreams realized and shattered, so how did I decide it would be brilliant to make this my gathering ground for income? I wish it had never been discovered by modern man. I must use my skills in a better way for myself and for my surroundings. Maybe I'll learn something by coming here. Gathering my wits, I returned to my glorious job.

After two more weeks of this torture, which resulted in

numerous successful snags of illicit sharks, I slowly approached Bruno in his office.

"Morning, Bruno, how goes it?"

"Not bad, Dago, not bad. I gotta hand it ta ya, my friend. You are doing very well here. We have rounded up many idiots dat you have identified, and I believe the word is out dat we have a secret method of analyzing our players. So great job! What can I do for you?"

"It's been approximately four weeks, and since I've done well, I was wondering if I could wrap this up and head home?"

Bruno frowned and thought pensively. I remained quiet but zeroed in on his movements and emotional display. I felt reasonably safe for some odd reason.

"Matteo, I believe you have earned your freedom, but it bothers me dat I may lose you. May I offer you triple your original gambling earnings ta stay longer?"

It was quite shocking that this dangerous mobster would actually allow me to leave.

"Thanks, Bruno," I said, "that is very generous, but I really miss my wife and my other life. It's time for me to go, if you can permit that to happen."

"I'll make you a deal. Ya can go home, but in da future from time ta time, I may need your services, and I would need you ta swing back and help for a week or so. That work?"

This was one of those times where my answer could mean wellbeing or disaster for me, so I thought for a few seconds.

"That sounds acceptable. I would love to help you from time to time. And I would expect excellent pay, okay?" My armpits began to sweat.

Bruno grinned. "When did ya decide that it was a good

idea ta negotiate with me?" He laughed and continued, "That's fine, and of course, da pay will be great. Just one more thing. You may never, ever discuss what happened here with anyone, capisce? If ya do, and we find out, den you and all those informed will disappear from dis earth. That sound fair enough?"

Of course, I had no choice, so I calmly spoke, "Sure enough. Sounds very reasonable." I choked.

"Listen, Matteo, I've grown to like and respect ya, and you have been a great help ta me and my organization. Even Freddy sees your value! Also, I can tell your honesty prevails most of da time, so dat's good, pal. Gotta be honest, right?" He laughed.

"So, I will see ya when I need ya, and one more ting. I love your Italian name, Mr. Matteo Dago Ferrari, and dat has helped you immensely in your survival here! But I would have shot the fool who gave me that derogatory nickname, you know?"

He walked me all the way out, down the hall, and down the elevator and through the lobby, talking the whole time about food, and drinks, the casino, and other Italian lore, and finally about his family.

"A while ago, Matteo, I lost my two sons to a lengthy mob feud, and it devastated my wife and me. We still had a daughter, but we could never create a new son. Da other family suffered greatly as well. We eventually made peace with this warring family, and it has lasted through the years. Dat was in Sicily. Now my wife and daughter and I are here, tings have worked out, and we thrive. But I will always long for my two sons. It's so hard."

He really seemed genuine although I tried hard not to be swayed. He reached into his pocket and pulled out a huge stack of bills and peeled them off one at a time. It all added up to triple my original winnings, approximately sixty-six thousand dollars. I thanked him profusely and gave him a hesitant hug, and he squeezed me so hard I almost lost my breath. He slapped me on my back and wished me well.

As he walked away from me, he stopped, turned, and spoke. "Matteo, if you ever need my help, please reach out. Us good folks must stick together." And he laughed again.

I waved and hurried away shaking violently. That was a nice gesture, but under no circumstance would I call him for help! A wicked weight had been lifted off my shoulders.

SIX

APPLY THE EXTRASENSORY

Upon my return, Sweet and I caught up on all my escapades in Vegas. At the same time, I warned Judy of Bruno's Code of Silence.

"I'm relieved that you survived. Let's not do that again, okay," Sweet remarked.

"Never again. I learned my lesson. At least I came home with a nice wad of money. The alternative was not good."

"I still don't understand how you can be so successful pointing out the card sharks. Because of your skills?"

"I must have some instincts about human nature which compliments my intuition, or it's just plain good luck, right?"

"In your case, I don't think it has anything to do with luck."

"Uncle Tony wants me to help him solve cases. Maybe I should try that?"

"Why not? But how would you help him?" she asked.

"Not so sure, but I'll find out." It was a bit of a white lie as I knew perfectly well how I would help. "I'll probably be asked to do various, boring research." I was happy that I had informed Judy of my ability a while ago because she never questioned it and never thought I was strangely out of sorts.

Next morning, gathering my wits and a hot coffee, I headed over to Uncle Tony's office for my appointment with him. Sitting in his office while waiting for him to exit a meeting gave me time to reflect and delve into the complexities of the vanilla life I desired. Sometimes I wished that I did not own my clairvoyance. My life would be simple then! But that was not the case, so in my overanalyzing way, I resumed my embrace of it and maybe, I thought, Uncle Tony's job would be exhilarating.

SEVEN

EMPLOYMENT

Over the next three years, I dedicated myself passionately to assisting Uncle Tony with solving crimes, some of which had gone cold, and I embraced them as specialties for me. My uncle would reopen them, and I solved about 70 percent of them, bringing me satisfaction, self-worth, and the praise of my uncle and his superiors. The pay was excellent, and my daughter, Rose, approached her fifth birthday which added pleasure to my hard work.

One case assigned to me, which I solved, involved a spree of retirement home robberies and murder. All four incidents occurred at the same retirement home, which should have been easier to solve, but Uncle Tony and his crew struck out. The crimes were conducted in broad daylight with no clues. The facility had cameras installed at every possible location that monitored the situation to no avail. The home started to hemorrhage financially as worried clients began to yank out their elderly loved ones.

The mayor met with the police chief due to the

brutality of the crimes. All victims had been bludgeoned to death with a sharp blade or object. At this point, the attacks stopped since it appeared that the perpetrator was aware of the intense scrutiny. Months went by as the investigation of the entire staff proved fruitless as well. Finally, my uncle threw me on the case as he was forced to put his men on other horrific crimes.

Uncle Tony, even though he knew it was illegal to tamper with evidence, took me to the police room where they held all the evidence and set me free to do as I pleased. I gathered personal belongings of the four deceased victims, things such as clothing, strands of hair found in their beds, and cheap jewelry. All the expensive jewelry had been stolen. I put as much as I could stuff into my backpack. From there, I ventured to my favorite nature spot, the top of a large boulder just inside the forested area above the city.

Days of excruciating analysis with my eyes closed produced many results, but only a few kept repeating themselves. The color yellow, the familiarity between the victims and the killer, and the intense feeling that the crimes had been committed by someone inside the facility made me wonder. I narrowed it down to possibly a staff member, but I suspected the other elderly residents in the facility. This made my skin crawl, indicating that I was on the correct path.

Seventy-four old folks originally lived at the facility at the time of the deaths and robberies. Methodically, I investigated each and every one and inspected their rooms while they were at lunch. One day I entered a room, and it made my senses soar as I stared at a room decorated with different shades of yellow! I had my man, but upon further investigation of the room, I concluded that a man had not committed the murders, but an old woman named Betty Watson was my gal. I sat down at her yellow retro kitchen table where my mind flashed back to a time when I was seven. We had the exact same yellow kitchen table where we ate our meals daily. I remembered my mom serving homemade meatloaf with mashed potatoes and a salad smothered with Wishbone ranch dressing. The tabletop was that yellow cracked ice glossy laminate with a two-and-a-half-inch metal edge, and all of it was supported by those art deco tubular chrome legs. It made me smile to be sitting at this replica. I was seated at our yellow retro table when my dad gave me his many unsolicited thoughts on relationships with women. I was twelve at the time, and I always remember his telling me—

Son, women never look as good with their clothes off.

I slowly ate my peanut butter and jelly sandwich in confusion while thinking to myself: *Why would I want to see them naked?* I laughed because that was the silliest memory I ever had sitting at our kitchen table!

I looked around at Betty's trinkets and collectables scattered throughout the apartment and realized with apprehension that all these pieces did not fit together, almost as if they had been gathered from a high-end flea market and thrown together in this place. All these items had been stolen from the folks she had murdered, and I sat in the middle of them. I stood and carefully examined the rest of her small apartment. I came across an item that confused me at first because I did not know what it was, and then my eyes drifted to the box next to it. On the box it read, *Hatchet and Machete Sharping Tool.*

Feeling uneasy, I sighed and returned to the kitchen just as the front door slowly creaked open. In walked Miss Watson. She was not very big, probably five foot, four inches and a bit stout. She looked at me with dreadful anger in her sharp eyes, and then she morphed, like a chameleon into a calm state.

"Well, hello there, young man. I think I've seen you around these parts recently." We quietly observed each other. "Why are you in my private home?" she asked with concern.

"Oh, no big deal, Miss Watson. Management has me run fix-it errands throughout the facility, always at lunch. They said you may have a small leak in your kitchen sink, so I checked it out, and all is fine." I tried to smile convincingly but probably failed.

"Oh," she paused and looked at the sink. "I wasn't even aware of a leak. But thanks so much." Miss Watson stood quietly looking at me, and I could tell her sharp mind was processing a future move. "I'm going to make some hot tea and have a muffin. Please have a seat and join me. I'd love to chat with someone not as old as me. I'm almost eighty now!"

Against my better judgement, I slowly sat down and drummed my fingers on the kitchen table. As Miss Watson fussed in the kitchen preparing the tea and muffins, I thought back again to my earlier years, when my father taught me a valuable lesson that I've never forgotten.

"Let's go for a walk right after you eat this wonderful peach." And he handed me this perfectly shaped, beautiful peach that had just a touch of peach fuzz, making it even more delectable. I took a large, juicy bite, and immediately gagged and spit out the peach. It was all moldy, and rotten to the core. I ran to the sink and washed out my mouth.

"Guess the peach was rotten, huh?" He laughed. He led me out the door and down the sidewalk of our peaceful neighborhood. We came to a house down the way that had a gorgeous Siamese cat sitting in the driveway, and I asked if we could go pet it.

"Sure, go ahead," Dad said, releasing my hand. The cat came to me with a meow and rubbed against my leg. I reached down and began to pet the cat, and without the slightest warning the cat grabbed my hand with his claws and bit down hard. I shrieked and ran back to my dad.

"Apparently that cat was not friendly, huh?" he said with a smirk. Did he already know that? We continued to walk and came across a nice young woman who stopped to say hello to us, and as we walked away, my dad looked at me and said, "Nice young lady, yes?" and I nodded. "Actually, she is not a woman, but a man dressed in women's clothes."

I stopped, looked back. Then looked at my dad.

"Son, have you learned anything from the peach, the cat, and the man?"

"They are all rotten?"

"I wouldn't say that applies to all three, but they are more of an illusion of something else. Life is not always what it appears to be, son. Don't ever forget." And we quietly walked back to the house. My dad's intentional lesson stuck with me forever.

Shifting back to the present, as I carefully and suspiciously watched Miss Watson shuffle around the kitchen, I realized that I must leave with haste and come back with the police. "Miss Watson, I must go, so I'll pass on the tea and muffins. Thanks so much but duty calls."

Miss Watson turned around and walked toward me with a plate of muffins and when she was close, she threw the plate at me, surprising me, while exposing a dangerous hatchet in her hand, one with a sharp blade on one side and a spike on the other. She lunged toward my head swinging with surprising quickness and strength. I blocked the swing with my arm, and the hatchet buried in the laminate top of the kitchen table. I sustained a small cut but quickly overpowered her and held her face down on the floor. She continued to struggle and curse.

"Stop, Miss Watson. It's over." She quietly succumbed and began to whimper. She certainly was not what she appeared to be — a cute little old lady. This horrific person had lived decades as a serial murderer and thief, and I shuddered to think how many people had died at her ruthless hands. After tying her hands and legs, I stood and stared at the yellow kitchen table. Oddly, I was disappointed that this fabulous yellow retro table had been destroyed by the blow of Betty's ax. But soon I wised up. It could have been my head.

Case solved, and I turned everything over to a deliriously happy Uncle Tony, who took it from there.

After a few days off, my uncle handed me another case. Eight young girls and boys, ranging from ages seven to ten, had disappeared in the same general vicinity, and they were found about seven days later wandering the streets. Especially disturbing was that all the children were missing parts of their bodies, such as toes, fingers, and even ears. None had any memory of the events. All had been sewn up in a professional way. Obviously, the perpetrator had experience with the application of stitches. This was an extremely confusing case, and I was thrown onto it after four months of investigation by Uncle Tony and his crew.

Gathering the necessary articles impounded from the investigative division for evidence, I headed out to my boulder and searched my intuition for clues. Nothing presented itself in a repetitive way, so in frustration, I took a couple days off and started again with some other evidence. Orthopedic surgeons and podiatrists kept coming up, but Uncle Tony had already investigated all those with no positive results. Did the kids have anything in common? My focusing on all aspects resulted in one common trait. All were the offspring of established doctors, mostly orthopedic podiatrists. Nothing made sense to my analysis. But visions of failure drifted through my dizzy mind, things such as failed tests, bad grades on homework, and destroyed written exams.

Anger and resentment also presented themselves in various ways. I was on some track, and soon an angle presented itself. Uncle Tony and his staff were investigating licensed, practicing doctors. But I believe our suspect may have failed medical school and did not practice at all. Running background checks on everyone who had failed medical school for the past ten years presented a rather large list, but upon narrowing it down by zip code, only two popped up in the area of the victims. Bingo! I gave the two names of those suspects to Uncle Tony who looked at me with astonishment.

"How the hell did you do this? You are truly gifted." In short order, Uncle Tony arrested the prime suspect, a male, and the case was solved.

I wondered why this guy had cut off toes and fingers and ears, but I suspected it had something to do with his jealousy of those doctors who had graduated. Eventually, Uncle Tony did verify that the guilty man had failed medical school. During that time, he had been bullied by several fellow students. Those students, now doctors, had been the parents of the children who had been abducted and damaged by the guilty man. There were other questions I had as well, but I lost interest immediately following the arrest. On to the next one.

A variety of cases, some big, some small, came across my desk. I developed a deep dedication to my work since it helped me apply my aptitude toward something worthwhile and advantageous to society. My life was settled with work, with family, and with friends.

But then, my next case rocked the world around me and changed my life forever.

EIGHT
THE RAVEN

On Tuesday, three days after solving my last cold case, Uncle Tony called me at nine- thirty in the morning.

"Morning Uncle, I'm just wrapping up coffee with Judy. What you got for me?"

"Not entirely sure yet, but we have some missing kids. Even though this is not cold, I'd like you on this one. I don't like the smell of it, so all hands on deck. See you at the station in twenty." He hung up.

"Got to go, Judy, I'm on a fresh case this time! Did Rose get off to school okay?"

"Yep, I put her on the bus thirty minutes ago. Good luck and call me later."

I dressed and rushed out the door. As I was backing out of our driveway, Judy rushed out and screamed my name.

I slammed my brakes on. "What?"

"You forgot your lunch." She smiled and gave me a big wet kiss as my heart settled down.

"You scared the heck out of me!" I laughed and headed out while thinking how much I adored Sweet Judy.

Shortly after, I sat in the back of the situation room at the police station as Captain James Burns spoke. "Got some missing kids and some frantic parents as well. About seven little girls did not show up at school this morning. We are still gathering information on how the school realized seven were missing all at once. Seems odd because an overwhelming number of the kids are dropped off by their parents. We should get a call from the principal soon. Hang tough while I wait for that call."

Uncle Tony gathered his detectives and shared coffee, donuts, and cigarettes while discussing last night's Dodgers-Giants game.

"That Ron Cey and Bill Russell both had great games," one detective said.

"To hell with the Dodgers. I'm sick of their 'nice guy' image. Just a bunch of wimpy bums," another said.

"Yeah, but they win a lot."

Captain James got off the phone and said, "Okay, fellas, listen up. The missing kids were all on the same bus, which failed to show up at the school. So, let's head out to search the route of that Jefferson School bus. We should have that bus number soon."

My cup shattered as I dropped my coffee and donut on the floor. Everyone turned toward me and stared. "My daughter, Rose, takes the bus to Jefferson!"

"Let's try to stay calm, Matteo," the captain said. "There are at least five small buses servicing Jefferson School. The principal will call me soon with the bus number and the names of the girls. Let's hit the road." Captain James clapped.

Not being a true detective, I stayed behind and waited

with the captain. Minutes felt like hours as I paced back and forth from the coffee machine. I called Judy and alerted her. Now both of us were frantic. She said the bus number was forty. Judy stayed near the phone while I waited with Captain Burns for the call.

Soon the captain's phone rang, and he chatted with the principal. After he hung up, he looked at me. He calmly said, "The bus number is fifteen. Rose is not one of the missing seven."

I called Judy. After informing her of the good news, I said, "Hey, I'm coming home now. I think we should pick up Rose from school today since there will be too much chaos on campus."

Judy agreed.

As I headed home from the station, an unexpected strong gust of wind jolted my car but dissipated quickly. *That was strange*, I thought. I looked up at the trees — the very tops swayed left and right furiously even though the wind no longer blew my car. Slowing for a red light, I waited in deep thought, but my reflections were interrupted by a large black bird landing on the hood of my car.

Just a crow, I thought. However, upon further inspection, I saw that the bird was a large, jet-black raven which was a rare sight in our area. It cawed three times while focusing directly on my face. It hopped around on my car for a few moments and abruptly flew off. Another odd occurrence. And then a wave of premonition struck me and disappeared as fast as the raven had.

Taking some deep breaths, I pulled over to the side of the road to gather my senses. Ravens could be a sign of ominous events, a prelude to something negative, or a loss of some kind. But I also knew that ravens are highly intelligent, and their meanings can be complex, often indicating positive traits as well, such as a rebirth in some capacity. They can represent wisdom from ancient times and often they're tied to transformations of sorts, even in the spiritual realm, which of course, fit perfectly into my clairvoyant and intuitive skills. I reminded myself that I must go to the library and research this hooded, dark clown further.

I picked up Judy, and we headed to the school, arriving within fifteen minutes. Many parents had the same idea, so we all waited out in front while teachers escorted the kids to their parents. For twenty minutes there was no sign of Rose which prompted us to approach her teacher.

"Where is Rose?" Judy asked.

"She isn't here."

"But she was not on bus number 15."

The teacher watched us in shock and paused before speaking. "Didn't you hear? There wasn't just one bus, there were two! Number forty is gone as well. Was Rose on that one?"

Judy screamed, and I gasped for air. The news disabled Judy and me for a few long seconds before we could gather our senses. We raced into the school to use the phone, and I reached Captain James.

"Yes, I got the news a few minutes ago, but I had no way of reaching you. I'm so sorry, you guys. But I got my men all over that bus route, and we should have something soon. Come down to the station so you can stay up to the minute with me."

Judy and I drove to the station in shocked silence, suffering through pangs of sorrow, fear, and helplessness. And above all, of guilt. Why hadn't we escorted our daughter to school ourselves?

Rose had excitedly wanted to ride the bus, so of course

we let her. Who would think a ride on a school bus could be hazardous? We huddled with the captain at the station and waited yet again. I wish the raven had not confronted me, but now I believe he was warning me. The station phone rang.

"Yes, okay, let me write that down. And the other bus? Oh, okay, and the drivers? Shit! Got ya. And the names of those at the two sites? And the missing? Okay, thanks, be there soon at bus number forty. Don't touch anything." Captain James hung up, sighed, and spoke to us.

"Rose is not one of the dead."

We sighed and exhaled deeply.

"That's the good news. But she is one of the missing."

Judy shrieked, and I grasped her tightly.

"Each bus had five girls. On your bus, three are missing and two are dead, the driver too. On the other bus, three are dead as well as the driver, and two are missing. A total of five missing."

"How did they all die? Was there an accident?"

"No, the buses were attacked by someone, and all the dead had been stabbed through the heart with a sharp object. Makes no sense. But I need to head over there, and you need to come, Matteo, and start your own personal approach to this ASAP, okay? I'm sorry, Judy, but you cannot come. It's a crime scene, and I cannot allow it. But stay home, and Matteo will call you as soon as he can."

Judy begged to come, but the captain would not relent.

"Do your best, Matteo. And use all your powers to solve this. I know you can do it," Judy said with intermittent sobs.

Clearing my own tears, I jumped into the captain's truck, and off we sped.

NINE
THE SCENE

The bus-40 scene was beyond description. I was not allowed to touch any of the evidence. Just observe the chaos. The bus was off the road about twenty yards, resting in a field of grass. The bus driver was outside the front entrance, stabbed once and lying in a pool of his own blood. The two young girls were inside the bus on the floor in the same condition as the driver. But Rose and the other two girls were missing. It was a murder plus kidnapping crime that all of us found agonizingly confounding. Making all the necessary mental notes to help me in my process, I continued to assess the entire site inside and out without touching anything of vital concern.

"Captain, I must handle some of the evidence to realize the full impact of the situation and to awaken clues," I said, trying to keep my wits.

"All bodies must be taken to the morgue and following the pathologist's inspection, you can do your deal. I'll drive you there when the medical examiner's van takes them away. And you will be the first to enter the evidence cage at the station. We are in the process, right now, of blocking off all exits from this area. I hope we are not too late."

I drove with Captain Burns to the morgue in a state of shock and drifted into a meditative trance with hopes of applying my clairvoyance to the fullest extent.

TEN
THE PLAY
1975

All five lay flat in perfect uniform order, with blooming, white flowing attire, appropriate for this unique play. Arms along their sides and legs straight. Peaceful, as if they were in a practiced ethereal dream, getting ready for an expanded part in the school play guaranteed to affect all parties concerned. Each had silky skin with outfits in order with serious calm in each matching demeanor. An occasional bruise was evident, common to all young players of similar age and current state of attraction. The children were between five and six years old.

It was a rather serene, quiet setting with a crowd applauding in silence, and the only sound was that of shoes touching the clean, smooth floor before the curtain rose. Their hair was proper for the most part, with one more tangled than the others. Fingernails were similar, some with polish and some plain. Four of the five were Latino and African American. The other was white, overweight, and with evidence of some health issues. All five could have been friends with all the physical and mental states in common, yet so different. Same approximate age, and all were female.

And now! In precipitous motion the curtain rose, the silent music began, and the crowd awoke. The play had begun! Anticipation! As the bright lights illuminated the sterile stage, I staggered backward, and my trance stopped. I entered the present moment. All five had one unnerving distinct characteristic. All were dead by a violent stab to the heart. As reported earlier, there were ten missing, but these five souls were all who had been found. My daughter, Rose, was one of the five missing, and time was of the essence. My skills had to be applied with speed and accuracy.

Gathering all my senses, I moved from girl to girl collecting hair samples, parts of broken skin, and dried blood, as well as the residue beneath fingernails with hopes that some physical part of the murderers had left its mark on the girls. I meditated while holding the cold hands of each poor soul lying before me. When I was finished, I drove at once to my special place on the boulder at the edge of the forest, and I began my cerebral search for clues.

While I did this, Judy retraced the path of the bus and searched tirelessly through the surrounding areas close to the crime scene and farther, as did the group of investigators. Nothing of significance turned up. It was as if they had all vanished into thin air. Roadblocks produced zilch, and frustration seeped through the minds of everyone.

Returning home that evening, I found Judy curled up on the couch in rightful despair. I joined her, and we stayed on the couch intertwined as one. Consoling each other helped little.

Judy said, "Any results from your mental search?"

"Nothing yet. Not even a remote clue has surfaced. I was able to talk briefly with the other five stricken parents and discovered that all five of the missing were white, blonde females. This could take all my efforts, so I'll be at it all day again tomorrow." That was not the exact truth, but I refused to alarm Judy with additional negative news.

This was the first time during my employment with Uncle Tony that I had failed to gleam *any* substantial information from all the evidence which I found troubling. Maybe just a bad day, so I resolved to attack it again, as always.

One week later, I sat by myself at the edge of the forest, sunk into the realization of my failure. Not only did I not come up with any information regarding the crime, but also I was incapable of predicting or solving *anything*. It appeared that my skill had temporarily abandoned me. Many years ago, my parents taught me perseverance, to excel at accomplishing attainable goals. I refused to learn to ride my bike while others were racing around our neighborhood. One day my mom, in frustration, took me to the top of our driveway, and shoved me down the hill on my bike telling me to avoid the cactus at the end of our driveway. In horror, I managed to keep the bike straight, but I struggled with the brakes. I approached the cactus rapidly and instinctively swerved around and crashed into the harmless bushes.

"See!" yelled my mom. "That wasn't so hard."

I laughed, picked myself up, repeated the exercise, and calmly swerved around the cactus and applied my brakes. I overcame my doubts and took the lesson forward in my life. I blamed my current Rose dilemma on intense stress, and I vowed to solve this puzzling crime.

ELEVEN
CESSPOOL
1977

Over the next five years, Judy and I dedicated our lives to finding Rose. The other parents who had also lost their daughters joined us regularly in order to help us all maintain our composure. We hired private detectives and notified all other police departments up and down the state. Judy and I hired professional therapists to help us grieve and recover properly. After years, all the parents felt exasperated and helpless. We all had fallen into an ancient waterless well that cratered to the center of the earth. I had begun to recover slightly at this point, forcing myself to try harder at work while trying to recover my skills. I thought that Judy and I had come to terms with the final conclusion. Rose was gone forever, and what hope we had faded away. Judy, unfortunately, could not shed any of her guilt and sorrow. We did try for more children, but we were not successful. Judy and I became inseparable through the grief, and we realized, even more than ever, that our love for each other was strong and eternal. I continued to work for Uncle Tony but with almost no results. My skill had vanished. I believe he felt so sorry for me that he could not find it in his heart to release me, but I knew that day was approaching, especially because Captain Burns had mentioned the cost of keeping me was becoming somewhat noticeable to the financial team.

The following year, I was informed that the police department would no longer need my services. I wandered home and sat on our porch pondering my next steps. Because of my love for nature, I started up a gardening business, and it helped to pay our bills. But Judy struggled.

She continued to skip from job to job, and her mental state deteriorated slowly. The episodes of anger, guilt, and loneliness increased noticeably and were becoming more debilitating. Our parents suggested that we exercise on a more regular basis, advice that we immediately implemented. But Judy had to stop when she began to experience severe headaches. We headed to the hospital.

After a battery of tests, Judy was diagnosed with an inoperable brain tumor and given less than a year to live. How could this happen? Did I ignore the signs? We both were shocked by the diagnosis. Could it have been prevented? No one knew, but the doctor revealed that on occasion he had witnessed people becoming extremely sick due to intense stress. Both Judy and I settled into creating the most comfortable setting in a gloomy environment. We spent hours sharing all the memorable good times we had with each other and especially those with Rose. Even though her time in our lives was short, we recounted endless wonderful moments, making us both smile and laugh. We spoke about Rose's first birthday party when Rose and her little friends crawled all over the floor and furniture and played like bunny rabbits. Adorable. We joked about Rose and her preschool since she would never let us leave after her morning drop-off. We had to sneak out the back door while she was playing. But when we came back to pick her up at two, she didn't want to leave. Many more childhood Rose experiences kept Judy focused on the positive, but she needed to rest many times throughout her final days due to headaches and sorrow. I always lay with her, and when she woke, I massaged her feet, back, and finished with her head.

Both Judy's and my parents visited often bringing food and household necessities. They tried hard to help, but in the end, nothing worked.

TWELVE
MORBID DELIRIUM
1981

On April 2, 1981, the true love of my life was laid to rest, and my future now stood me alone. Could things get worse? Following Judy's demise, I fell into a coma-like state. Like being constantly drunk even though I rarely drank, but when I did, well, look out people. I fell off the edge of the world and wandered on other planets, as far away as possible, to places like Pluto. With Judy's death and Rose's disappearance, everything surrounding me evaporated except for me. I wanted to die. Death would halt my misery.

My parents continued their emotional support, allowing me to have a small semblance of worth. But I became an emotional strain on all my relatives, and many avoided me. I continually emitted negative vibes to everyone. My mom and dad, bless their hearts, continued to try, but even our conversations became cursory and meaningless. It was almost as if my parents were dying along with Judy and Rose. We continued to meet with the hope that enough recovery existed to help my charade of normalcy in this game of life.

The next year, due to relentless bad dreams and ghosts, I rented out my house and moved into a studio cottage in Uncle Tony's backyard. Every day, seven days a week, I ran my landscape gardening business and maintained a mundane, boring existence. It was perfect, I guessed. No stress, no worries, no responsibilities. Just support the lush foliage of my clients' yards. I found that when you have trouble accepting the actions of life or of other people, go immediately to gardens with clippers in hand and give the plants a haircut, making them smile with beauty. It's restoring not only to the plants but also to one's heart.

Nature rules!

One day sitting at my not-so-happy place, I realized that there was only one thing worse than death: disappearance. Vanishing into thin air. Poof! Gone. Never knowing if they were dead or alive, hoping for the latter, yet there could exist no closure, ever. Wandering back to my cottage, I created meals I did not like, I washed dishes and clothes that were not even dirty, and I watched idiotic TV shows.

The days dragged on forever. I lived like this for months. Sometimes I struggled to remember the details of Judy's face as my memory was blocked by the incessant horror, depression, and guilt pounding in my brain. There was no more room in my brain for growth. I was in lockdown, stagnated by grief. It made perfect sense that I had lost all my intuitive strength due to the overwhelming stress.

One day, Uncle Tony came to my cottage, took a seat at my couch, and said to me, "Hey pal, seems like you cannot dig out of your rut, so I have a suggestion."

"What? You've already done enough for me," I said.

"How about we go fishing, just like old times? I have a good friend who lives up north, and we can shack up with him. Let's have a little fun and slap you around a bit. What do you say?"

I looked at my uncle and said, "Okay, I'm game. Where to?"

"Juneau."

THIRTEEN
CHUCK
1983

The most exciting event in my last four years was approaching since tomorrow I would fly on a large plane and for a long way to boot. I had not flown for many years, and when I did, that one flight was short. Having no idea what to pack, I threw everything important into two large duffle bags for a simple four-day trip, which resulted in a good laugh by Uncle Tony.

"You plan on never returning?" my uncle asked with a chuckle.

"I know, it's pathetic, but hey, I'm prepared for any scenario." I grinned.

Wide awake on the plane, I sank into deep thought as my uncle snored away, in peace, right next to me. The hum of the plane drowned out any distractions allowing my emotions to rage through me. I was flying away from not only the scenes of my life's remorse but also from all the positive memories of Judy and Rose, creating an emotional, long-lost sensation — a previously unattainable feeling which now presented itself as relaxation. In my prior healthy life, this is where my intuition and clairvoyance would rise and take over, but no more. At thirty-three, I didn't know what lay ahead. I fell asleep.

Upon waking, I peered out the window into a vast never-ending forest surrounded by gigantic mountains topped with snow, all of which took my breath away. I had never witnessed such a magnificent sight. After landing, we were picked up by Uncle Tony's friend, a stout man of good humor and sarcasm with hair that shot up in all directions. This was the glorious Chuck. His old red '57 Chevy truck accentuated his celebrity.

"Chucky, this is my nephew, Matteo. He needs to have some fun and fishing."

"You got it, Tony. I'll make you guys dinner tonight, and we'll get out in the morning with poles in the water," he said.

I watched with wonder as we approached Chuck's massive log cabin built with real logs, not with fake siding. This looked like a perfect place to hang and recover from life's maladies. The cabin was all on one level with five bedrooms and various bathrooms, a game room, and an expansive rustic kitchen sharing space with an inviting family room. There was lots of wood throughout with high ceilings in every room.

We had a delightful evening of jokes and stories, and somehow Chuck, without knowing me very well, managed to make me the butt of many of his jokes. Impressive, to say the least, and it distracted me from all my negativity with laughter and goodwill, something I had not savored in years. I noticed that my cheeks were sore from smiling. I realized how little of that I had experienced in recent times, and obviously my cheeks were out of shape. We all drifted off to our rooms around midnight.

At 7:30 sharp, Chuck entered my room, cupped his mouth with both hands, leaned back, and yelled, "Hey, Oh! Up'n at 'EM. Rise and shine, princess. Breakfast in twenty!" He rushed out.

I just about had a heart attack. Twenty-five minutes later, I staggered into the kitchen while the smell of bacon permeated his large cabin.

"How's my Sleeping Beauty?" Chuck handed me a cup of coffee. "Damn, Matteo, even with your thick hair sticking straight up, you are still a handsome young man. Should have lots of women after you. How can this fella be related to that ugly Tony?"

My uncle laughed and shrugged.

"Is Chuck always like this, Uncle Tony? All fired up early in the morning?"

Tony nodded.

"Thanks, Chuck, but I'm not so young anymore, and there are exactly zero girls who match my desires."

"Your uncle tells me you were quite the Sherlock at solving difficult cases. That takes some talent."

I looked at my uncle. He shrugged indicating that my secret power, or lack of it now, had not been discussed. I'm sure Chuck would have dissected that right into the toilet.

FOURTEEN
THE TONY AWARDS

"Okay, boys and girls, or whatever your persuasion may be. Here's all your poles, spinning reels, and lures. Got some Mepps, Rooster Tails, and Panther Martins, and I've clipped off the barbs so we can throw back all the fish except the two or three we will keep for dinner, alrighty?"

My uncle and I gave thumbs ups.

"Also, Matteo, your uncle created a friendly competition years ago, and since he was close to that high-falutin' Hollywood, it's called The Tony Awards. You earn points for fishing buffoonery, such as falling in the water or losing the most fish as you reel them in, or catching the smallest fish of the day, and lots of other antics preventing you from catching fish. Whoever has the most fuckups, earning the most points, is declared the loser at the end of the day. This lucky soul must buy drinks that evening. Got it?"

Once again, I agreed, figuring this should be a cake walk victory for me. No way a 275-pound slob like Chuck would prevail. Off we marched about a mile and half to Mendenhall Lake.

"Chuck, what kind of fish swim in these waters?" I asked.

"An assortment of rainbow, cutthroat, Dolly Varden, and Coho salmon. Probably some others as well. Lots of sizes so we each will sport twelve-pound test."

When we arrived at the lake, the beauty of the awe-inspiring scene shadowed by Mendenhall Glacier blew me away. It was a perfect painting. After shaking off the sensation, I tied on a Mepps with my trusty slipknot and yelled,

"Hey, losers! You can't catch fish if you don't spend time in the water!"

I launched out my first epic cast of the day and watched in disbelief as my lure kept sailing far beyond my cast, splashed into the lake, and then sank to the bottom where it would rest for eternity. My knot had not held. I quickly gazed at the guys to see if they had noticed my foolishness. Both were staring at me, then they broke into belly laughter and yelled together.

"Well done, idiot! That's one point!"

Nothing like starting your fishing excursion already in the hole. And that about summed up my stellar performance for that first day. Back at Chuck's cabin that afternoon, we sat around on his front porch.

"Okay," Chuck said, "so I earned three points. Tony, you earned five points. Matteo, you amassed a staggering twelve points. Congrats! You are the proud winner of today's Tony Award! Did you really fall in the lake twice?"

I nodded. "And I snagged tree branches snapping my line, hooked rocks in the lake snapping my line, hooked my pants, wrapped my fishing line around the button on top of my baseball hat snapping the line, and caught the least fish. While trying to take a piss, I stepped on my rod and damaged it beyond repair. And finally, in complete utter frustration, I threw my entire rig into thorny bushes, and as a result, I took twenty minutes to retrieve it. Any questions?" I asked before swigging my beer.

"Well, that will suffice, and I can taste the free, high-quality bourbon slipping down my gullet," my uncle said with bountiful laughter by all.

That evening we celebrated my epic win at a bar called the Rusty Canteen where my wallet became much lighter by the evening's end. In the morning, all of us were a bit slow, so we headed out for day two of fishing later. I managed, with exaltation, to finish second this day with my uncle securing last to win the not-so-coveted Tony Award. This time we headed to the famous Red Onion Saloon for libations.

As the evening progressed, Uncle Tony said, "For Christ's sake, Chuck, are there no good-looking women in this godforsaken town?"

Chuck laughed. "Nope, but come to think of it, there is one, but she doesn't like men."

"Geez, Chuck, you always tell it like you know all. The world according to Chuck," I said with cheer.

"I only speak the truth."

We ordered more drinks and food to boot.

In the morning, Uncle Tony and I began to pack since our trip was ending. I sat in my room looking out at Mendenhall and realized that the depression was seeping back into me with the thought of returning to the scene of the crimes. The smell of all the fresh wood that helped construct this cabin gave me the strength I needed, and I strolled into the kitchen and spoke to Chuck.

"Would it be okay with you if I stayed a little longer?

Being in these lush forests has been great therapy for me, but I still have much repair ahead of me."

"Hell yes, Matteo! You can stay as long as you need. I'd love your company, and besides, I don't enjoy drinking by myself." He laughed.

Well, that certainly vindicated my existence to know I was wanted for a worthwhile cause: drinking. Uncle Tony wished he could stay as well, but his work called for him with many crimes to solve. We escorted my uncle to the airport to see him off to the grand parts of California, and Chuck took me to town to set me up with some wading gear to fish the Montana River.

Entering Juneau, we parked Chuck's rickety old Chevy truck on beaten Front Street. After walking a couple of blocks, we turned right onto an even older paved street that eventually turned into gravel. Two blocks down we arrived at Chuck's favorite spot, Eddie's Tackle Shop. As we entered, two surly men walked out, and I said hi to them, but they gave no reply. One was heavyset and ugly as sin, and the other had a daunting fierceness to his gaze, and I noticed a large scar that reached from his left earlobe all the way to the edge of his mouth. Disturbing to say the least.

The tackle shop was an adult candy shop of fishing paraphernalia, mostly for men like Chuck. I immediately enjoyed it. Chuck bantered with Eddie, introduced me as his "son" with a little explanation, and we looked around in his shop. At one point I asked Eddie, "Boy, those two guys exiting your shop were a bit eerie. What's up with them?"

"They are French Canadian miners who operate with others deep in the Yukon and are to be avoided. No fun and dangerous. They, like all miners, prefer not to be disturbed while mining. They think that others may steal their gold."

An hour later, we wandered out with a lovely Loomis rod for me and a classic 1955 Fenwick rod for Chuck. In my other hand I held a high-quality Shakespeare spinning reel and Chuck had a Shimano DUX.

"Chuck, don't you already have enough fishing gear for yourself?"

"Of course I do, but a man never has enough fishing gear. And besides, this is my happy place. I'm like a fashionista in a high-end clothing shop. I must buy something. I'd be grumpy if I only bought something for you." Chuck slapped me on the back, and we headed home.

FIFTEEN
MONTANA RIVER

Next morning I organized the equipment that Chuck had so graciously purchased for me and headed out the door toward his Chevy truck. Even though I loved the new fishing gear, I really wanted to indulge in fly fishing. Chuck said no because I was a rookie at that style of fishing. He mentioned that I would need lessons. Chuck came out as well and handed me one more item.

"You should have this for protection." He handed me a .44 magnum pistol with a chest holster. "You probably will never need it, but just in case. If a bear approaches you, fire the gun in the air once. That should scare it away, but if it's a female with cubs, then you may be forced to shoot her, okay? Don't hesitate."

"Shoot her? I'd hate to kill a bear."

"Better her than you, Matteo. Chances are slim but you never know. Usually by the time you see them, it's too late anyway." Chuck laughed. "There hasn't been an attack in years. Catch us some dinner, pal!"

"You sure you don't want to attend this fine excursion into the wilderness?"

"Nope, but thanks. I've been down that fine path many times with various successful fishing trips in my portfolio. But I'm a little too fat these days. Enjoy." He waddled off toward the house.

As per his instructions, I checked all my gear and did not bring any food with me as that would attract unwanted beasts.

Driving down the dirt road, I passed the time admiring the immensity of these forests and the grandeur of the trees. Magnificent! A sense of calm engulfed me, and my hope was to restore my lost form of intuitive clairvoyance. No luck so far, but I kept faith in its reclamation.

I ventured about five or six miles and finally reached the spot that Chuck had described so vividly. Just ahead a broken sign leaned to the left with the words: *Enter at your own risk.* I wondered why that would be posted. Chuck told me that was just to keep the illegals out, or at least an attempt to block them with fear, and for the bear action in the area.

I sat quietly on the tailgate and prepared my spinning gear with a small Mepps attached, a favorite lure of mine back in the days. Chuck told me to go after the trout that follow the breeding salmon up stream. If I caught a salmon, then release it because it was breeding. With the .44 strapped to my chest, I charged through the bushes and instantly tripped and fell over. I laughed to myself and gave myself an obligatory "point". After I cleaned off, I continued toward the meandering river.

Standing close to the river, its beauty and charm gave me goosebumps and a decent hope for a rebirth of all my lost abilities. Smiling, I concluded that maybe this is where I should live. I prepared to fish as I wondered if Chuck would rent me a room in his vast cabin.

SIXTEEN
THE RANGER

A woman flew out of the bushes making as much noise as possible and scared the living crap out of me. I thought I was going to die a miserable death in the jaws of an angry bear.

"You have a fishing license?" she asked, pointing at me.

A forest ranger.

"Wow, you scared me! I could have shot you; you know?"

"Right, then you would have been written up for murder instead of fishing without a license."

"Good point. Lucky for you I didn't shoot. I *do* have a fishing license right here." I rummaged through my chest pockets. "I know it's here. I just got the license about a week ago." After what seemed an eternity, I sighed and dumped out the contents of my backpack all over the rocky shore. My license was gone. I glumly said, "It must be in my vehicle."

"Are you aware that the license has to be not only in your possession but also exposed in a clear, visible location on your body, such as attached to your hat or fishing vest?"

"Yes, I'm aware. I screwed up probably because I was so excited about fishing." I found it ludicrous that she didn't care about the exposed .44 strapped across my chest.

She looked me up and down and calmly said, "Let's go to your vehicle and, if it's there, I'll let you off. Follow me."

I trailed after her as she climbed back through the bushes. She was wearing a very baggy Smokey Bear outfit, but even that frumpy outfit looked good on her. A shapely female ranger in the middle of nowhere. I laughed at the randomness of that and smiled since I had failed to take meaningful notice of a female human being in numerous years. In short order, we arrived at the truck.

"This is Chuck's truck, isn't it?" she asked.

"Yes, I'm staying at his place for a few days. He was gracious enough to lend me his red truck. A beauty, huh?"

She looked at me with suspicion, possibly thinking that I had stolen Chuck's truck. As she placed her hand subtly on her gun, she said, "So, tell me a little about Chuck and how you know him."

"My uncle met Chuck many years ago when I was younger. Chuck was in our area to speak about a project he had dreamed up in Juneau. My parents and my uncle attended his speech and took me along. My uncle ended up giving a donation to his project, and they became friends. He always invited my uncle to visit, and so here I am as a guest of my uncle, many years later."

"What was his project?"

"He had a grandiose vision of constructing a gondola that would attach Juneau to some point high in the mountains, and—"

She cut me off. "Okay, okay, that's legit. But he is

having trouble getting that approved. Taking a long time with a lot of opposition. It makes sense *not* to do it because local folks around here want to keep it peaceful with a limited number of reckless tourists."

"Yes," I said in agreement with a personal goal of avoiding the fishing ticket. "Seems like a rather farfetched dream."

She looked at me without emotion. "Where is the license?"

I began searching throughout the truck but with little success, and I realized that I had left it conveniently on my nightstand. "Hey, I can't find it. I'm pretty sure I left it at Chuck's place. Can we go back and get it?"

Looking at me with utter disdain, she calmly spoke again. "Are you serious? I'm obligated to write you up. We have salmon poachers around here, and the need to clamp down is important."

I slumped down on the tailgate of the truck and watched her unfold the ticket book and write. She asked for my driver's license and resumed.

"Do you have to issue me a ticket? I'm not one of those bad guys you mentioned. What did you call them? Prancers?"

"No, poachers. I'm trained to do my job regardless of who I encounter, Mr. Ferrari."

"Well, good job, Smokey."

She looked at me in disbelief and said, "You wish for me to arrest you?"

"No, no, sorry. I'm not very polished with someone like you."

"What sort of person am I, Mr. Ferrari?" She placed her hand on her pistol.

"A woman. I don't speak much with women these days."

"Well, you're speaking with me."

"Good point. Wanna know why I suffer so much with the opposite sex?"

"No."

I leaned on the side of the truck bed and watched her scribble out the ticket. This was no ordinary park ranger. She had stunning thick sandy blonde hair partially tucked under her goofy Smokey hat. Her large eyes glowed with shades of green and blue and brown. Her skin was tanned to an olive, silky smoothness. Surprisingly, I enjoyed her presence. Sweet, while near death, had encouraged me to live my life and not mourn her too long. That had not worked over these numerous years. I loved Judy so much and distancing her memory was just about impossible for me. I chuckled some because this remote ranger had spurred my lackluster interest.

"And what is so funny? You enjoy getting tickets?"

"Oh, nothing in particular, just laughing at myself for such foolishness with my license," I lied.

She grinned a little which made her glow. She tore off the ticket and handed it to me.

"While I appreciate your dedication to your work, I wish we hadn't met in this way, two folks wandering in the wilderness." I laughed.

"First of all, I'm not wandering, but you may be. Second, you should not be out here by yourself as it can be problematic with bears and poachers, the latter being worse."

Realizing that she was not lightening up, I said, "What do these tickets cost nowadays?"

"They can be quite costly, but it will be considerably

less if you round up your license and take it to the ranger station down the way." She pointed to the right.

"I guess my gun doesn't matter, huh?"

"Not really. It's smart to have it with you."

Keeping up the conversation, I said, "Where are the good spots to catch trout?"

Perhaps deciding that I was not too dangerous, she rolled her eyes and then pointed down the river. "There are some falls that way and soft flows below it that house the salmon and the following trout. But you cannot go there."

"Why not?"

"No license." She rolled her eyes again. She was clearly frustrated.

I laughed and slapped the side of my head.

"And there is another reason not to go there by yourself."

"What is that?"

"Bears swarm that area in search of the salmon as they run upstream. Venturing there by yourself is ill advised."

"Maybe you can escort me to it, so I'll know where to go in the future?"

Shaking her head, she said, "No, I have to go find more fools without fishing licenses. It's my job today." She turned and walked toward her truck swaying from left to right in a naturally feminine fashion.

"Love your Smokey Bear outfit!"

She paused, turned back slightly, and then shook her head. A moment later, she jumped into her truck and started up the engine.

"One last question, can you recommend a decent place for a good steak and a glass of Pinot? I want to take Chuck out in appreciation of his generosity."

"Not really. Good luck and behave yourself," she said and was gone.

Depressed, I plopped down on the tailgate of the truck and stared out into nature. Did I really need this type of treatment after all I'd been through? At least it was a nice day, even if the ranger was a jerk. I wondered what her name was. I sighed and looked down at the ticket resting in the palm of my hand. Written properly at the bottom of the ticket was her full name — Gabriella Valentina. Two Italians wandering in the woods. I laughed.

SEVENTEEN
JUNEAU NIGHT

Upon my return from a fruitless fishing extravaganza, I cleaned up and sat with Chuck in his spacious living room. We chatted about life with its ebbs and flows. Chuck had been married but lost his wife to cancer, so we had a comparable life disaster, but my loss was double. Chuck acknowledged that.

"I stand proud of you, Matteo. You have survived those thoroughly unfortunate events. Hang in there, my friend. It shall pass."

"Sorry, Chuck, but this is not passing. I don't have faith it ever will. How can it?"

"Not sure, but I just feel that it will. Go grab some ice for the gin and tonics, and then you can tell me about your day."

"Sounds perfect. Where is the store?"

Smiling, Chuck said, "Our ice store is right over there." He pointed straight out his living room window to the magnificent Mendenall Glacier.

I jumped into his red truck with an ax, provided by

Chuck, and headed toward the glacier. As I approached the towering wall of ice, my body felt enchanted by its sheer grandeur. My spirits soared and my senses rattled my body in ways I hadn't experienced in ages. Maybe this was the heaven on earth that would restore the powers that had abandoned me?

I chopped off a small chunk of Mendenhall, gathered it in my hands and sat on the cold ground, crossed my legs and began to focus. Minutes passed in agonizingly slow motion. Nothing came other than some flashes of light that faded into obscurity. I set the ice on the ground and looked to the skies through the still treetops for some sort of sign, but zilch happened. Staring at the sheer grandeur of Mendenhall Glacier was almost a religious experience, even though I was anything but religious. It resembled the work of God or something far beyond the simple minds of human beings. I realized that this massive mountain of slow-moving ice was formed by the smallest and most delicate item of all — a snowflake. I'm sure these epic earthly statues of ice have a connection to the meaning of life on earth, but in what way? I had no clue. It sat as great food for thought, and I committed to further research of glaciers upon my return from this vacation.

Tears came to my eyes as, once again, I had been shut out. Could anything end this exasperating search for my clairvoyance? Deciding to stop my self-pity, I jumped up and hacked off another hunk of three-thousand-year-old ice, threw it in the cooler and headed back to Chuck and our waiting drinks.

Gazing into my gin and tonic, I was impressed with the clarity of the hard ice. No imperfection and no air.

Chuck clicked my glass. "We will be able to make at

least two or three drinks using this ancient ice. Impressive, huh?"

"Yes it is, Chuck, yes, it is."

"So, tell me why your day didn't pan out."

"Well, the day didn't even get going far because I forgot my license, got busted by a ranger, had to come back and get the license, and then find the ranger station to prove that I actually had a license, and got the fine reduced quite a bit. That all took so long that I had to abandon fishing for the day. Besides that, the ranger warned me about being out there alone. She said there were too many bears and poachers, blah-blah-blah."

"She? Did you get written up by Gabriella?"

"Yep, that's the ranger. A little cold, that one."

Chuck laughed. "Yes, she is tough and goes by the book, which is good. She is not easy to read or approach, as many have found in these rough parts. She is the one looker we have, as I mentioned the other night, but stiff as a dried-up piece of my homemade jerky."

"Anybody know why?"

"Nope and many a-man has tried to court her with zero success. She hangs out with just a few oddball women and a couple of old local miners from Skagway. But what should we expect from all you queer Californians? You folks all want to marry anything but what God intended. Heck, she probably is married to her pet goat. She is colder than Mendenhall Glacier." He laughed and pushed himself up to make another drink, grabbing mine on the way. Chuck was quite entertaining with his inappropriate chatter. He created laughter wherever he went and made a joke of anything and everyone.

"Chuck, I didn't realize that the bears were much of a

problem up here. You had me take the .44, and the ranger warned me too. Why all the worry?"

"To be perfectly honest, we haven't had an issue for a while. But a couple years ago we experienced several deadly issues with grizzly bears, but we all think it was just one specific bear. This bear killed various poachers and a couple of criminals running from the law, but no locals. He was spotted a few times and has a distinctive marking — a long narrow streak of blondish hair running along his back. He was affectionately named Golden. His size was another disturbing characteristic. He was much larger than your normal grizzly. Close to twelve hundred pounds. A real brute and smart to boot. The local hunters attempted to track and shoot him but were unsuccessful. Anyway, he disappeared, and most folks assumed he had died or wandered off to more remote areas. Best to never meet him," Chuck said with a devilish grin.

"That's a little scary, so the .44 makes sense. Hey," I said, changing the subject, "I want to take you out for dinner and a drink tonight. Got any recommendations?"

"I like Ruby's Saloon. Great fish dishes and fresh salads for you grass eaters."

"Sounds good. I love meat too, so pipe down, you old miner."

The laughter and storytelling continued for another half hour, and then we headed out to Ruby's.

Bouncing along the old road in his shockless red truck, I asked, "How are things going with the gondola project?"

"It's moving very slowly with numerous delays because of local concerns, which I understand. But we really need this to help Juneau prosper. Could be another five years or more." He slammed his brakes on suddenly as two small grizzly cubs wandered onto the road. They were unbelievably cute.

"Shit," Chuck moaned. "The mama must be right here too." He put the truck in reverse and slowly backed away when a large thump shook his truck. The mama had attacked our truck! He kept backing up with the snarling bear following.

"Don't look at her. That's a challenge that she won't particularly like." After about fifty yards of reverse, the bear stopped and returned to her cubs.

"Christ almighty! That was a bit harrowing."

"All fine. We just need to stay calm and always remain in the vehicle. It happens around here. It's not like the love-child hippies in California. It's real life here." He laughed again. "Besides, I have Old Betsey right here." He pulled the .44 magnum from under his seat. For the next thirty minutes I didn't relax much. I kept a keen eye on the road's edge.

Ruby's was near the water and packed with people, which was a good sign. It reminded me of Judy's old stomping ground, The Chart House, but more rustic. We got our names on the wait list and bellied up to the bar. Chuck got his usual gin and tonic. I mixed it up and ordered my favorite California drink, a margarita with Cuervo Gold.

"How can you drink that shit, Matteo? Taste like a worn-out Mexican Senorita."

"Chuck, you're disgusting, you old fart."

We both laughed, and he gave me a big bear hug.

"You know, Matteo, I love you like my own son, but he has been gone for a long time. So, you are in his place."

"Didn't know you had a son, Chuck. What happened to him?"

"A couple few years ago, he got really sick and passed away before I could get him professional help. It was some sort of cancerous blood disease. The doctors said there was little I could do for him anyway."

"Damn, I'm so sorry," I said. "I had no idea. My uncle didn't tell me."

"That's because I didn't tell him. But you have just as much suffering, and more with your two losses, Matteo. So, we drink in their memory." We cheered and teared up. "Since you arrived, I've had this feeling that you are kind of like my surrogate son. I know that's foolish, but it is how I feel. No harm."

"I have no problem acting as your surrogate son, but I won't tell my parents. They will be jealous."

As the hostess led us to our table, we passed by many folks all having a raucous time. And then my gaze landed on someone familiar as she sat with a couple of friends. The ranger Gabriella. I smiled, nodded, and waved. She tipped her baseball hat to me.

I stopped and looked her straight in the eye and said, "So, we meet again, under more favorable terms. I guess this is the best spot in town, but then again, you wouldn't know, right?" I smiled.

"Haha, no I wouldn't. This is not the best spot according to my girlfriends here. Did you get your license over to the ranger station?"

"I did and that paid off. Thanks for the kind recommendation."

"Catch any fish after that?" she asked.

"No, I also took your advice about fishing alone."

"Good, we would hate to clean up what's left of you after the bears got done." She smiled infectiously.

Chuck walked back to her table. "Well, hello, Gaby. You

need to go easy on my son here. He is one of those sensitive Californians like yourself." He chuckled mischievously.

"Is he really your son?"

"No, just my adopted son for me. Not sure he would admit that."

I wrapped my arm around his large frame and gave him a big kiss on his fat cheek. The women at the table all laughed.

"So, you're from Cali too," I said "Where?"

"From L.A., around Laurel Canyon area."

"That's great. I'm from Santa Barbara."

"Yes, I know, saw it on your driver's license today."

I nodded, and after brief introductions to her friends, Irene and Rosanne, Gabriella gave us her candid cue to move on. "Hope you two have a wonderful evening, and good luck on your adventures, Matteo."

We waved and followed our hostess.

* * *

GABRIELLA

"Why did you scare him off, Gabriella? He is so handsome. I'd ravish him in a second," Irene said.

"I didn't scare him off. I wanted to be with just you two," I explained.

"Sure, sure, Gaby. This happens all the time," said Rosanne. "We bring you along to attract the guys, and we all get nowhere! What in the world is your issue? You won't look this good forever, you little picky princess!"

They laughed.

"Just not interested. It's been that way for a long time.

You two know my story, so clam up and have a little fun. Nothing is stopping you from jumping guys on your own."

"Yes, we do know your story, but no one is going to feel too sorry for the forlorn beauty queen!" Irene smiled. "We will still invite you along because you make a perfect troll, and we don't mean for freshwater fishes. Can you just try not to be such a bitch? Maybe Rosanne or I could have bedded that hunk Matteo, you know?" she said assuredly.

They all laughed and drank up.

As the meal progressed, Gabriella thought to herself, have I really been that unsocial and disassociated all this time? Is there something permanently wrong with me? I'm depressed about everything, but I just adore this environment surrounded by nature, its offerings of wilderness, wildness, vast forests, and the separation from the harshness of city life, and I embraced the transcendent thought that little else mattered. I'm not that peculiar, but still searching for an encompassing, peaceful existence. Negative experiences have taken their toll on me, but that one enormous event kept me in lockdown mode. It wasn't my fault, but now I owned it, so it was my responsibility alone. The concept that all things shall pass had yet to materialize in my world. I came to and rejoined my perennially upbeat, and in heat, girlfriends! They were my joy.

EIGHTEEN
DREAM A LITTLE DREAM

Chuck and I finished up an entertaining meal and conversation and headed toward the exit. I took a quick look back at Gabriella and her friends. She looked up and gave a halfhearted wave. Irene and Rosanne turned and waved furiously. I smiled, waved back, and off we went. What a perplexing wild alley cat Gabriella was. I almost felt like I should wander back in the woods to perhaps get busted by her again. I drove back as Chuck snored in the back seat.

Chuck was not the easiest person to escort from his truck to his bed. I needed a forklift. Eventually the mission was accomplished, and I crawled into bed, and drifted toward memories of Judy and Rose. This, being common most nights, made falling asleep a tedious task. But tonight, all the drinks aided in achieving a comatose state.

Later, as always, I rose restlessly and gazed out my bedroom window into the dark night. A slight breeze rhythmically rocked the treetops while the lower part of the forest lay still, black and foreboding. No moon tonight, yet the dazzling stars lit the sky. Throwing on some warm clothes and gathering a flashlight, I headed outside for a midnight stroll but not before snagging the .44 magnum, as counseled by the ranger, while ignoring her secondary admonishment — never wander alone in the wilderness.

The evening was beautiful with stars aplenty, with multiple shooting ones racing by. Following Chuck's homemade path, I arrived at the lake's edge admiring the silhouette of Mendenhall Glacier. A great horned owl serenaded the stillness, repeating its mating call in intermittent rhythm. Breathing deeply in my favorite Qigong pose, I shut my eyes creating an environment of uninterrupted focus with hope of resurrection. The owl suddenly stopped.

Opening my eyes in suspicion, I slowly turned to see a dark object jogging down the path toward me. It looked like a figure of a woman, but as it approached, it morphed into a larger more robust object of fur and teeth and claws. Nothing looked particularly positive in its approach, so dropping my flashlight, I drew my .44, and pointing it to the sky, I pulled the trigger…*Click*…I pulled the trigger again…*Click*…

Fearfully I realized that I had unloaded the gun on returning from fishing. Screaming, I sprinted along the lake shore with the huge beast, a bear I assumed, in hot pursuit. I was losing this race rapidly, so I saw no other choice but to run directly right into the dense forest and shrubs. Falling numerous times, I bounced off abundant trees and shrubs, scratching myself endlessly. Soon there was nowhere to run, and I launched myself into some low-lying branches. My feet were swept off the ground trapping me in place. I turned and looked back in terror and screamed again as the great bear arrived. With snarling teeth he ripped through my legs and crushed my bones.

"Wake up, wake up, Matteo! What's all the screaming about? You woke me up from my drunken stupor!" Chuck continued to push me till I became conscious, sweating profusely and gasping for air.

"Shit, horrible dream. Sorry."

"When you can wake me, then you are making some real noise, my son." He laughed. "What was the dream?'

"I was attacked by a huge bear by the lake while getting stuck in the trees."

"I don't think you should ever drink again."

"Shut up, Chuck! Ironic that such stalwart advice comes from a certified alcoholic such as yourself."

We laughed while hugging each other.

Chuck went back to sleep as I toweled off staring into the mirror. What a wild dream, and could the power of it be a prelude to something significant? But exactly what was it? The lake, the shrubs, the forest, the sky and stars, the bear, or the human figure? I shook my head realizing the extent of my headache. After guzzling water to wash down two aspirins, I collapsed into bed and fell back to sleep.

NINETEEN
A NEW DAY

n the morning, a searing screech woke me suddenly, and I feared the attack in my dream was recurring. Looking through my window I noticed a huge soaring bald eagle gliding through the skies, and I was relieved and excited to witness this majestic creature. It circled a few times, glided down, and perched on a branch close to my window. She stared directly into my eyes with unnerving confidence and shrieked twice before flying off. It was as if the majestic bird was telling me something, and I smiled. A sense of calmness enveloped me. Sighing, I rose, arranged myself and went to the kitchen where my surrogate dad already had my coffee prepared.

"How are you feeling, Matteo?" Chuck asked.

"A little frazzled to be honest. Obviously, I didn't have the most fruitful sleep."

"You should learn to drink responsibly, like myself!" Chuck exclaimed.

"Okay, I'll take note." I told Chuck about the eagle, and

he mentioned that no eagle had ever perched so close to his cabin.

"You must be something special to that bird." And he continued, "Today, I'll take you to fish with me. I have some sweet, secret spots unknown to others, including any park rangers."

"Sounds good, but I was kind of hoping to get busted by Gabriella again." I smiled.

"No such luck, my boy, no such luck with that fine lady. What a waste," Chuck said while stirring the eggs with cheese and onions.

The thought had never crossed my mind until Chuck had reminded me twice now. In high school, one of our friends, Peter, was gay, but no one knew about it until years later. It seemed just fine to me, but I quickly learned that mainstream society rejected this lifestyle, often with violence and disregard. My parents were firmly against such behavior, but then again, they were also extremely unhappy when I brought home Mukasa, my African American soccer teammate, or Ebony to me, for a weekend break from Berkeley.

Both of my parents were unadmitted racists, but it was more a sign of their time and upbringing. I was never apologetic about Ebony and did not allow my parents any sort of victory by heading back to Berkeley early. I loved my parents anyway. Their issues had been home grown for generations. Through thick and thin, they remained committed and supportive of me. They knew why I escaped to these remote lands in my troublesome effort to reset my brain and recover from twin losses. As a result, Gabriella didn't alarm me, just disappointed me for some remote romantic reason. I enjoyed our brief encounter and ensuing talk, and I resigned myself to that simple pleasure.

Besides, my chances of actually seeing her again were similar to my surrounding environment — remote.

"Let's go fishing, Chucky Cheese!" I yelled.

Eight grueling hours later, I dragged my exhausted ass into Chuck's kitchen, sat at his counter, and slammed a beer. He made his standard gin and tonic.

"Not a bad day, Matteo. At least you caught a couple fish. More than yesterday."

"I caught exactly two small ones, and you caught at least fifteen, some quite large. What the hell was I doing wrong?"

"Look, I've been fishing this river for the last fifteen years. I know it like the back of my hand. Also, you must pay more attention. With this spinning gear, it really isn't that hard. Have you ever tried fly fishing? Now *that's* hard!"

"No, never tried that, I'm sorry to say. I do like your spinning gear, very high quality. It's just me, I assume."

"Yes, some of it is you, for sure. If you ever want to try fly fishing, you must first take a few lessons and be guided. But tomorrow, we will work on your spin fishing. But now we drink."

"What shall we do for dinner since you released all the fish?"

"I'll take you to another spot I love called The Red Dog Saloon, where they display Wyatt Earp's gun from Nome. Outstanding fish and steaks. Good bar too."

I realized that keeping up with Chuck and his party habits could be a rather challenging task, but I was game.

"Okay, let's get cleaned up and roll," Chuck said.

TWENTY
NIGHT MOVEMENT

Chuck and I plopped down at The Red Dog bar. I ordered a Bud and Chuck his usual. I smartly decided to avoid the hard stuff.

"You know, Matteo, life will throw you fastballs and then curves, and then a sudden knuckleball. Which one will you hit out of the park?"

"I can hit the fastball," I said.

"Well, that's not the one pitch you will get. You must learn to hit them all. Then you survive." Chuck burped. "Learning to predict each pitch is paramount. And most folks cannot do any of that. I cannot do that. Wish I could."

I wanted to tell Chuck about my long-lost skill but figured he would just laugh at me. But he was correct. I needed to regain it to survive.

"I want to venture far into the wilderness to straighten my crooked path. Any suggestions?" I asked.

"I do have an old buddy who owes me a big favor, and he is a hunting guide. You interested?"

"I don't hunt, but I could watch or fish while they hunt. Why does he owe you?"

"Let's just say that I provided his sorry ass with a safe haven from the authorities many years ago. He has been indebted to me ever since."

"Sounds perfect. Can you set it up?"

"Will do. He works out of Skagway, just up the way. I can fly you up in my little four-seater plane. Great way to see the sights too."

"I'm in. What did this fella do to upset the law?"

"Oh, nothing much. Just killed someone who deserved it."

I almost gagged on my beer. "What?"

"It was self-defense, but the law disagreed," Chuck said.

"Maybe this isn't such a good idea."

"The guy is harmless and wouldn't do a thing to you. He knows that would bring my wrath. He has behaved very well for years. He doesn't drink much anymore to my knowledge. Besides, it wasn't his fault. Leave it at that. If you want to venture deep into the abyss, then he's the guy."

"When I go, may I request the possession of your .44?" I sighed.

"Sure, just remember to leave the bullets in the chamber." Chuck laughed and gave me a hug.

"Order me another, *Matteeeeo!*" Chuck got up and headed to the restroom.

His absence allowed me to question my impending excursion with a criminal guide, apparently wanted by the law, to lead me into the wilderness. Seemed foolish and unnecessary. Surely there were supplementary, decent guides in the vicinity. When Chuck returned, I was speaking with the bartender about reordering, and I said, "Hey, Chuck, I…" I stopped mid-sentence.

To my surprise, sitting comfortably in Chuck's seat was an attractive woman. It took a few seconds to realize it was Gabriella with her long, lovely hair pulled back into a pony and a touch of makeup. She perched on Chuck's barstool in her Wrangler jeans with a mountain blouse of blended colors and a Levi corduroy jacket. Stunningly grounded.

"Hi, Matteo, is it okay that I sit here?" she asked somewhat nervously.

"Um, sure. It's actually Chuck's seat. He's in the little boy's room."

"Oh, sorry, I will move on. I saw you sitting by yourself, so I wanted to check on your fishing success today." Gabriella began to rise.

"No, no way. You stay right there. My choice is obvious. Shall I take the three-hundred-pound drunk and smelly Chuck or the mysterious, groovy ranger?" I smiled as Gabriella reassumed the seat while managing a partial grin. "As far as fishing goes, let's just say that I need some work. I caught two rather small ones, while Chuck landed at least fifteen lunkers!"

Gabriella laughed. "Chuck, the river, and the fish are all well acquainted with each other. The fish know that he is kind and will release them all to see another day, even with barbless lures on spinning gear."

For the first time, her face was only a couple feet from mine. I was mesmerized for a few, brief moments by her eyes, which glowed with tones of bright green and deep blues, by her thick sandy brown hair which flowed down beyond her shoulders in her thick pony, and by her skin which radiated the immaculate bloom of youth.

"Hello, Matteo. Are you okay?" she asked as I was at a brief loss for words.

"Oh, yes, just a little tired from today," I said.

Suddenly a gruff voice growled, "Well, well, well! If it isn't little Miss I-Hate-Everyone, and she takes my seat as well!" Chuck proceeded to hug us both at the same time.

"You old, sanctimonious bastard. That's not true. I do like you," Gabriella said as she punched his arm. "You can have your seat."

"I'll tell you what. I'll grab a table and chat with my buddy Josh over there, and you two Aquarius grass munchers take your time and join me for a bite soon, okay?"

"Sounds good. Thanks."

He waddled off yelling, "Hey, Josh, bring your drink, and let's catch up!"

Josh raised a thumbs-up from the end of the bar.

Gabriella laughed. "Grass munchers? Never been called that before. Lots of other things, but not that. Are you a vegetarian?"

"Not in the least. Tried once but started feeling bad quickly, so I went back to eating everything. I do try to avoid too much junk food," I said.

"Yes, me too," she said looking away from me.

"Would you like something to drink?"

"Sure, a glass of red wine, any kind is fine."

We sat in silence as we waited for her wine.

She looked at me and softly said, "Hey, I just want to apologize for my rude behavior last night. I'm sorry for asking you and Chuck to move along so quickly. I've used the same technique a million times up here. My girlfriends were ruthless on me for such behavior." She sighed.

"You must be quite popular to use the same line so

often. No big deal, Gabriella, it didn't affect me at all. I just cried all night about it."

She laughed. "I hope you had enough Kleenex to get you through all your sorrow."

"Also, I'm sorry for my rude behavior while writing you a ticket. In my defense, you would not believe some of the awful characters I've encountered. It's scary."

"So, you immediately assumed ill intent on my part because of my scariness?"

"I must be careful, but I could tell you were somewhat safe and handleable. Especially when I saw you trip and fall over."

"What makes you so sure you could handle me? I am larger than you."

"I could take you, if required." She smiled.

"Oh really? Want to arm wrestle?"

"No, I would be forced to embarrass you."

"Funny girl! Somehow, I believe you, but you should always have your guard up when alone in these woods."

"Often times we Rangers patrol in pairs, but on occasion my partner will be called away, and my job must continue. When I'm alone, I check out the culprit from a hidden distance before I approach. I have drawn my gun before and made arrests, so I'm comfy with it."

"Ever shot anyone?"

"No, not yet." She replied with a smile. "So don't push your luck. May I ask you a question?"

"Sure, fire away. No pun intended."

"What brings you up to these parts from Santa Barbara?"

At this moment, I decided it would be best to tell her the whole complicated story. "You got a couple hours?" I smiled wryly.

"I might, but a condensed version is fine too. Whatever works for you, Matteo."

Trying to keep things as simple as possible, yet understandable, I described my whole life from youth to arriving at Chuck's. I walked her through the Gargoyle Squad, high school, soccer days at Berkeley, girls, my marriage to Judy and Rose. I added my time in Vegas and employment with Uncle Tony, and the loss of Sweet and Rose. And much, much more. Including my escape to Chuck's in Juneau.

Looking directly at Gabriella, I noticed some wetness in her eyes, and I said, "Sorry to barf on you, but you asked."

She exhaled. "They really called you a Dago?"

I smirked. "Sure did, and I liked it. It did not bother me, although my parents hated it. But it had a nice ring to it."

"Did you not feel demeaned in some way?" she asked.

"Nope."

"Wow, quite a journey, Matteo. I'm so sorry for your losses. That's devastating." She was genuinely moved.

I decided to fill in the story because it didn't make full sense without an explanation of my rare skill. I had never told this before, so here I was about to expose my quirkiness to a stranger. Oh well, what did I have to lose?

"One more small detail, Gabriella, of how all this ties together. Are you confused yet?"

"Yes, just a little bit, such as how you helped your Uncle Tony so well? And Vegas? Just a good guesser?" she suggested with disbelief.

So, without further ado, I described my ability in detail for the first time. It took a while, but in the end, Gabriella just stared at me.

Finally, she commented gently, "That is so ridiculous that it must be true, I guess. Next, are you going to don a cape too, and fly away like Superman?" she said with a smile. "This is not some line you use, is it?"

"Not at all. All my lines are much more direct and usually fail." I laughed. "Yes, Gabriella, I'm strange, but it is all true. I've never voiced it because of what you are doing right now. Not believing it. But that's okay, it was good for me to release the pressure off my chest. Only my parents and a couple more know, and they were amazed by it. Now you, a virtual stranger, knows."

"I'm starting to believe you."

"Good."

"So, you still have not retrieved the power? And that's why you have escaped up here?"

"You got it, and I plan to achieve my goal. Years ago, I was at my best with all the clairvoyance when hanging in nature." I smiled.

She spoke with a sigh, "Geez, so sorry again. Suffering through those losses is beyond words. And your power is lost as well." She rubbed her forehead.

"So now you see why being labeled a Dago is low on my totem pole of stress," I said. "I've come to accept the losses of Judy and Rose because their return is impossible. Moving forward from that has been a sticking point for me, but I hope to regain my intuitive skill. I begin my journey here to instigate a rebirth of my soul as well."

We sat in silence sipping our drinks, pondering every-thing and nothing. I gazed back at Gabriella. "I guess the long-winded version wore you out."

"No, no, that's fine. I'm just amazed. Thanks for confiding in me. I won't tell anyone."

I looked at Chuck and Josh as they were engaged in discourse and laughter.

"Our options are limited to interrupting the two drunken sailors, or just remaining here," I said.

She smiled and pointed her finger straight down. She grabbed a menu, and we looked it over together, her face close to mine. Her pleasant aroma encompassed me, and I shook myself for being so foolish. At least she had loosened up and participated in an engaging conversation. I had no female friends in my bizarre post-Judy and Rose existence and gaining one would prove worthy.

Grinning again I said, "You know this place. What do you recommend?"

She sat upright. "I usually go for the steak sandwich with grilled onions and Swiss on sourdough with Heinz 57 or A1 Steak Sauce and french fries."

"No grass munchers here. Let's make it two."

After ordering, I looked at Gabriella. "So, may I ask what your story is and why you are here?"

She looked at me with a pause and pensively remarked, "It's a struggle for me to discuss, so maybe some other time? You wore me out with your gut-wrenching tales. It's remarkable that you are still functioning, I must admit."

"I just spilled my entire guts all over the bar, and you get to say nothing?" I affectionately nudged her. "A famous writer once said, 'You may talk, and I may listen. And miracles might happen.'"

"Very touching statement. I'll take note of that simple advice. Who was the author?" she said.

"Ernest Hemingway."

"Perfect! I love Ernest. Speaking about such a great writer reminds me of something about me that I don't mind sharing. It's kind of silly, but when I was in high school, I loved to write poems. When I was alone at home,

I would scribble assorted poems, some with rhymes and others without. Many would make no sense to anyone but me, and I made a big mistake because I didn't save any of them. It breaks my heart, and I've tried to recreate them, but I'm locked in a space that blocks my writing ability."

"Sounds like a familiar windowless closet to me. My space is dominated by fear and guilt, but I think both of us can navigate these scary tunnels someday, and Gabriella will write new poems."

Much laughter and idle chatter ensued as we ate our fabulous steak sandwiches. Time flew by and before we knew it, the saloon was practically empty. Chuck staggered up to us and said he would be in his truck and to come soon. He slobbered goodbye to Gabriella, and off he strolled.

"Quite the guy, that Chucky," she said. "He has a good heart, but I hope it holds up. It's supporting a bunch of weight."

"I must drive home soon. May I give you a hitch?"

"Okay, but it's not that far, so I can walk."

"No way, Jose! Let's go."

We split the bill after a light debate about who should pay. Half a mile later we arrived at her adorable, quaint house.

"You weren't kidding about living close by," I said. "Great location, walking distance to all the happening spots."

"Thanks, I bought it upon arriving here with my savings just to grab something. Gave me immediate purpose. It was quite run down, but I fixed her up. How long are you vacationing in Juneau?" she asked.

"Good question, and I'll stay as long as it takes for me to get back to normal. I have no timetable since Chuck granted me an indefinite stay. If he had a choice, I believe he would take me forever. He also arranged for his friend to escort me to the wilderness via Skagway. Flying in his plane day after tomorrow."

"Oh, my! I'm going there as well, but I must leave tomorrow for work the following day. Takes awhile to drive there."

"Well, maybe Chucky would be willing to fly you up along with me if you can wait an extra day. Hey, Chuck," turning to the back seat, I asked, "can you fly Gabriella up to Skagway too?"

He mumbled something incoherent and resumed snoring.

"I'll take that as a *yes*. Thanks Chuck." We both laughed and she said,

"I'm not convinced that Chuck knows what he just committed to."

"I'll deal with him. You are in, groovy girl," I remarked with a grin. "How shall I reach you once I verify everything with Chuck?"

"Well," she thought with hesitation and continued, "I can give you my number. I seldom answer, but I have an answering machine." She milled around in her purse for a pen and paper.

"You seem a bit pensive about this, so if you prefer, I can give you Chuck's number."

She paused with her hand stuffed in her purse while pondering for a second or two, and finally said, "Yes, that's probably the better idea."

"Sure, no problem." Being agreeable, I shared Chuck's number with her.

"Gosh, what is that smell in the truck? It's not me. Is that Chuck?" Gabriella asked.

"Yes, it's his breath! I've had to endure it a few times driving him home in his drunken state."

"Thanks, Matteo, I had a wonderful time tonight. A great break from my pushy girlfriends who I do adore. I think you felt comfy speaking with me about your life and traumas." She said, "After all, I'm just the strange, introverted ranger who wrote you up."

"Strange? Not the word I would use to describe you. Well, now you know all about my bizarre life, and I only know three things about yours. Gabriella owns a cute house in the woods, she loves grilled steak sandwiches with Heinz 57 sauce, and she is an aspiring poet. Come to think of it, that is quite strange."

She nudged me in fun, and out she jumped. Strolling away, she offered up a casual wave and a smile while entering her house. Driving the inebriated Chucky back, I wondered about the complex nature of Gabriella, and how reluctant she was to discuss her life. A hard nut to crack, yet she poked my imagination, something not experienced by me in some time. Rubbing my forehead, I concluded how foolish I was to be falling for a woman like Gabriella, but maybe she would develop into a safe companion. My only other option was Chuck. Once again, I dragged him to his bed.

TWENTY-ONE
THE MORNING SUN

The sun beat through my window. The warmth on my face sent tingles all over my body. I stretched, yawned, and sat up. Straight out my window stood an astonishing large moose casually eating the low-lying branches of a tree. I always wanted to see a real wild moose. Chuck said I would at some point, preferably avoiding the fierce creature face to face. I snapped a couple of pictures and as I dressed, the animal wandered back into his forest.

After a healthy breakfast of everything greasy under the sun, Chuck and I discussed Gabriella's desire to ride along to Skagway on his plane.

"I'm sure I can fit her cute ass on my plane, if required." Chuck grunted. "What's the purpose?"

"She has work in Skagway. Are you always such a gutter mouth? Maybe it is just a nice gesture to help her get to Skagway? Besides, I enjoy her company, even on a casual basis. I have zero friends up here except you, ya stinky old bastard," I said with endearment. "Gabriella said she would call you today to verify. I don't have her number."

"I have it." Chuck strolled off to find his address book. On returning, he gave me Gabriella's number, but I thought better of it as she had mentioned she would call. I spent much of the day packing all the necessary camping equipment. Chuck lent me his tent, sleeping bag, and sundry outdoor items, along with his far-out Kelty pack, a name brand I had admired for years.

In the early afternoon, I wandered out into Chuck's massive yard and discovered a large boulder down toward the lake, which I climbed enthusiastically. At the peak, a scenic view of Mendenhall Glacier emerged, stoking my strength. Peacefully, I sat cross legged, as usual, and relaxed my hands onto the spiritual rock supporting me.

The ancient glacier became my focus. I knew this stunning sight had formed approximately three thousand years ago, and it reminded me that my time on earth was nothing more than an indiscernible blip on the world's historical graph. During time, what other animals, birds, or lizards occupied this identical spot with this staggering view? All of us are just an unnoticed flash in the eternal universe. The spacious glacier dominated my thoughts, resulting in flashes of light and sparks shooting by my closed eyes. As usual, nothing more came to me.

I opened my eyes and searched the skies, yet again, beyond the majestic trees for a clue to the entity that had inspired my telepathy in the past. I pleaded for its return. I drifted into a meditative state, revisiting positive thoughts of my escape to these northern parts, a wild and unforgiving wilderness. An image of Gabriella appeared, and despite her issuance of a fishing ticket, she still gave my spirit a lift. I looked forward to seeing her again. My thoughts were rudely interrupted by the irrepressible, unmistakable, and obnoxiously endearing voice of Chuck.

"Hey, Matteo! I've got Gabriella on the line. Come chat with her."

"Be there soon." I crawled down the boulder and jogged into the kitchen where Chuck handed me the phone. "Hi, Gabriella. How goes your day?"

"All right, sometimes packing all my bags for these trips is annoyingly difficult. But it's coming along. What did Chuck say?"

"He's fine with it."

"Stellar! When do you guys leave?"

"I believe around eight a.m., but I can verify and let you know. Hold on." I yelled at Chuck, and he called back to me verifying nine a.m. "You hear that, Gabriella?"

"Yes, how can I miss the husky voice of Chuck?" Gabriella said with a giggle. "I'm so thankful, Matteo. Saves me a lot of time and gas to fly up there. Should I offer Chuck some cash?"

"No way, he enjoys doing this. Gives him an opportunity to show off his flying skills. We can pick you up on the way to the airport. His truck has plenty of room for the bags. Sound good?"

"Absolutely. See you in the morning."

"Gabriella, Chuck and I are grabbing an early dinner at Sally's Grill. Would you like to come?"

"Gosh, I'd love to, but I have too much to prepare before tomorrow."

"Shall we bring you an order to go?"

Gabriella paused and then answered, "Yes, that would be totally awesome. I appreciate that, really. I'm starving."

"We are going shortly, so you call in your order, and we will deliver it to you soon."

"Will do, and thanks again. See you in a bit." She hung up.

"Chuck, let's go. Gabriella is hungry, and we must satisfy the deity, yes?" I laughed.

Gabriella

On hanging up from my call with Matteo, I looked around my house and realized not one man had visited my house, only women, and the place was a mess. I instantly had regrets but abandoned the ridiculous thought and scurred around cleaning up the place, grabbing socks and under-wear scattered all over. I called in my order and began vacuuming. Maybe I should have said no, but in some ways, having them stop by was uplifting. Not sure why.

I am so stuck in the frazzled past of my life. One that began with shock and awe, then drifted to grief and anger, and now at this current point, it had finally settled into a lingering sadness and isolation that enveloped most of my soul, but not all of it. My fears did fester occasionally in my dreams, turning into nightmares where I envisioned myself drowning after falling off Mendenhall into freezing water, or plummeting over an endless mountaintop, or shooting myself. Over time, these visions became less frequent, to my relief. Living in nature helped calm my frayed nerves.

I threw on some jeans and a T-shirt and combed my ratty hair. Looking in the mirror, I realized the radical difference between my showy appearance in L.A. and this humble look in Juneau. Sighing heavily, I managed a smile, and reminded the mirror of my past confidence, and I said, "I will retrieve it!"

I got back to cleaning up. Lastly, I sniffed my armpits, which I had not washed or shaved in weeks. I gagged on the smell. Laughing, I rinsed off with a washcloth in my sink and threw on some deodorant. Why am I doing this? Then the doorbell rang.

MATTEO

Gabriella opened the door and gently said, "Hello, fellas, and come in. Sorry the place is a bit of a wreck."

"You kidding? This is the Taj Mahal compared to Chuck's joint." I laughed as Chuck scowled. I handed the food to Gabriella while she showed us around.

"Thanks so much for the food." She handed me some cash, but I waved it off.

"Chuck's treat. He never lets me pay anyway. Right?"

Looking at us, he rolled his eyes and said, "You kids are all spoiled. But what the hell, I can't take it with me to the grave. And you are my son."

"You're his son?" Gabriella asked with shock.

"No way, just his surrogate son in his quirky mind." I slapped Charles on the back. "Our food is on order, so we have to bail. Come with us if you'd like."

"Oh, thanks, but I have to pack. You guys have fun."

Off we went as Gabriella waved and shut the door.

Gabriella

Leaning on the back door, I sank down to the floor and held my head. What was that? I clean up, and even vacuum, and then don't even invite them to have a seat? What sort of shit ass hostess was I? And I should have accepted Matteo's invitation.

I screamed and teared up. Obviously locked in my shell, I stood and realized I must make a better effort to shatter this self-imposed cage that surrounded me. But I had attempted that many times before without much luck.

I wolfed my food and continued to pack while chastising myself from time to time, slamming cabinets and throwing more clothes on the floor. Eventually I sat down and cried.

Matteo

Chuck and I settled into our chairs at Sally's and enjoyed our meal of steak and potatoes with a trip to the salad bar.

"Did Gabriella seem a little discombobulated? Almost nervous, would you say, Chuck?"

"Yes, but you find that odd? Having us men in her house was unnerving for her. You know, no one that I know has ever been allowed to set foot in her house, especially men. I've known her for a couple years, and she is always cordial, but never reveals too much. She has those two crazy girlfriends of hers. Then you show up, and she accepts the food and allows us in. What's up with that? But it was ever so brief."

"She did listen to my pathetic life story the other night, so maybe she feels sorry for me, or she just plain wants me. Ha!" Chuck shook his head and laughed.

We finished our meal and headed back to the cabin for an early trip to bed.

TWENTY-TWO
INTO THE WILD BLUE

At approximately 9:00 in the morning we pulled up to Gabriella's house. I jumped out and ran up to her door. She opened it before I arrived.

"Hi, Matteo. I have a few bags."

"No problem." I went in and began to gather them.

Gabriella said, "Hey, I want to apologize for my lack of hospitality last night. It was rude of me to shove you guys out the door. Not sure what I was thinking."

"Oh, shoot, Gabriella, no big deal. However, we were disappointed because we had sprouted a sleepover plan of spending the night on your couches," I said smiling.

Slowly Gabriella caught onto the joke and laughed. "I guess I deserved that, Mr. Dago!" She smiled.

"Chuck snores like a freight train, so neither one of us would have slept anyway."

Gabriella loosened up considerably as we grabbed her bags and headed for the tiny airport. I did notice that all her actions made me relax.

Bumping down the road in Chuck's shockless truck, I

said, "Chuck and I made three breakfast burritos with the works. There's one for you."

"Thanks, gentlemen."

"You may call Matteo a gentleman, but not me," Chuck said. We all had a good laugh.

At the airstrip, we climbed into Chuck's six-seat single-prop plane and loaded all our baggage in the last two seats and some in his co-pilot seat. Gabriella and I squeezed in the second row. I tried not to show any excitement, but I was thrilled to sit so close to Gabriella.

"I will fly the scenic route, if you don't mind. It's not direct but the view is staggering, okay?"

We both agreed, and my heart soared in anticipation of witnessing the vast wilderness from so high up.

Chuck fired up his plane, which promptly stalled. This unnerving procedure repeated itself numerous times until the engine started humming. Gabriella and I looked at each other in distress.

"Everything fine with the engine, Chuck? It sounds a little questionable."

"This happens almost every time. No big deal. Besides, I once had to glide down to earth, and I made it," Chuck said with cryptic laughter.

"Not sure about you, Gabriella, but I've only flown on two planes in my life, and they were both substantially larger than this putt-putt," I said.

"About the same for me, Matteo, but I guess Chuck has made it so far, so here we go." She leaned nervously into me.

We motored down the bumpy runway and then up into the wild blue. The sky was clear without any wind as the rising sun cast golden sunlight across our view. Chuck took us over Mendenhall Glacier, an awe-inspiring perspective of this grandeur. Even though she had visited the glacier on foot, Gabriella was shocked by its size and beauty. Chuck continued through other valleys and raced over majestic peaks, astounding us with every rise and fall.

We were like kids in a Froster Freeze. As we continued this epic journey of natural beauty, I morphed from amazement to analysis of this delicate moment with my usual foolish, cerebral drifting.

Gabriella noticed my disconnect. "You okay, Matteo? You seem off in space. No pun intended."

"Oh, yes, I do this quite often since the losses from my earlier life. I overanalyze everything," I said with a smile.

"Tell me your thoughts."

With Gabriella positioned snuggly next to me, I began. "Well, I was exploring the significance of our plane and what it provides for me. This motorized flying vehicle allows me to separate from Mother Earth and all her trials and tribulations below. Daily struggles become minute compared to the eagle's nest on which I perch. I look down and absorb the awesome scale of the universe not only below, but also above, and this perspective can change my vision of life, or not. For me it does. I don't just half look, I begin to see with wide open eyes, you know? It could motivate and direct me, giving me aspirations and the ability to soar above the muck. It represents freedom and independence from everything with no boundaries, especially as we glide through these peaks and valleys. At any moment I can crash in a ball of flames, or my life can take a hard left, ditching all the simple minutia while moving toward something grander, even mystic. While inspiring, it forces all my fear to take a back seat as I journey toward a possible change or a simple peacefulness. Because we are so far up in the wild blue sky, it creates a sense of superiority above everything else. I know I don't speak like this in normal conversation, but it's how I think when I'm in one of my cosmic zones. How's that for heaviness, Gabriella?" I chuckled.

She looked at me in astonishment. "Quite impressive, Matteo. It makes plenty of sense. Amazing how you come up with this on the drop of a dime. Never thought of it that way, but I don't think I have your creative-thinking gene, and I'm not sure all my fear can fit in this back seat."

"Sure, it can. You must just let it, which is easier said than done. It's a metaphor for taking control in some sense, and I believe we are both on that journey. Are you on that path, Gabriella?"

Sighing, she nodded in approval.

Looking at her with hope, I said, "Tell me, what does this small irrelevant window mean for you?"

"Well, let me think, because it obviously must have some deeper meaning than just a window on a plane." She scrutinized its shape and felt the window with her hand. "It's a rare portal that gives us the required view to this new life?"

"That sounds perfect. Yes, a gift from the heavens, like a black hole to somewhere else." I smiled.

"Matteo, thanks for sharing your thoughts. They were stimulating. Not sure I can keep up, but I'm going to try."

"Or I'm just crazy, and it's my way of ignoring the fact that I'm scared shitless of our grand height in this flimsy plane."

We both laughed.

She poked my ribs. "You are funny in your own self-deprecating way, Matteo."

"The silent one has a sense of humor," I said rubbing my ribs.

"There are reasons for my lack of sociability, as you know, but was I not engaging at dinner the other night?" She quizzed.

"Of course, Gabriella. You're a poet and don't know it. Very enjoyable for me for sure, and to be perfectly honest, I'm not any better than anyone else with this whole friendliness thing. Over the past four years, I've come to dislike people," I joked. "But I love animals and forests. And you know what really bothers me? When humans hurt the animals that love us so much and rely on us for their survival."

She agreed, and we laughed, and we turned our attention to the great unknown beyond our window.

Chuck took us low to earth through the next valley where I caught a glimpse of a moose and a small pack of wolves. My heart jumped with joy as I grabbed Gabriella's knee and pointed to the wolves.

"Right on, Matteo, that's the bomb," she yelled patting my hand.

Her touch caused goosebumps while igniting my senses. Once again, I was thankful for my rediscovery of an attraction toward a female. I took it as a positive toward my overall healing. I smiled widely.

Gabriella took notice of my satisfaction and asked, "Why the big smile, Matteo?"

"Not only do I enjoy the wildlife on the ground but also the one in the sky right next to me. I enjoy your company, even with all your disillusionments of life, and your self-professed spiritual imperfections. Other than that, you are perfect in my foggy eyes, just like me." I gave her a smile and the okay sign.

"Well, thanks! I am regaining my confidence at a crawl. I'm thankful for your patience. I'm not an easy subject matter, as I admit."

"It might help me if I knew more about you, but you will share all that someday, if you want to. No pressure. As you know, I have my issues," I said lightly. "What would be great is revealing just one of your nicknames. That would be somewhat fun, yes?" I said with hope.

"Okay." She sighed deeply. "Let me think about that."

Things went silent for a while.

Then she spoke with some hesitation. "They all are demeaning, so it doesn't matter. So, he're two — Chesty and Sweet Cheeks," she muttered staring at me.

I chuckled a bit saying, "Those are nifty, and while I understand Chesty, I don't understand the Sweet Cheeks one. I assume that is about your face?"

"No, it refers to this." She pointed to her rear.

"Well, okay then! I get it. Those nicknames are flattering, aren't they?"

"I guess that would be in the eyes of the beholder. I suppose, in a demented way, they are a form of a compliment, but I did not see it that way, and the others are far worse. You may not have those."

"So, when you were younger, you were labeled with those nicknames, as well as others unknown to you?"

"Correct, professor."

"I'm a regular Einstein, aren't I?"

"When I was in my teens, I learned that no one chooses his or her nicknames. They materialize out of somewhere, for some reason, and someone picks up them, and any personal choice is shuttled. Does that make sense?"

"Yes, but I still can't believe Dago did not bother you."

"No, not really. At least Stinking Dago didn't stick. My parents always repeated a silly little saying whenever I got bullied by others: *Sticks and stones will break my bones, but words will never hurt me.* I hated that saying, but it is applicable when needed. Dago is just a word like Sweet Cheeks and Chesty, right?"

Gabriella sat quietly for a second or two and then said, "Do you think those words are an accurate assessment?"

I realized I was being baited. The correct answer was obvious not only for her sake, but also precise for me. "Obviously, I don't know firsthand, but if I had to take a stab, my answer would be yes, you possess an attractive shape. That's a plus in most worlds, wouldn't you say? A gift from Mother Nature, so good for you. And for those you recognize the attribute. It's all good fun. That's the way I look at it."

"Yes, I know what God intended for me, but I struggled to force a change to that, even though I was born this way. I have shaped two additional skills that do not use my genetic intention. Being a ranger and flyfishing. What good is my rear end except for attracting demented, slobbering men?"

"Let me see," I said as my erratic mind raced in circles. "Your above-average fanny is also good for sitting comfortably in a chair or even on a toilet seat without bruising. It also allows you to run faster due to its athletic shape and strength. Are you a fast runner?"

"Yes."

"Aha! My ridiculous theory has some validity. Your nice fanny can provide a place for different clothing to be modeled. Slick underwear and skimpy bathing suits may find a good home on your fanny."

"How do you come up with this so rapidly? If it wasn't so funny, I would cut you off at the knees."

"Okay, I'll stop. Wait! What do you call a Ghost's Butt?"

"Scary?" she said.

"Nope, Boo-ty"

Gabriella laughed.

"What do you call a Zombie's ass?"

She shrugged.

"A dead end," I said.

She smiled.

"What do you call a magnificent fanny, such as yours?"

"Big and fat?"

"Haha! Nope, wrong answer."

"Enlighten me, Mr. Dago."

"Ass-tounding."

Laughing even more, Gabriella said, "Okay, that's enough, Mr. Humor. You truly are slightly damaged, Matteo! But, for some reason, I enjoy the stupidity and the lack of relevance to anything meaningful. Shall we move on to something more intelligent?" She punched me in the arm.

Rubbing my arm, I said, "Hey, you need to know that you are stronger than you realize, so try not to bruise me anymore."

She smiled.

"You know why I'm going to Skagway. Why are you?" I asked.

"When I have breaks from my ranger job, I indulge in a recent passion of mine. I guide folks into the wilderness on instructional fly-fishing trips," she said confidently. "I also tie my own flies."

"That's bitchin', Gabriella. I'm impressed! I am going into the wilderness with a friend of Chuck's."

"You mean Dick?"

"Yes, the hunter, even though I don't hunt. Chuck has arranged for me to tag along. Honestly, I'd rather learn to fly fish with you. Maybe I could switch to your trip?" I said sitting up.

"That would be great except that I am fully booked. I can only handle two people at once, and these two are rookies. It will be difficult work. Possibly another time, though?"

We quietly gazed out the window. I was disappointed but decided it wouldn't be wise to show it. After all, she did break the ice with the revelations of her nicknames.

⸻

GABRIELLA

I sat bewildered by my insensitive comment, knowing perfectly well that I could accommodate an additional person. It's not the recommended number for a successful instructional guide, but I could manage it. What a spaz I am! I wasn't sure the other two would appreciate another member, as they all knew two was my maximum.

Also, upsetting Chuck's plan with Dick wasn't very nice either.

Keep on trying to justify things, Sweet Cheeks! I continued to block entry into my soul, and while it was perplexing, it also did not surprise me. Been doing it for years. What a mess I am!

Matteo even assessed me correctly, with humor, in identifying my social ineptitude. I believed he unknowingly still possessed some of his intuitive skill. I took a sneak peek at Matteo as he surveyed the outdoors. While the lens had always been focused on all parts of me, here, stuffed into this little vehicle high above the soaring trees, I found myself dissecting this stranger next to me, Matteo the Dago. He was right, it was an endearing nickname. Even with all its negative connotations, it still had a fancy ring to it! He really wasn't a complete stranger, I told myself.

His thick hair was sandy brown, a little darker than mine. His facial skin was unblemished and evenly laced with a four-day growth. His large eyes were protected by long lashes complimenting his green-brown eyes and dark brows. His hands housed long, strong fingers, and I suspected a similar strength to his clothed six-foot two-inch frame. I was five-foot nine inches, and he seemed much larger than me. He certainly was all man with moral fortitude, but his self-worth was lost because of his family tragedies. I'm sure he realized his attractiveness. He had great humor, but that may be a defensive position. But of course, I existed in equal turmoil, I told myself with self-pity. At least I felt comfortable around him, and I could use a good male friend. I continued to watch him as his chest ebbed and flowed with each breath.

***

Matteo

As I watched through the plane's window, the sun shifted, and it exposed a reflection of Gabriella's face. She was staring at me. I smiled and turned to her. "Did you like what you saw?"

She turned bright red, looked away, and laughed. "How did you know?"

"Your reflection was crystal clear in this 'portal to the cosmos.'" I pointed to the window.

"You are such a sleuth," Gabriella said. "Yes, I am guilty."

"Hope you enjoyed the view," I said with a smile.

"Hey, do you think Chuck is listening to our silly talk?"

"Not a chance, he has his headgear on. So, what if he did?"

"Just my paranoia at work," she said jesting.

Chuck waved at us and pointed down to the seaside town of Skagway as we began our descent. After gliding over the quaint town, we landed safely, to my relief on the nearby airfield. I had survived the gorgeous flight in the company of the beautiful Gabriella.

"Thanks for allowing my tagalong," Gabriella said while patting Chuck's shoulder. He flashed a thumbs up. "And thanks to you too, Matteo, for the delightful flight and discussions. You appear to have rescued some of your skills with all your in-depth analysis."

I grabbed my bags. "Thanks, but I am nowhere close to my earlier intuitive form. If I were, I could predict the color of your underwear," I said with a flimsy whim and walked away.

Gabriella laughed and shook her head in disbelief, grabbed her bags, and upon catching up with me said, "What makes you think I'm wearing any underwear, smarty pants?"

"Aha! Gabriella, good comeback! I guess I'll never know, but the visual was entertaining."

We both laughed and hurried after Charles. One of Chuck's compatriots, Hank, met us with his ginormous truck and drove us to Skagway obnoxiously lecturing us on the history of this frontier mecca.

"Did you folks know that this area was inhabited by

the Tlingit, which were a bunch of aborigines, and it meant People of the Tides?" Hank yelled.

"Goddamn it, Hank," Chuck said. "They weren't aborigines. They were indigenous people of the Pacific Northwest. More like ancient Indians."

"Well, maybe you're right. It was the Tlingit word Skagua that eventually morphed into Skagway, which means 'place where the wind blows.' It was founded in the 1890s resulting in the formation of the gateway to the Yukon and Klondike goldfields. Isn't that wild?" Hank said with enthusiasm.

We all mumbled in agreement.

"Became a real city in 1900. A wild boom town that catered to miners. And with miners, what tags along?" he asked.

No one said a word, and then Chuck whispered it to Gabriella.

She yelled, "Prostitutes!"

"Correct, my dear. And they say this place has more bars and brothels than Vegas has strip clubs," Hank said with pride. "The oldest brothel was the Red Onion Saloon. And guess what? It's still here, but now it's a great place for food and fun. The first large ship to dock here was the mail steamer, *Queen,* in 1897. What else would you like to learn?"

"All good for now, Hank," Chuck chimed in quickly as we all smiled.

We pulled up to the Skagway Inn for Gabriella, and Hank said, "This here hotel has been around for a long time, and each room was named after a renowned 'Lady of the Night' such as Essie, Kitty, Ida, and Grace, to name a few."

I helped Gabriella take her bags to the front porch, and

said, "Chuck and I are heading to the Red Onion at seven. Like to join?"

"Sure, I'd love to."

"We will pick you up just before seven. Bye for now." We gave each other a hug.

As I walked toward Hank's truck, Gabriella yelled out from the porch of the Skagway Inn, "Hey, Matteo! They are red with little pink doves!" Then she disappeared inside.

I laughed out loud and climbed into Hank's truck.

"What was that all about?" Chuck asked.

"Just a funny story, and maybe I'll fill you in later. She is coming to dinner with us, okay?"

"Good luck. You are wasting your time."

"It's never a waste of time to upgrade or increase the quantity and quality of your friends, Chuck, and I have only a few and none are female. Maybe Gabriella will be my first great female friend."

"Sounds like a good plan to me," Chuck said while slapping my shoulder. We drove toward the other ancient resort, the Golden North Hotel.

We picked up Gabriella at six-thirty and headed to the Red Onion and met the other hunters and fishers being guided by Dick and Gabriella. Davey and Rob were the hunters, and Gus and Mel were the fishermen. An entertaining group of folks, and Dick and Gabriella were especially close, which I found odd. They seemed like old friends. Perhaps that would become clearer someday.

In the morning, the hunters piled into a truck driven by Dick, and the fishermen went with Gabriella in another vehicle. I wished I was in Gabriella's car, but technically, I was one of the hunters. Stuffed with gear, our little caravan headed out to the frontier town of Atlin.

TWENTY-THREE
WHITEWATER

After spending one night in Atlin and fueled by a hearty breakfast, we scrambled in the cold morning loading everything we had into the two large rubber boats to motor down the Yukon River to the secret camping spot established years ago by Dick inside the Yukon Territory. The trip would take about two days and would span almost a hundred miles, but apparently the fishing and hunting was well worth the trip, not to mention the dazzling natural beauty of the surrounding wilderness.

While loading the boats, Dick educated and entertained all the fishermen and hunters about the river excursion and about the do's and don'ts while traveling the white-water sections.

Gabriella whispered to me, "Dick loves standing on his soapbox and scaring folks about the river hazards, but there is absolutely nothing to worry about. It's all easy. However, you'll find it quite entertaining watching Dick captaining his boat."

"Aha! Okay, thanks, Sweet Checks." I said lightly.

Gabriella looked at me, shook her head, and gently slugged my arm with youthful affection. "Not much hope for you, is there, Mister Dago?" she said in jest.

When Dick was done, Gabriella stood and concluded our education with a bit of history. "We will boat from Atlin past Whitehorse and on to Lake Laberge, and then to Dick's camping area. Lake Laberge was named for Michael Laberge, from about 1866, who ventured along the Yukon River to discover a telegraph route and happened upon an extra-long lake, now named Laberge. It is thirty-one miles long and about two to three miles wide. Whitehorse was a small town christened due to the nearby river rapids which resembled the manes of white horses."

It was chilly motoring along the river, yet Dick wore only a ratty T-shirt and stood in the back of the boat with one hand on the throttle and his other hand hanging freely. During all this wild navigating through the river, he was singing.

He looked back at Gabriella and shouted, "Keep up, girlfriend! Don't want you to get lost! Weehaah!"

I laughed and looked back at Gabriella, and she smiled while twirling her finger in a circle at her ear. So, this was Dick's sideshow that Gabriella had whispered to me. Some laughed and some commented with consternation, and in short order we all wondered if Dick actually knew what he was doing. Probably he'd end up leading us over a gigantic waterfall! But, to our relief, that never happened. The spiritual aura of the magnificent river settled around us.

My mind roamed free with wide open eyes. Birds flew up and down the river pursuing multiple species of insects. Abundant fish darted beneath us. On land many deer, a rare moose and playful beavers entertained our group as we drifted. Everything flourished in and around the river. Mother Nature's harmony accented the magnificent trees and mountains. This river felt like the main artery in this pulsating body called the Yukon. If there ever was a place for me to regain my previous strengths, well, God Almighty, it would be here!

My only wish was how nice it would be to have Judy and Rose experience this with me, causing me to slump backward into sadness. I shed a couple of tears, but I erased the feeling quickly and gazed back at Gabriella who impressed everyone with her professional approach to maintaining speed with Dick while adhering to the safety of her passengers. Gabriella certainly showed a little different approach than Dick, I thought. Soon she spoke to me quietly so that the others could not hear.

"Matteo, the more I think about it, I can easily handle one more in my fishing group, so would you like to switch and join my flyfishing?"

"I would love to, but that may hurt Dick's feelings, so maybe it's not a good idea, for his sake."

"I'll take care of Dick. He never takes anything personally with anyone these days, especially with me. Besides, he always does what I want. I'll clear it with him. You want in?"

"Yes, and thanks so much. I'm excited! I was never much of a hunter anyway."

As it began to darken, Dick and Gabriella pulled over and made a quick camp with a premade dinner, and we all bedded down early, for rising at the crack of dawn was mandatory for one more full day of travel on the Yukon River.

In the nippy morning cold, we burned through hot

coffee to defrost our chill while we hurried through breakfast. With the sun beaming and our boats comfortably arranged, we slipped upon the clear, clean Yukon water for day two of river travel. This serene setting glowed like a Claude Monet painting, gently saturating my mind with forever images of rugged tenderness. I stood in the boat (which was forbidden), smiled from ear to ear and howled like a wolf. The whole group turned and stared at me in astonishment. I turned various shades of red with embarrassment until Gabriella saved me.

"It's okay, folks, just Matteo expressing his long-lost hidden desires. This happens often to those needing the pleasures offered by this heaven called Yukon!"

The entire group rose and began to howl followed by laughter. But only one continued to howl, Dick, of course. as he remained standing, yelping and howling until Gabriella interjected.

"Dick, Dick, *Dick*! It's time to stop, and let's get motoring!"

Dick looked like a beaten dog and slowly guided his boat into the heavy current.

"Thanks, Gabriella, I drifted into my wild state without thinking of the others."

"Didn't know you were a wolfman, Matteo. Do you bite?" she quipped as she motored her boat into line behind Dick's.

I laughed and gave her a thumbs up, and she smiled and nodded. Deciding this could be another great happy place for me, I settled into my seat and chatted with Davey and Rob while traveling down the river.

While I loved all aspects of this beautiful river, something strange occurred. While perched in the bow of the boat, I watched two large, white-headed birds coming up the river directly at us. They flew over Dick's boat, circled ours, and began to fly away when suddenly one veered back, scanned our boat, and then swooped down and perched next to me. Amazingly it was a bald eagle, just three feet from me. Everyone gasped in wonder. This splendid raptor stood about three feet tall and stretched out her wings to six or seven feet.

Some in our boat murmured words of fear, and Gabriella immediately told everyone to remain silent.

With fierce yellow eyes and a look that could melt ice, the feathery bird stared directly at me and quietly examined me from head to toe. She then let out three straight screeches right at me, forcing me back into my seat holding my breath. Gabriella stopped the boat slowly and pulled out her trusty instamatic camera and shot a few classic shots of me and my eagle. Oddly, I now felt at ease with this bird of prey, and we calmly watched each other. Was this the same eagle I had met at Chuck's cabin? She let out a few more screeches and soared off. Everyone clapped with astonishment at this fabulous event.

Gabriella laughed. "I believe she liked you, Matteo. I snapped some great pictures."

Continuing down the river, I began to suspect that this great bird had spoken to me, just like the raven had so many years ago. What did this eagle signify? Slipping into one of my spiritual moods, I thought that possibly this raptor, with all its beauty and grandeur, must signify strength and courage and even pride. Maybe something different than the raven. Freedom came to mind since I realized the bird became the symbol of the United States during the Revolution. The bird could represent a new beginning for me without many boundaries aiding the growth out of my stagnancy.

I snapped back to reality and told myself to enjoy this special moment.

Near the end of the day, we arrived at our campsite nestled among the trees, shrubs, and boulders of the Yukon wilds. It was beautiful and secluded. Gabriella gathered us at the center of the camp area.

"As we face the river, on the far right, on its own, you will see the campfire spot. We keep it separate from our tents to prevent being smoked out while sleeping. In the middle and to the left are many spots for your tents. Choose as you please. The trail to the left meanders about a mile to the mountain edge where it ends without farther passage possible. The trail to the right follows the river's edge from whence we came for a mile or so, and it too ends in a thick forest. That's why we travel by boat since there really is no easy way out. If you choose to walk the paths, please do so with a partner, just for safety. Above our site far up is a flat, small meadow surrounded by large pines. It's a lovely place to expand your view, have a drink and relax. Enjoy your setup and please look forward to a few days of hunting with Dick and to fishing with me! Tonight, Dick will cook up some venison burgers with corn and potatoes by me, all starting with snacks by Rob and Davey and drinks by Gus and Mel. Then we wrap up the evening with S'mores and coffee by Matteo! Let's enjoy!"

It was nice to see the elusive one so content in her apparent happy place, the wild. I felt like the fifth wheel since Rob and Davey were friends as were Gus and Mel, so reluctantly I picked a tent site at the edge of our camp among the boulders and shrubs, a perfectly silent and isolated refuge.

Following my setup, I decided to check out the Meadow above, and I found Gabriella setting up her tent.

"Need some help?"

"Oh, thanks, but I got it."

"I'm going to go up to the meadow above, and wondered if you could be my partner?"

Gabriella looked at me and didn't smile. "Did you ask any of the others? One of them should be able to accompany you."

"No, didn't ask them. I wanted to go with you, our fearless guide."

"I'd love to, but I have too much to do here. But the meadow is so close, you really don't need a partner. Go for it. The hill is steep and treacherous, so be careful."

I wandered off to the hill, slightly disappointed but not surprised. Gabriella being Gabriella!

GABRIELLA

I stood and watched Matteo walk away in his handsome way, and I realized the extent of my rudeness. How hard would it be to go along with him? My dysfunction had won again. I walked into my half-built tent and cried softly, but just for a few brief moments. I felt much better releasing my emotions, and I exited my tent telling myself to grow up and conquer my demons. I wiped my eyes just in time to watch my tent collapse in a heap, causing me desperate laughter.

Matteo

It was a good struggle getting to the top of that hill, but it did open up a wonderful view of our site below and of the Yukon River. On the far side a path began with a fork to the left and a fork to the right. The meadow was covered in ground cover sprouting tiny yellow and purple flowers. A lovely mediative spot! I leaned up against the largest pine and began a spiritual search for something or anything that could pique my skills. Closing my eyes, visions began to race across my shuttered eyes, which was a good sign.

First a raven, then an eagle, and last a great bear. As fast as they arrived, they disappeared into thin air, leaving me sweating and breathless. What did it mean? It was excellent news to me that something triggered my clairvoyance, though fleetingly brief.

Standing up I wandered around the edge of the meadow, and something white caught my eye. I parted the bushes and to my surprise some white bones were scattered randomly. It jolted me briefly, but it must be some wild animal remains, perhaps. Heading back to the camp, I knew what the raven and eagle represented to me, but the bear was something new. He must symbolize the strength and fearless confidence I needed to overcome the obstacles blocking my path toward redemption and fulfillment. I smiled and gazed at the guiding skies while passing Gabriella.

"Well, you look happy. The meadow on the hill is inspiring, huh?"

"Oh, hi, Gabriella. Yes, it's a happy place filled with mystery! I did find some bones scattered about, just FYI."

"Yes, not surprising here in the wild. I'll check them."

TWENTY-FOUR
MORNING, RISE AND SHINE

n the chilly early morning dew, I struggled to leave my sleeping bag. I managed and exited my place of solitude and a fictional protector, my illustrious tent. Why do we continually feel so comfy and safe in our easily penetrable tents where any wild animal or ill-intended human could breach with ease? The tent's only true guard was against the Yukon mosquito, which seemed as large as a small hummingbird with the viciousness of an angry wasp. And when they attacked, they approached like a large squadron of WW2 Hellcat fighter planes.

Masterfully, I created a small fire at the main site and boiled enough water for the group's coffee. This was one of my two daily chores along with creating the S'mores for the evening dessert. Sitting quietly on a stump warming my hands and staring into the mesmerizing fire that engulfed me in its warmth, I drifted into one of my analytic stages and came up with this: The campfire is the center, or even the heartbeat of the campsite. The flames can begin life, sustain it, and end it brutally. All our motions and reactions revolve around it. It was living and emulated a bond between humans and nature. Even over-cooked hamburgers or charred hot dogs tasted fabulous. Sloppy, burnt S'mores satisfied the palate more than those prepared at home. The smoky haze was the secret sauce unmatched anywhere else. Awaking slightly from my drift, I felt the wilderness seep into my bones creating the sensation that my journey so desperately needed. I felt progress had been achieved in my travels toward regaining self-normality from my previous ten years of wandering from double losses. The power of my emotions was strong but uncontrollable. Tears came to my eyes as a voice broke my trance.

"You okay, Matteo?" Brightening my morning and glowing through the hazy morning air in her typical mysterious way was the pretty face of Gabriella.

"Yes, I'm fine, just considering the loss of Judy and Rose so long ago. It still grabs me."

"So sorry again, Matteo." She sighed and sat down. "Some events can be difficult to release, and often they can last what seems a lifetime. It's about learning to exist with sorrow or loss and to plod forward through all the muck and disillusions of life while finding a place of peace. But, as you know, I suck at implementing my own soapbox advice."

I stared at Gabriella in amazement at the depth of her interaction and her release of such emotion. "This is why you, too, ventured to these northern parts, to escape?"

Gabriella smiled. "Yes, it is why I came here."

I began to speak, but Gabriella interrupted. "But more important, today is fly fishing lesson day! Time to roust the troops." And she grabbed a cup of coffee and swayed away with elegant courage that confounded me. She showed more confidence in this particular environment, yet what had happened to this beautiful person that she could not speak of it? Once again, she had avoided the issue.

TWENTY-FIVE
THE LESSON

Following our hearty breakfast, we all gathered the assortment of disassembled rods and reels and proceeded to build our instruments for fly fishing. I assumed this would be relatively easy because of my years of successful spin casting. I hastily finished my assembly and proudly showed Gabriella.

She took one look, and a slight smile appeared. "The reel is on backward which is a common mistake the first time. Go ahead and fix it," as she moved on to the next participant.

Well, that was a fabulous start. That would earn a 'point' in Uncle Tony's fishing game. In a short time, we all claimed readiness and followed Gabriella to the edge of the graceful, meandering river.

We all sat on the stumps that had been placed for our comfort. Gabriella stripped off her water-resistant outer shell and stood before us near the river flow. Without her frumpy ranger outfit, she was an enlightening experience. She wore slightly form-fitting wick-away cargo pants and a teal Patagonia quarter-zip shirt that allowed her full unrestricted motion. I was hardly paying attention to much else. A far-out angel had dropped from the sky, and she was in her element. I gazed up to the blue sky as the top of the trees swayed gently in the wind.

I looked back at Gabriella, and she turned her back to us and began the cast. Her right arm moved effortlessly forward, slight pause, and back behind her, and another slight pause. Repeating this motion, she spoke of the necessity of fluidity in the entire process, emphasizing the ease of it all. Her hands, arms, chest, back, fanny, and legs were all in a relaxed, congruous motion as she had instructed us. Slowly, she released more line with her left hand and continued to cast. Twenty feet, thirty feet, forty, and more.

Her final forward cast floated through the air, and the dry fly gently embraced the water surface a second before the entire line lay upon the water's surface without a single splash. She looked back at us to continue her lesson, and without notice, something struck her fly with power and purpose. Gabriella quickly lifted her rod with a peaceful, yet distinctive, flick of her wrist, but the beast was gone.

She giggled and said, "This was an excellent lesson on exactly what *not* to do as the fly connects with the water's surface. Never look away! I turned to speak to you all and removed my eyes from the fly. This is a big mistake as you will only have a split second to set the barbless hook before the fish is gone. That's all they need to identify the fly as counterfeit."

Gabriella continued the lesson for the next fifteen minutes, and then lined us up to practice some casts. Thankfully, and probably arranged on purpose by

Gabriella, there were no trees or shrubs behind us for a good distance. Feeling good about that, I began my casting and instantly wrapped the line around my neck. Recovering from my buffoonery, I cast again and while improved, I still hammered the water with my line with brute force. Whatever fish were there scattered. Sighing, I continued and made progress, but this was not as simple as spin casting. At about noon, we all took a welcome lunch break and sat on our stumps as Gabriella served up some turkey sandwiches.

"No steak sandwiches on sourdough?" I jested.

She smiled. "Not today, but maybe later." She winked at me.

I melted.

We ate as Gabriella continued her fly-fishing lecture.

"I'd like to dive into the aspect of fly fishing that many folks simply don't identify, and it's hard to accomplish in other solitary sports. As one dedicates more time to this event, the spiritual pull and solitude of something as simple and timeless as fly fishing emerges. With spin casting gear, one is trying to muscle out a huge chunk of metal or fake cheese in an effort to kill everything that attacks the terrible treble hooks. Fly fishing is an effortless, spiritual, meditative event that embraces all that is calm and correct in life."

"There exists a primeval attachment between the water, the barbless fly, the fisher, and the entire experience. It has the power either to frustrate the mind or to soothe the soul with healing, transformative effects all in the same breath. It requires ultimate patience and concentration in a pleasant connection with nature."

"Meanwhile, all other aspects of nature swirl around you in support, the sky, the wind, the trees, the birds, and much more. As a captured fish is gently released to see another day, I think of it as a rebirth of sorts. With the practice of *catch and release* the fish can, unbeknownst to you, encourage you to take risks, be kind to all, and follow your dreams in similar fashion."

I sat there starring at her in amazement, with a full load of a turkey sandwich in my mouth. Pieces of turkey and bread fell randomly out of my mouth. What else could this girl do? Now she was a bitchin' philosopher, too?

She continued, "Also, there is an intense spirituality to the fish itself. And this goes far back in history. Fish, through fly fishing, are unique to different cultures. The fish, as I mentioned earlier, can be seen as symbols of rebirth. They multiply randomly and rapidly. The fish reflects notions of intelligence and potency, and they represent a symbol of restoration and security. Just depends on the culture."

"Many people fly fish to connect to the celestial. Many cultures also view the fish as riches and plentitude in their lives because it is found in the lifeblood of all nations, the rivers and lakes filled with fresh water. The fish that we chase are the trout, and to me they symbolize hope, love, and community. They swim with their group and protect each other. The majestic breeds have remarkable patience in their hunting methods."

"So, to catch one requires patience from you, the fisher, as well. We also keep only the fish that we must consume for survival. When we catch some, I will clean and prepare them with my Buck knife which I keep strapped to my ankle. A handy tool to keep close. You never know when you might need it. I will interrupt all my babbling with a famous quote: 'Many men go fishing their entire lives without knowing it is not the fish they are after.' Anyone know who said this?" Gabriella quizzed.

None of us could guess the correct writer, but we certainly threw out a few, such as Hemingway, Fitzgerald, Hawthorne and others.

"Henry David Thoreau," Gabriella said with a sigh. "I have one more quote, and this came from one of our presidents:

'Fishing is much more than fish. It is the great occasion when we may return to the fine simplicity of our forefathers.'

"Any guesses?"

I raised my hand and said, "Theodore Rosevelt."

That was wrong, so a few others took a shot, but we all missed the mark.

"It was Herbert Hoover," she said with a smile.

I think she liked stumping us.

"But I will say that Matteo's answer is the most popular choice over all my fishing expeditions. And it makes sense since Teddy was such an avid outdoorsman."

Following lunch, we reloaded and continued to practice with multiple failures and a few successes along the way. Gabriella did assist each of us individually, and I took note as she gave personal attention to the other two before coming to me.

"Your casting, although it eventually makes it out there, needs to have a gentler touch. Your motions are still too severe. This is a common error for first timers. No need to self-flagellate too much."

She came up behind me and grabbed my hand while pressing onto my back and began the motion. She instructed me to just relax and let her do the movement. Her final forward cast allowed the fly to land peacefully.

"This make sense?" she whispered.

"Yes, it does," I said exhaling, but what really made sense was her proximity to me. So kiddingly I said, "I think it would be best if you keep doing this with me for about the next thirty minutes. Yeah, that would be great."

She pushed me gently and moved on with a chuckle. We practiced all afternoon and then wrapped up the day back at our camp where I dutifully prepared the smores for the evening delight. We all participated in the preparations and had a scrumptious time of overeating. Some bourbon drinks appeared magically, probably from Dick. The hunters and the fishermen shared their stories. Gabriella was relaxed in this environment and told some enthralling and joyful tales of her previous trips to this area as well as some dangerous ones. Dick did the same, and let's just say that Dick's tales were rather cryptic but laughable. Things began to wind down, and I presented my smores to many cheers. Eventually, folks wandered off to their tents.

Gabriella and Dick were the last to leave and wished me a nice evening and were gone. I stoked the fire and decided to hang on for a while and to enjoy the calm by myself.

GABRIELLA

Settling into my tent, I curiously peeled back the opening just enough to glimpse the dwindling campfire and Matteo holding his head. I hoped he was okay since he had been under some duress earlier. I allowed the tent flap to drift closed, and I lay there staring at the tent wall, overanalyzing everything and unable to sleep. I tossed back and forth. I jumped up, got dressed, and exited my tent.

TWENTY-SIX
CAMPFIRE

Staring into the iridescent flames, I began to drift back again to my morning excursion and into the meaning of the campfire and its surroundings. I laughed and wished that I had just another small nip of the bourbon which had evaporated with Dick and Gabriella's exit. Closing my eyes, I allowed my imagination to run, and a few sparkling lights flashed before my eyes. My spirits lifted as these strange lights were often present during my days of intuition. I sat up straight and focused intently on the lights and tried to press more out of my thoughts. But things stalled as thoughts of Judy and Rose interrupted. I held my head in my hands and teared up. Looking up, a haloed figure approached but was blurred by my watering eyes. Coming into focus, I could see that it was Gabriella, waving.

I waved back and said, "Oh hi! Did you forget something?"

"I couldn't sleep. May I join you for a while? Or would you rather be alone? You look a little sad."

"No, no. You are welcome. Have a seat as there are plenty here." I extended my arms left and right. "I was just drifting back to my campfire analysis from this morning and was interrupted by thoughts of Judy and Rose. It's always a good thing, but it does sadden me. Hence my tears again."

"So sorry." She sat down and slumped forward to stoke the fire. "May I join in the campfire assessment?"

"Sure, it's nothing more than a rather childish game I dramatize. You sure you want in?"

"Sure! Groovy." She clapped her hands and pulled out a flask.

"Well, what does Gabriella have there?" I asked. "I thought Dick provided the bourbon, but it was little Miss Fly Guide herself!"

She laughed. "I am the guilty one for sure, but I like it when others blame Dick. Care for a little?" She handed it to me.

I gladly splashed a shot into my cup, and we enjoyed good cheer and a sip. Why didn't I think of bringing some libations? Always an excellent choice around a campfire.

"What kind of bourbon is it?"

"It's Maker's Mark, a rare select brew," she said with confidence.

"Excellent! I'm impressed with your taste and selection."

"It's one of the few things I consistently got correct in my life."

"Alrighty. So what does the campfire mean to you, Gabriella?"

"Well, I would say…" She thought seriously and still hesitated.

"By the way, there is no right or wrong answer," I said.

She said, "I'd say that the campfire is a symbol of hope and happiness throughout the world." She raised her hands high. "How about you?"

"The campfire is the sun and everything else exists because of it. Did you know that the calcium in our bones comes from stars? Carbon, iron, and even oxygen originate from exploding stars that shoot their elements in all directions helping to form everything we see today, including our bones. The endless stars connect us all. For some, stars are small bright lights, but for others, stars are symbols of something far greater, something spiritual, perhaps even a guiding force, possibly even the entity I'm trying to identify. We have kinship with all these moving things."

"That is so boss! I love your answer way more than mine," she jested.

"Both our explanations are fabulous, so the campfire is the sun with all hope and happiness orbiting around it." I laughed. "What about other items in our camp?"

Looking around, Gabriella said, "I believe all our log seats are planets, what do you think?"

"I like it! I had the same conclusion, so it's a done deal. The log seats are planets. And the different size rocks?"

"Those must be asteroids, correct?"

"Yep!" I agreed. "And the millions of stars? Those are fascinating. What shall they be?"

"Maybe those can be all our friends and neighbors shining down upon us. Or possibly the force that guides you?"

"Good analogy," I said. "I know this is somewhat silly and the answer seems obvious to most, but not to me. These vast heavens are brimming with seemingly endless stars that shine light which travels forever without stalling or expiring, right? So why don't the skies shine brightly twenty-four hours a day? I mean, I understand our sun is on the other side of the world half the time, and that's why it's dark, but what about all the light from these zillions of stars? Shouldn't they light us up some? I'm just saying…"

"I don't know how to answer that, so let's go to the library again when we are back and research it. Or maybe we are being too naïve."

"Okay, sounds like a plan. How about you and me? What are we in this game we are playing?"

Gaby wavered and deferred to me to lead on this one.

"Since you move so elegantly, I'd say…" I paused for a moment and decided to go ahead. "You are a gorgeous shooting star, racing across the heavens." I smiled.

She clasped her hands together, and smiling she said, "Thanks, I'll accept that." With a blush, she continued, "And what should Mr. Dago be?"

I laughed and appreciated that Gabriella suddenly became this blossoming flower that had been locked in for a long, cold winter while she embraced this silly game with passion and enjoyment.

"Well, that answer is in the hands of the shooting star."

Gabriella pondered pensively while twiddling her fingers and staring into the fire. The flickering light of the fire struck her at just the right angle so that her face shifted between shadows and light depending on the strength of the flame. I quickly fanned the fire to maintain the glow on her. Watching her think, her face was endlessly youthful, even though she was thirty-five. Flawless preservation sat before me. The wavering firelight penetrated her eyes just at the right angle so that they lit up like sparkling diamonds for just a moment.

And then she calmly said, "I think you will be a stellar, handsome spaceman flying to save the world!" She smiled and blushed again as she grew silent thinking that she had blurted out too much.

"That makes me smile since no one has called me handsome in a long time, except for Judy. I'll gladly accept the label and even a spaceman to boot. Maybe space cadet would be more appropriate." I chuckled.

"You are handsome, Matteo, that's why I said it. It just came out, so it is true."

"Thanks." We both paused and watched the essence of life, the flickering fire.

For her sake I changed lanes and said, "What should the trees and sky be?"

We bantered back and forth in good cheer and came to a unanimous decision.

"The trees are the almighty gods of the universe, and the sky is the illustrious home for all of us." She spoke euphorically.

"Nice, Gabriella. We have created our own eclectic world that rotates around the star of all stars, the bomb campfire."

We both clapped. We clicked our cups in a gentle cheer and then rested quietly absorbing the warmth of the fire. Neither of us spoke, and it felt calmly relaxing. Previous tension did not exist between us now, and it was natural, at least to me.

Gabriella moved her gaze to me. "What are you thinking? You seem deep in thought."

I didn't want to scare her back into her rabbit hole, but I went ahead with the truth. "I was enjoying the moments spent with you and how relaxing it all appears. No judgements or requirements laid on each other, other than that I must improve my fly casting."

She smiled.

"Also," I said, "I was beginning to think back on some predictions that occurred earlier in my life."

"Such as?" she asked.

Our discourse came to a halt as a wild, deep roar resonated from the distance.

We looked at each other and Gabriella said, "It's a bear, probably a grizzly. Many live in these parts. We are not their food of choice, but they will eat us occasionally."

"Isn't it rather dangerous at night when we sleep?" I asked.

"Dick doesn't sleep much, so he stays up and stokes the campfire with his firearm cocked and ready. We're safe. In all the trips I've guided, nothing has ever happened."

"Famous last words, they say." I laughed.

"So, let's ignore the bear and return to my question about your earlier predictions."

I sat up straight on my log seat and reflected, "Not sure at what age because it was a while ago, but at some point in my youth at the height of my intuition, I predicted that the world order would change over the coming four to six decades, possibly with the rise of the more plebian sector, such as the Hispanics and Asians and other subgroups. Dominant nations may exchange places with lesser ones, with some being eliminated entirely. The last part of my vision encompassed the role of the female human being since that group would morph toward some level of grandeur in many places but would collapse in others. When I look at you, my thoughts and foresight become blurred yet begin to focus on something." I sighed.

"And what, pray tell, is that Mr. Dago?"

Smiling I replied, "You know, when you speak my nickname in your glorious way, it has an individual twang to it that is slightly sarcastic, yet affectionate. I enjoy the fun of it."

Engrossed, she reached out and took my hand. "What are your thoughts about me?" she repeated with curiosity.

Thinking more and looking directly into her wide eyes, I said, "You belong in the future. Through all your trials and tribulations, you have developed, it seems to me, far beyond your peers. I'm not aware of female fly-fishing guides other than you, and frankly, I've never met a female ranger either. You should have been born sometime in the present moment instead of thirty-five years ago." After taking a sip of bourbon as Gabriella took a bigger slug, I continued, "In some way you will be a leader in the advance of women, a trendsetter so to speak, I think. Possibly through education or lecturing or even the fashion world? If I still possessed all my strength, I could grasp something physical of yours and probably gather a more accurate appraisal of you. But alas, we will just have to wait until I retrieve what I lost. By the way, you are squeezing my hand quite hard."

Realizing her faux pas, she released it and said, "So sorry. I was transfixed, and my hand is sweating profusely." As she dried it off on her pants, she said, "I've never had a sweaty palm before!" She pulled back.

I examined the sweat on my hand, and I stroked it on my other hand creating an electrical pulse through me. Shutting my eyes, I said, "I see various cameras, lots of photographers pointing at something or someone. Maybe you were a photographer, or being photographed in your earlier life? You enjoy taking pictures of people and places?" My thoughts vanished as fleetingly as they arrived.

"Looks like I retrieved my power for a few brief

seconds there. Maybe there is hope for me," I said with excitement. "Any of what I said correlate?"

Staring at me with her lower jaw slightly dropped, she muttered, "That's pretty good, Matteo. You are on some correct course with this. I guess you really did own something incredible before your losses. Matteo, what happens if you never retrieve your influential skills?"

"Then I will perish in the process," I said "But I will try my hardest. Besides if I do fail, I must say this is a fine country to be laid to rest in, surrounded by massive forests and all they have to offer, including your spiritual grayling."

Smiling gently, she said, "I would be sad to have you pass, so you need to get to work even harder and find what you're looking for."

"It's nice to have someone believe it other than my parents. How did my thoughts compare to your life?"

"Gosh, that could take a while and hey, big day tomorrow as all you fishermen will be on your own while I observe. Maybe another time? Thank you for the enlightening conversation about the magnificent universe, our campsite. Campfires rule!" She lifted her fist to the sky, gave me a big hug, and sashayed off to her tent. She avoided her life again, but whatever, I was getting used to it.

I rose as well and started to turn toward my tent when I noticed Gabriella's bourbon cup at the side of the fire. Looking from side to side, I reached down and grabbed the cup, surrounding it with both hands. Sitting on the ground with my legs crossed I held the cup firmly, closed my eyes, and focused on Gabriella's cup. Concentrating on her DNA with all my effort toward an extension of my recent intuitive connections, my mind remained steady except for a few bright flashes of light that raced across my eyes. Even though that was a good sign, nothing more occurred with the same unfortunate conclusion. I was still stuck in a different time. Disappointed, yet hopeful, I sighed and strolled to my tent.

It was a bit colder tonight, so I dumped my clothes in a pile next to me and bundled up in my sleeping bag surrounded by my impenetrable fort, my tent. Ha! I thought briefly about the campfire fun with Gabriella and began to drift off when suddenly a shuffling noise outside my tent aroused me. Listening carefully, I suspected a bear.

Without hesitation I grabbed the .44, and a soft voice spoke, "Matteo, are you awake? Gabriella here."

My heart jumped, and I unzipped the tent. "Hey Gabriella, I almost shot you! What's up?" I asked.

She was rubbing her arms in the cold, and said, "I was thinking a little, which is dangerous in my case, and if you are up for it, I'd like to talk to you further."

"Of course, I couldn't sleep anyway," I fibbed. "But you are freezing, so come inside. There's plenty of room."

"Okay, let me get something warm, and I'll be right over." She ran off.

In a rush, I cleaned up some of the mess in my tent, like old underwear and socks, and brushed all the dirt to the side to make some relatively clean room for her.

She entered my tent clothed in her pajamas with sleeping bag and pillow in tow. "I know what this looks like, so I'm sorry to just barge into your tent, but it's all innocent. You sure it's okay?"

"Absolutely. But don't think you can just take advantage of me so easily just because I'm almost butt naked in my bag," I said cheerfully.

She waved her finger at me in a playful way. "I want to

apologize for being so evasive with my story, but I've only been able to discuss it with a few close girlfriends, and they have all sworn secrecy. I know speaking of my story may help me in coping, but I have not been able to bring it to real life yet. You have been more than accessible to yours and have no fear of it. May I speak of my life, and can you accept my silly terms of silence?" She smiled.

"Well, how formal of you. Of course, I've been waiting with bated breath. I am Italian, so we WOPS capisce the Code of Silence, eh?" I shrugged with my arms out. "I'm all ears, and by the way, I still have plenty of fear from my past."

Gabriella slipped into her sleeping bag and began.

TWENTY-SEVEN
THE GRACEFUL MAJESTIC ONE

Gabriella paused, looked at me, sighed deeply and remained quiet. I smiled at her and said, "Just start, and it will flow like the river." I attempted to illuminate things with the knowledge that losing this rare moment was a possibility.

GABRIELLA

"I lost both my parents when I was young, around eight. I lost my mom to a car accident. My dad was driving, but he suffered only scratches and bruises. The accident was his fault."

MATTEO

I contemplated touching her arm in sympathy but refrained from such, not wanting to interrupt her monologue.

GABRIELLA

"My dad fell into a deep depression because of his guilt and his responsibility in mom's death. It devastated me as well. Dad began to drink excessively, and darkness began to envelop us. He became aggressive and often senseless and babbling. He lost his job as an engineer and began to circle the toilet. And then he began to strike and abuse me with his fists and belt. I had no choice but to run away. I feared for my life and ended up at my neighbor's one night, and they notified the authorities, and Child Services came to whisk me away. I wanted and needed my old dad back, but he never materialized. He drank himself to death shortly after." Gabriella welled up with tears. She took a couple of sips of her water.

Matteo said softly, "This is devastating. I guess we both suffered a double loss. Unimaginable. So sorry."

She nodded and wiped her tears, and after a few brief moments, she continued. "I had no siblings or grandparents or uncles or aunts that I was aware of, so I was fostered for a while. Various folks were interested in adopting me, but nothing happened, and I was not told the reasons why. I felt as if there was something wrong with me. Prospective parents came and went.

"I was skinny, gangly, dorky and spoke infrequently when interested contenders would interview me. I refused to even look in my mirror. Earlier in my life, my mom and dad noticed that I had a worthy voice, so I took some singing lessons. While in foster care singing helped me cope. But it just was not enough. I came close to running away from foster care when suddenly it was announced that I had a home and some new parents, ones I had met weeks ago. They were an older couple, Robert and Elaine Atterbury.

"They lived in a beautiful house in Beverly Hills with gardens and a dog named Mona. I missed my parents so dearly, but this couple helped me adjust while I began to normalize in a limited sense. Not sure I ever truly recovered from my trauma, as you know full well, Matteo. I attended the local school where I met some nice girls and boys, but I was a nerdy type, so I engrossed myself in all my classes and subsequently became a voracious reader. I loved my English class with Miss Collins. She became my surrogate older sister and helped guide me when my life fell apart, as it did on numerous occasions."

Pausing, Gabriella took a drink of water, smiled and continued. "Over the next year or so, I continued on this straight and narrow path. I did not attend parties or school sporting events. They seemed interesting, but I could not pull myself out of my box and participate. I found that I enjoyed greater strength than all my girlfriends, and they encouraged me to play sports on their teams, especially soccer, but I refused. I was a fast runner, but I did not care. It seemed like an overabundance of pressure to me.

"I know I'm weird in that sense. But that was me. Just

enjoyed the studies and, of course, I got all As. Then one day I discovered something that helped me navigate through hectic times in high school. Poetry. I would isolate myself and write verse after verse. Although much of it seemed senseless and silly, it made me relax and smile. As a result, I happily accepted an A in my creative writing class.

"At around twelve to thirteen years old, things began to change. Over summer break, I morphed toward womanhood in a hurry. I really didn't understand it much because no one had educated me about these changes. Especially menstruation. That was frightening, but my stepmom helped me through all the pit falls and educated me without question. Both my stepparents began to compliment me on how pretty I was. It didn't make sense to me, but I loved the attention. Parts of my face grew into perspective with my skin clearing up from pits and pimples. The most alarming thing was the transformation of the rest of me. I grew from a skinny five-foot four-inch stick to a five-foot-eight-inch woman. My chest grew dramatically to the point of embarrassment.

"Elaine got me some bras, but I outgrew them promptly, and she would say *Oh my, Gabriella, you are one healthy girl,* and she would run out to get me a larger size. My legs, butt, and hips filled in proportionally, but all my clothes failed to fit. Robert told Elaine to take me shopping for something that would fit properly. A whole new wardrobe came my way. How fun, I thought. I even started using some of Elaine's makeup. She enjoyed showing me the process, and I loved it.

"I returned to school that fall, and things began to change there as well, not particularly for the better. Some of my girlfriends became jealous of my looks. I was embarrassed to some extent because some of them still had not changed. My best friend, Lucy, would say, *Gosh Gabriella, you look so hot! What happened? And you have nice boobs! I want some.*

"At around fourteen years, the boys and bullies emerged, and my nicknames grew. No longer was I just Gaby, but more outrageous names popped up, like The Rack, Chesty, Boobalicious, and Sweet Cheeks, which referred to my fanny, but you already know that one. But I will still save you from the worst ones. Without even going on one date, which I refused anyway, I was labeled the class Hose Bag.

"This was tough to handle causing me to pull back yet again, and I dove only into my books and poetry, avoiding class dances and other events. Boys asked me to go to these functions. I refused.

"I became adept at writing and reading to the point of entering contests at school and winning some. But I did not wear form-fitting clothes just so I could focus without interruption… until one day. While loading up my locker with books, one of the bully boys, Zack, walked by and goosed my ass with vigor. I jumped forward and hit my head on my locker door. Jerking around in shock I saw Zack and his buddy walking away laughing. Lucy said, *Those guys are such assholes!* and my blood raced, and, running up to Zack, I yelled his name. He turned, and I slugged him directly in his face and watched him crumple to the floor bleeding while holding his face. I shook my hand because it hurt while realizing I had never done anything like that before. Lucy cheered me on, as did some other students, and they mocked Zack for getting hit by a girl. In short order, I landed in the principal's office along with Zack and his bloody nose.

"As we sat quietly in front of his desk, Mr. Plambeck shuffled some papers around while occasionally looking up at us. Eventually he stopped and asked me to explain.

"I explained that Zack had grabbed my ass hard, and I hit him.

"Mr. Plambeck confronted Zack for verification. Zack lied and refused to comply with the truth. I mentioned that Lucy and others had witnessed the event, and Zack eventually broke down and confessed. He was confused and admitted it, thinking I would like it. And here's the troubling part — *Mr. Plambeck asked me if I had liked it!* I paused at the absurdity of his question and replied that I had not. Zack began to cry, and I felt sorry for him, but only for a few seconds.

"The principal told him that his behavior wouldn't be tolerated, and he would be calling Zack's parents. Zack did apologize as he left the office. But then the principal told me that I couldn't get away with hitting someone. I was suspended for five days. I began to protest when Mr. Plambeck asked me to calm down and then asked—

Are you sure you didn't tease him with all your curves?

"At that point I realized the epic fruitlessness of my complaints. I asked if I could be excused, and Mr. Plambeck waved me out.

"Before going home, I went by Miss Collins's office and sat with her for a while and unloaded my day's trauma. She helped me get through it with some thoughts to ponder, like how there are good men out there; they are just hard to find. She educated me with the confusing thoughts that often embed themselves in the minds of very young men. Their actions reflected a bizarre way of showing affection, but without any remote sense of suitability. And she continued with a bit of blame on Zack's parents for a lack of proper training as well.

Can't live with them, can't live without them.

"She went on to explain that all of us have been through it and very few emerge unscathed. What Mr. Plambeck had said about my curves was grossly inappropriate, but she explained that there was nothing to be done about it.

You are learning about boys and men, huh?

Live and Learn.

"I never forgot those two statements from Miss Collins."

"She gave me a big hug, and feeling better, I headed home to inform Robert and Elaine. They were fine and, at my request, they did not take it any further with the school. I wanted it all to fade away, to disappear. As I lay in bed that night, I realized it was a compliment, in some bizarre way, that Zack had grabbed my fanny instead of any of the other girls'.

"Within six months, I ventured out of my box out of sheer boredom, and I was tired of touching myself."

"By year's end, I lost my virginity with another classmate who was part of the basketball team. Jeffery was his name, and we dated for a while but drifted away from each other due to his philandering. It was an educational experience for me that will have a permanent home in my soul, for better or for worse." Gabriella stopped and drank some more water. "How's that for a start? Now you've learned something about me, yes?"

"Very interesting and quite the beginning. The sudden loss of your parents is beyond comprehension, but you are plowing through well, it seems to me. Also, I learned how popular you were with the boys, which makes plenty of sense. And now I have a few nicknames for you. But I'm curious, what are the exceptionally bad ones?"

"Maybe later." She laughed and sighed.

"Well, you could have been labeled a Dago."

"If I was, would the female version of that be Daga?" She grinned.

"I have no idea." Matteo laughed. "But good question. When we return to Juneau, we can explore the adaptations of Dago at the library."

"Would you like me to continue for a little while longer?"

"Sure, go for it."

GABRIELLA

"At home, my parents kept saying how beautiful I was, and they took many pictures to record their theory. I remained shy about all this because it all felt foreign and intrusive. Eventually I began to like the photos, and some made me smile. One day, my parents came to me and said a magazine photographer wished to speak to me. I became suspicious, because how did a magazine photographer find out about me? I asked my parents if they were responsible, but they denied it. After some hesitation, I agreed to call her back, and the next day I met Carly, the photographer.

"We spoke for about thirty minutes and in the end, I was completely comfortable with her. She did say that one of the teachers had informed her about pictures from our yearbook. I could only think of Miss Collins, and it made me smile. So, at the tender age of sixteen, I began to sell my face, through Carly's photography, to large companies for ads. My lips were used by Elizabeth Arden, and Max Factor, and my eyes for makeup by Maybelline and by Covergirl, and my thick hair was used by Johnson's Baby Shampoo, White Rain, and others. All parts of my face were employed, and I was paid handsomely for these rather simple jobs.

"I concentrated on my studies to finish the school day in time for my afternoon photo shoots with Carly. I ignored all further extracurricular activities at school, such as parties and sports. I only wanted to do my job of standing there to make money with my face. I saved most of it to help pay for college, as advised by my stepparents. They were extremely giving but could afford only so much. It increased my confidence to save my pay.

"One day, Carly asked if I would care to expand my repertoire with full body shots in bathing suits. Of course, I had hesitations and spoke with her about those, and told her I would think about it, deciding that speaking with Miss Collins would help with my decision.

"Miss Collins readily expressed mature opinions, as always, encouraging me to stay focused on studies while working and to be certain to get an agent. She advised me to protect my money while reminding me that I only have one life to live. Sometimes it can be uncomfortable employing a part of me that wasn't on my radar. Miss Collins repeatedly encouraged me to remember that I happened to be gifted in a few ways, including straight A's in school. She told me that my good looks wouldn't last forever, so go ahead and use them without compromising my integrity. Miss Collins was always there for me.

"I returned to Carly telling her about the guidance from Miss Collins, gave an affirmative answer, and my work expanded. I still had disturbing issues with ignoring my mind through this physical process but plugged on. My photo shoots expanded from mountain hills to the sandy beaches of Malibu and Newport Beach, and even up to your hometown of Santa Barbara. I met other gifted women, and we shared some of the same positives and negatives of our glorious jobs. We all felt fortunate.

"We were born this way, so embracing it became our way of life. I also took night classes at the junior college in creative writing and foreign language. I learned French and Spanish since they stimulated my brain, something I desired in opposition to my physicality. After about six months, I was selected to be in the *Sports Illustrated Swimsuit Edition*, and my income soared. I became known as *the* supermodel of our school, but I seldom attended school anymore.

"I need to visit the little girl's room, the bushes. Be back soon."

Matteo

The entire forest was our bathroom, and that made me smile, but our forested bathrooms did not have showers, and I realized my smell was increasing with each day. I wondered if Gabriella noticed, but crap, she probably smelled too. Gabriella returned and snugged up in her bag. Just her simple motions were graceful.

"Do you and Dick bathe somewhere out here, or do we suck it up until returning to Skagway?" I asked

"I wash off in the river, but we have a requirement that someone on shore must stand guard with a weapon, just in case of trouble. But there are no other women on this trip, so I'll wait until we resume civilized life."

"Like which threats are most common?"

"Varies, but the usual suspects are wild animals, miners, mountain men, and the occasional deranged Indian. Things are relatively safe these days."

"Well, since there are no other women, I can watch for you. Promise not to look," I said with jest. "I would love to wash off as well, but you wouldn't have to return the favor. I can get Gus or Brad."

Gabriella gazed at me, thinking, and then said, "I'll take it into consideration. God knows I could use a bath as well. Gus and Brad are against guns, so I doubt either one has ever shot one. I wouldn't want to arm them without instruction. They might shoot you." She laughed. "I can spot for you too, if required. I'll continue my story another time, okay? I'm sleepy now."

"Sure, whatever works. I've learned a lot about you and look forward to learning more about Sweet Cheeks!"

Gabriella rolled her eyes, punched me with demented approval. "I think this is a good time to stop. I'm worn out recounting everything."

"Not a problem, but it's good to listen to you here in the woods, so I assume things all worked out. But, sure, I want to hear the rest at your leisure."

"I apologize for the long, winding road, but it just kept pouring out." Gabriella sighed.

"It's getting late with a big day of fly-fishing tomorrow, so let me escort you to your tent."

Gabriella looked at me. "I'm a little frazzled and don't want to be alone. May I sleep in your tent?" she said shyly.

"Sure, whatever makes you feel relaxed," I said without showing my pleasure in her stay. My sick mind thought of a way to lighten things up, so sitting up with a straight and serious face, I proceeded, "I do have one perpetual, non-negotiable requirement of all the single, attractive female guests who choose to invade my tent."

Thinking that she should return to her tent, Gabriella said, "I won't sleep with you, Matteo, so save it."

"What makes you think I want to?"

"Hmm, you're a man?" We both paused and then she said with remorse, "Sorry, that was inappropriate. I take it back."

"It's okay, you are correct. I am a man, I think," I said.

"I can't imagine what the requirement is but go ahead and enlighten me with your rule."

"All my uninvited female guests may not, under any circumstance, *fart*," I said seriously.

Gabriella raised her eyebrows momentarily and immediately broke into hysterical laughter with a futile attempt at remaining quiet, and said softly with tears in her eyes, "That's a rough requirement." On that note, Gabriella proceeded to laugh and snort loudly and suddenly, without warning, unloaded a monster fart.

We both had a difficult time keeping quiet as we buried our heads in our sleeping bags in a useless effort to calm down. Eventually we emerged waving our hands to clear the air.

Gabriella said, "Apparently, I'm not one of those attractive females that swarm your tent."

"Not true, Sweet Cheeks. But it is nice to know you have imperfections. On *that* fragrant note, is there anything else before we try to sleep?"

With a serious look Gabriella said, "It's all your fault."

"Huh? What the hell is my fault?"

"Your S'mores caused me to poof." She began to laugh again.

"Poof?? Is that even a word? Good night Gabriella, and if you don't calm down, you could earn a swift spanking," I said dryly.

Smiling a bit she said, "Yes, sir, Mr. Dago."

We both slipped away to sleep. My dreams that night included memorably vivid intimacies, a first in many years. Throughout the night, many beautiful women drifted down from the heavens into my sleepy illusions.

Waking a little later, I noticed Gabriella was snoring soundly as drool slipped from her mouth, and I smiled as it pleased me to see her content. Transfixed by Gabriella's peaceful demeanor, I knew that I was falling for her, even more than before. Imagining Judy's spirit hovering above me, would she approve of my draw toward Gabriella?

Shaking my head, I attempted to ditch the thought as I knew perfectly well that falling for this woman was nothing more than a lark. I needed to pee, so I exited the tent and found a bush. While going, I gazed up at the trees as they shadowed the peeking half-moon. The treetops moved subtly in the light breeze, and I took a deep breath absorbing the smells of the powerful pines. The fragrance soothed my soul creating a powerful euphoria that made me stumble.

Gathering my senses, I returned to the security of the almighty sleeping bag thinking briefly of my evening with Gabriella, and I concluded that she was the graceful, majestic one, unlike any other. As I still searched for what squired me on these far reaches of civilization, could my elusive, unappointed, spiritual guide be Gabriella? I drifted off to sleep and fell into my dreams.

TWENTY-EIGHT
MINERS

Upon rising in the early morning, an eerie mist crept through our camp, leaving an uneasy feeling in my bones. I justified the sensation to a distinct lack of sleep and prepared the campfire. In the wee morning hours, Gabriella had snuck out of my tent like a bandit on the run, just so rumors wouldn't fly through our camp. Although I enjoyed the thought of such mischievous scuttle-butt. Much chatter and hot coffee spread through our group, and following a hearty breakfast, Gabriella prepared us for the first day of fly-fishing on our own. She would be there to help when required, and in my case frequently, I hoped.

Fully outfitted and raring to go, the three of us followed our illustrious guide along the path to the river in order to walk along the flow of beauty. I breathed in the cleansing air and admired the sky dotted with colorful clouds and teeming with flying wildlife. I smiled easily at this special scenario.

Two gunshots interrupted my beautiful vision.

"No worries," said Gabriella calmly. "Most likely just the hunters with Dick chasing their prey. Let's hope they feed us well tonight."

We all agreed that adding a few graylings to the menu would make it a feast. My first few casts frustrated me no end since I caught a tree branch in my back cast, and my second cast snagged on the bottom of the river, snapping my line. But with the professional Gabriella around we all began to perform adequately, landing some fish, and the thrill of it enlivened us all. I caught my first wild grayling fly-fishing with a dry fly, which looked like a mosquito. It sent me soaring with pride, a sensation my existence had abandoned over the last ten years. Smiling and laughing, I cast out again, albeit not a good cast but a cast, nonetheless. Gabriella wandered over to me as I headed up the trail.

"It appears that you are experiencing some pleasure all by yourself, my tent friend."

"Yes, but I've gotten used to entertaining just myself over the last decade."

"So, you see the value of fly-fishing? While it's the hardest style of freshwater fishing, it is also the most gratifying, isn't it?"

"Yes, I understand your message about the connection with nature not many have experienced. Thanks for allowing me to join your group, and Dick didn't mind?"

"No, being inherently a little lazy, he encouraged it."

"Sweet Cheeks, I wanted to say how invigorating my conversations have been with you not only around the campfire but also in my tent. It's been forever since I've had such conversations with a woman. Knowing more about you explains a lot about your devastation."

She smiled and both of us quietly looked at the mesmerizing river with its gentle, hypnotizing flow.

"Gabriella, do you ever dwell on your purpose in life? I mean, what are you here for?"

"Gosh, I've never thought about it. I've spent a good deal of my life avoiding everything, you know? When I was a little girl, I wanted to get married and have kids, something Mother Nature intended. But, of course, that failed to materialize for various reasons, so now I think my appointment on earth is to teach folks how to fly-fish successfully," she said with conviction, "And to stop those without a license." She laughed while nudging me. "How about you?"

"Oddly enough, you've hit upon what I've come to believe. We have all been plunked on this dazzling earth for one big reason, other than propagation, of course."

"What? Fly-fishing?"

"Yes, in a circuitous way, but when I was young, running around predicting and solving various puzzles, I did it unwittingly, but only for me. Through time, and trial and error, my brain eventually enabled me to distinguish my real reason for existing. To help others, to give them the best opportunity to better themselves in their quest, and you, Gabriella, are doing that in your own indomitable way, teaching others not only to fly-fish, but also to absorb the connections it has with nature, which ultimately heals us all. As I said before, it's why I traveled to these remote parts. I think a deeper connection with the wild may help me regain what I've lost," I said with a smile.

"Yes, I enjoy your approach. More than my answer. So, I'm helping others through fly-fishing?" She thought for a few seconds. "I do feel very satisfied when I watch my students flourish and smile, even Mr. Dago."

"Thanks, Gabriella. I'm slowly improving and if I fail, I'll have only my teacher to blame. I'll keep up my hard work and someday I'll show you how good I can get at this."

"Your thoughts make me wonder if we are also on this earth to help *everything*, not just other humans."

"Well, I'm not going to help a mosquito."

"Why not? Aren't they on earth for a purpose?"

"Like what?"

Gabriella thought and then said, "They act as a great food source for spiders, animals, and bats, and even aquatic predators, like the trout. And believe it or not, some mosquito species can help certain plants cross-pollinate."

"Brilliant! Did you major in the History of the Mosquito in college?"

"Very funny, but on a serious note and whether you realize it or not, you have helped me without question, since I now can relate a bit more than usual, and I believe it's a consequence of various chats with you," she said with a glow.

I nodded in agreement. We had unknowingly wandered away and out of clear sight of Gus and Mel.

"Shoot, I need to get back to them, so let's continue later. I'm sure they are tangled in the bushes."

Abruptly, our connection ended as shots and screams rang out, reverberating through the tranquil forest and causing all the birds to screech and bolt for the skies. Gabriella and I looked at each other with confusion.

"Gus and Mel! I must find them."

We started to run when Mel staggered around the trail corner stooped over holding his chest. He fell. We rushed to him and rolled him over.

He stared at us while spitting blood. He mumbled some incoherent words and continued to breathe harder and rapidly.

"What did he say?" I asked.

"Mel! What happened? We can't understand you." We both leaned close to his mouth while he gasped his last word. "*Run!*" He passed away.

I grabbed Gabriella's hand, and we bounded directly into the thick underbrush of the forest and dived face down hidden from view. We held each other and looked into each other's fearful eyes and took deep breaths to quell our trepidation. In a few brief minutes sounds emerged from the trail, only steps from us.

"This one is a goner as is the other, but it looks like there may have been other people just here. Look at the other footsteps." The man pointed to the ground. "Search the area." They rustled through the brush, and both Gabriela and I knew that we would be discovered. We sighed and decided it would be best if we just surrendered since the two men were slowly making their way to us, just yards away. We knew that shooting at them with our pistol would probably fail as both men were equipped with automatic rifles. To avoid being immediately shot on sight, Gabriella grabbed me.

"Please don't shoot! We are right here in front of you." We both sat up and waved our arms. Two armed men stood before us with large rifles pointed directly at us. Both men were large, overfed, and fearfully ugly. One had a dirty black bandana wrapped loosely around his head and the other had an old camouflage John Deer baseball cap. I recognized this man: He had that large scar running from his ear to his mouth. It was the same man I had met exiting Eddie's tackle shop in Juneau. Both were dressed in hunting outfits with military boots that blended with our forest environment.

"Lay on the ground," the bandana man said.

They tied my hands behind my back and secured a rope around Gabriella's neck. They removed the .44 magnum from my waist. One man, his name was Buck, grabbed Gabriella by the hair and dragged her, screaming, out onto the open trail. He kicked her in the stomach, and Gabriella stopped resisting and choked. The other scarred man, Pierre, laughed and shoved me out as well.

"Looks like we got a couple perpetrators, Pierre!"

"Let's take them to the landing spot above the river where we usually take the others and do what we need to do."

The other man barked, "Don't even try to escape."

We obeyed.

"Why are you doing this?" Gabriella said fearfully, "I've been here before. I'm a fishing guide…"

Buck quickly backhanded Gabriella across her face, causing her to spit blood while collapsing like a ragdoll.

"If you talk before we ask, you die." He continued to drag Gabriella along with me in tow.

"Hey, Buck, this one is a babe! Maybe we throw her in with the others for production back at the compound?"

"Maybe, Pierre. I think she is too old. But not for me," he snarled.

The trail led to a familiar open, flat, grassy area on top of a small hill overlooking the river. This was where I had hiked when we first arrived and discovered all the old white bones. My heart sank to my feet realizing what lay ahead for Gabriella and me. Buck held Gabriella down while Pierre tied me to a large pine at one end of the meadow. He punched me a couple times making me gasp for air, and he stood back. "Tell me why you are here, and are there others?"

"Just fly-fishing and hunting," I stuttered, regaining my breath.

He kicked me, returned to Gabriella, and they began to tear off her clothes.

"Fight, Gabriella, fight! Leave her alone, you pathetic assholes!" I screamed.

Buck turned to Pierre and said, "Go ahead and shoot him. He's bothering me."

Pierre stood, and while Buck began to grope Gabriella, he picked up his rifle and raised it toward me.

GABRIELLA

I lay pinned under this dreadful excuse of a man, and the fears and anxieties I had labored so long to expel launched themselves back into my soul. The old scenes from my youth reappeared with vengeance causing me to cry for a second. I had worked so hard, and lately my ghosts had not appeared as much as before. I was healing, but now all the evil came back. I knew, as Matteo had said, that I must fight, and while Buck's stinking, hot breath and horrific body odor made me squeamish, it also gave me the strength to resist.

I kicked, screamed, and fought like a honey badger. My strongest assets were my legs, and I lashed them out relentlessly to repel this scum. Buck, foolishly, released my right hand in an effort to control my legs, giving me a split second to grab my fishing knife from my ankle holster. While Buck waited for Pierre to shoot Matteo, I struck blindly and sank the sharp blade deep into Buck's upper inner thigh and forced it across this leg.

Buck released a loud howl and fell off me, staring at the knife in his leg. He began to spout blood profusely while weakening. Pierre failed to shoot when he heard Buck scream.

At the same moment, and unpredictably, a flash of brown fury exploded from the bushes to Pierre's left, and he turned just in time to witness his last sight on earth, the huge teeth in the snarling mouth of a gigantic grizzly.

At first it looked too big to be a grizzly, but in fact, it was. It was Golden, the famous large bear of Juneau lore with the blonde stripe down his back. I slid away from the injured Buck and removed the tight rope from my neck. Golden finished off Buck, and with a few violent jerks removed his head and threw it in Matteo's direction. As I stood, the bear stood at the exact same time right in front of me, ten feet of fury, shocking me to freeze. His six-inch claws wavered directly in front of me, and I stared into his dominant eyes; a breathless moment of fear encompassed me. These few seconds I knew were the last of my life. Inexplicably my body became calm, and my legs became heavy. It felt like my feet had grown roots. Suddenly, without warning, Golden released a deafening roar and swatted me off the meadow down the steep hill.

TWENTY-NINE
OUT OF THE MIST
POST ATTACK, 1984

Matteo

till in a daze of death, I drifted through clouds of either smoke or fog or something unknown, a foreign substance interfacing with a gel-like liquid, shifting from freezing to white hot. Do all the doomed experience this or was it unique to me? I saw shooting stars, one brighter than most, and I envisioned this as Gabriella, who also must be dead, filling me with sorrow. Maybe I would find her in this new medium.

My eyes were open, but viewed nothing other than purple haze, out of focus and claustrophobic. I suffered no pain, apparently a common thread among the dead. How can the dead feel anything? Yet I envisioned various disillusionments. Portraits of my dad, mom, Judy, and Rose sifted aimlessly through my purple space, and I tried in vain to voice their names, eventually succumbing because dead men cannot speak. The image of Judy continued in my dreamy, diminished state.

There she drifted right in front of me, smiling as if she had never perished. Trying to smile back, my arms reached for her but never moved. I tried to scream as the image faded. Drowning, burning, strangulation, shot, disease, depression are multiple ways to perish. The list is endless. Does this mean the dead will float through all mediums forever, feeling nothing, speaking silently, seeing everything through filters of this cloud? This may be Heaven, or perhaps a space below but above Hell, where we are attached to everything, but doomed to nothing. Lastly, I surmised that death may be a pleasant experience, not a dark hole of eternal falling.

Inexplicably, my eyes hurt, and I blinked and blinked, and the dryness began to moisten, the fog briefly separated allowing my tearing eyes to focus. Large trees appeared while a slight breeze jostled my hair, with pine needles and cones at my feet. Further in front of me lay the separated parts of the two dead men. I could not move since my arms were tied back against the tree. My lost memory returned, giving me the realization that I may be alive. Or?

My final recollection had been of Golden descending upon me in shocking fury. They say when violent death is inescapable, fear blinds you as you prepare for the end. Hearing something, I looked slowly from right to left and held my breath in horror as twenty feet away, curled up in a huge ball of fur and having a nap was the gigantic, peaceful Golden, snoring away the day. Perched on a branch just above the slumbering bear was that bald eagle I had encountered on the boat.

Scattered next to the bear were a few bones of the dead men, stripped clean of skin and flesh by the beast. I was alive? Maybe Golden was saving me for a snack later. I had no way of untying myself without waking Golden. I just slumped over wondering if Gabriella had survived. Exhausted and sore from the ropes, I passed out.

At some point later, I was jostled to consciousness by a snort that blew spit and hot breath into my face. As the saliva dripped down my face, I realized that Golden was merely inches from me. He began to sniff me all over, and I feigned my unconscious state, even keeping my eyes shut.

Instinctively, I did not react in the slightest, nor fight nor scream. I remember Gabriella instructing me never to look directly into the eyes of a grizzly, as death would be the reward. But I could not control the small amount of fear tears that seeped from my eyes, rolling down my cheeks. Golden sniffed them and proceeded to lick each drop until they stopped. He must have enjoyed the salt. The beast shuffled all around me, and after sitting down near me, he rubbed his ears with his front paws, moaning with pleasure at the extent of his scratch.

I was able to view this activity by opening my eyes slightly. Golden pointed his nose to the sky, sniffed the breeze, and casually sauntered to the largest nearby tree. Standing on his back legs he stretched out his two front paws and leaned against the tree. He pushed with all his strength. The tree moved slightly beneath his power. He turned around and rubbed his back on the bark.

It staggered me to witness his actions without his noticing me. Or did he? And then it began to rain, but it was not water but thousands of pine needles and cones flowing down enveloping Golden, and he rolled in them with a growling passion. Standing, he shook himself clean, sniffed the air, listened, and suddenly galloped off with a distinct mission in hand. The path to the right forked, and Golden took the left fork with the bald eagle following.

Somehow, I had survived without a clear explanation, but maybe it was an extended dream? I looked to the skies and watched the great trees sway ever so slightly in the wind. I struggled in vain to free myself from my shackles. I gave up, hung my head and rested again.

THIRTY
AWAKENING

GABRIELLA

hit the ground with a thud and felt pain on my left side where Golden had slapped me flying over the edge of the hill. The bear ran at Matteo, and I heard him yell, "Run, Gabriella!"

With abandon, I rolled down the steep hill unable to stop myself. Tumbling over and over, I glanced off trees and came to a rest far down the hill. I lay dazed and confused. Various sized boulders were all over the hill and at the bottom. Miraculously, I had missed all of them.

I had careened off a few trees and felt lucky, hardly able to move. I opened my eyes, lying face down in the dirt. Turning my head I looked straight into the eyes of a small white mouse that stood on its haunches looking at me while sniffing the air. He ran off, and I felt like telling him to come back. It reminded me of a time long ago when I raised pet mice, and they all became my friends. When I came home from school, they would all gather around the cage until I allowed them out to sit on my shoulders as I walked around the house. My stepmom thought I was crazy and was afraid of the harmless creatures. But I needed their company. And I wanted this wild mouse to stay with me now. I crawled to the nearest tree and leaned up against it. Checking my body, I had no serious injuries, just multiple bruises. Still in shock, I gazed up to the top of the hill and noticed the great head of Golden staring down at me. I reached for the .44, but it was gone, taken by the miners. I sighed, looked up, and Golden turned and disappeared from my sight.

I sat still for a while thinking of the tragedy that had just unfolded, and felt devastated that I could not help Matteo, a loss I did not wish to endure. Now that he was gone, my affection for him poured out, and I began to cry. I wished I had treated him with more fondness but was unable to ditch my emotional cage. Never had I met a man such as Matteo, so kind, so attentive, and always there for me.

What a fool, and now he was gone, and I must forge on, but I felt like dying instead. I thought for a few minutes and decided to climb back up and deal with his body. He would do that for me. If Golden was there, then I would perish with Matteo. Gathering my senses, I stood and began the arduous climb to the top. Trying to remain as quiet as possible. I rested every twenty feet, trying to maintain strength to avoid tumbling to the bottom again. I looked at myself. I was covered with dirt and pine needles, and I reached up and felt my hair. It was a rat's nest. I muttered to myself that I must blend in well with my environment.

Halfway up, I paused and began to think, which in my case could be dangerous. I had run from my past in a rampaging effort to locate something to fulfill myself. I did find extreme value and reward in learning the fine art of fly-fishing and becoming adept at teaching it. I'd studied and mastered the requirements of becoming a dedicated ranger. I'd learned to handle and shoot a gun, something this model never even imagined.

In so many ways, I had accomplished my goals and felt fantastic but was still unfulfilled. Yet often the answer is so obvious that it can't be seen by someone looking too hard. It's like someone must drop the proverbial brick on my head. Naturally, even obsessively, I searched and consciously avoided people and events countless times, dismissing everything and everyone while always seeming happy.

Perched on the side of this hill, covered in dirt and pine needles, it dawned on me that whenever folks act happy all the time, it means the opposite, sadness. Rubbing my eyes to clear the tears, I now understood the glaring solution to my frustrations, and it had been swirling around me over the past few weeks, making me laugh and cry with intellectual compassion and humor meshed with Matteo's own tragic tale. And now he was gone as fast as he had arrived. Pouring his personal life onto me was like pure mountain stream water bathing my mind of negativity and ultimately, and shockingly, it spurred me to enter his tent and reveal some of my discombobulated life.

Trying again to justify the fact that I had known him for only a few weeks failed miserably because something about him had eased my pain with the noninvasive power of persuasion. I had a chance to exorcise my demons by simply accepting this warm, blessed being who stood patiently in front of me, washing me with humor, with keen discourse, and with compliments. But no, I retreated again to my defensive position and screwed myself in the process while discouraging him at the same time. Although he still stood in front of my blinded eyes. Sighing, I began to climb again, quiet as a mouse. The task ahead of me seemed insurmountable and deadly, but I pushed ahead.

As I approached the hilltop, I sank into cold fear created by the realization of my impending end of life, and here I was about to experience it for the third time in one day! I knew bears seldom abandon their kills for fear of others pilfering their catch. I hoped the .44 magnum would be close as it would be my only chance. Stopping a few feet from the edge, I lay quietly in the dirt and pine needles, and oddly I felt remarkably comfortable. I smiled at the frivolity of my effort, sighed, and gathered my wits for the obvious mayhem that lay ahead. I had hoped that most of Matteo would be intact for a decent funeral, as it was his wish to be buried in the remote woods of our majestic wilderness.

My heart skipped a few beats as I cautiously peeked over the hill and first saw multiple body parts scattered about. I suppressed a scream and pulled back gasping for breath until I calmed down. Gathering my strength, I stuck my whole head up and scanned the setting. My heart jumped as my gaze settled on Matteo slumped over still tied to the tree! I noticed well-picked bones scattered near him, but no blood on Matteo, and no sign of the killer bear. I refrained from yelling at Matteo as I noticed a glitter to the right, the .44 magnum near the torn remains of our dead captors. After hesitating for a final look around, I bounded over the hill and rushed to the gun. No bear. I ran to Matteo, he looked up, startled, and I hugged him repeatedly.

Matteo

"How are you still alive? I'm incredibly happy, but I'm so sorry that I couldn't have helped more," she cried softly.

"I must still be in a dream. A vicious bear attacked me, I died, and now this Gabriella is hugging me. I must be in heaven with her," I choked with astonishment.

Gabriella laughed. "No, we are here on earth together somehow."

"Is this even possible? Gabriella, can you untie me? My arms are almost dead from the ropes."

"Yes, sorry, I was excited to see you." She raced around the tree and began to untie the ropes, and said, "What happened to Golden? Where did he go?"

"He took off in a hurry a few minutes ago. No idea why. Or why he did not harm me."

"I know this is a lousy time for explanations, but I found myself missing you terribly when I thought you were dead and eaten," Gabriella said.

"Maybe I should die more often," I jested and winced in pain. Looking at Gabriella I said, "You look quite camouflaged with all the dirt and pine needles in your hair." I helped her clean them out.

It took a few long minutes to regain feeling and strength in my arms. We both agreed to leave immediately. I walked the meadow and found Gabriella's Buck knife covered in blood and dirt. I cleaned it off and handed it to her.

"A great guide, like you, should never lose her most important tool."

Gabriella smiled and sheathed the simple instrument of her survival.

Making our way briskly to our deserted campsite, I said, "Gabriella, I always thought Golden was merely a myth fabricated by you and Chuck."

"Guess you now have firsthand experience with the most vicious beast in the west."

We arrived at our destroyed campsite, and I silently gathered supplies such as food, water, flashlights, and sleeping bags. Gabriella grabbed one fly pole, a reel, and some flies. After stuffing our small day packs, we ran to the river and our mode of escape, the boats. Standing defeated in shock, we saw that the boats were gone, taken by the attackers.

"We have no clear way out. I only know this journey by water," Gabriella said sadly. "We have no choice but to navigate the forest."

We stood quietly soaking in our dilemma, and I said, "Hey, Gabriella."

"Yes?" She looked at me with beautiful wide-open eyes that fluttered with subtle color changes.

"Thanks so much for saving me. I would have died tied so securely to that tree, especially in the cold of the night."

"I'm happy I could be there. And you know what? You saved me too. By screaming at Golden, you distracted him from me."

"We saved each other."

We hugged each other tightly. Her body braced against mine was so pleasurable it washed me with confidence.

"And now," said Gabriella, "let's get the hell out of here. Hopefully, we can find the others."

THIRTY-ONE
THE WILLOW

We started along the path next to the river. After a mile or so, we rounded a bend, and a hundred yards ahead of us came three armed men. We saw each other simultaneously. They shot at us.

I jumped. "Run, Gabriella!"

We ran in the opposite direction until we began to tire and noticed that the three men were gaining on us.

"This trail ends soon directly into the mountain, but we have no choice," Gabriella said.

Moving forward, we came to a dense area of multiple shrub-like trees that had canopies of branches hanging to the ground decorated with millions of green leaves. A willow grove of unmatched beauty. There were hundreds of these large willows everywhere, our path leading directly through them toward a dead end at the base of the giant mountains ahead.

"We have no hope of really outrunning these guys, so we should hide and wait until they disappear, and hope," I said. "Maybe in one of these umbrella-shaped willows?"

Gabriella nodded, and we made our way far off the path to the back side of one of the large willows and squeezed our way inside. Surprisingly, there was enough room for both of us to fit in, completely covered from the outside world. We sat and leaned against the trunk holding each other, silently listening. Gabriella gently set the .44 Magnum on the ground in front of us. It housed six bullets, which was the extent of our armory. We waited.

The eerie silence sparked my senses. I noticed a big spider crawling on Gabriella's pants and casually, but mindfully, I flicked it off with my finger. Gabriella mouthed thanks. The chirping birds seemed louder than normal. A slight breeze moved our canopy, muffling our ability to detect unnatural sounds, such as human foot-steps. Without warning, the bird sounds stopped, and human voices came into range. Their accents were foreign, and Gabriella and I looked at each other with confusion. If I had to guess, I would say French Canadian.

Gabriella whispered in my ear, "Miners."

But why were these miners chasing us in the Canadian Yukon? We had done nothing to them. I slowly picked up the .44 as the voices grew louder. Gabriella covered her mouth with her hands and closed her eyes. The chatter and scuffling outside grew as the men were looking about the grove of trees. It seemed as if they were arguing. Like a gift from Heaven, a great roar rocked the area nearby, and the men grew quiet for a few seconds. Soon they began to argue again, and as fast as they had arrived, the voices nervously faded away.

Gabriella and I sat as one, two separate beings molded into a single fleshy object glued together by excruciating fear while inexplicitly pacified by trust in one another.

GABRIELLA

Here in the land of the midnight sun, I felt oddly at peace on this long treacherous day so close to extinction not once, not twice, but three times. The sun's dying rays seeped through our canopy of safety, casting a kaleidoscope of colors around us. A gorgeous setting amid danger. I could feel his rhythmic breathing as all else washed away.

"Do you think the men are gone or just waiting for us to move?" Matteo whispered in my ear. His quiet, infectious voice tingled my body, surging familiarity through my bones assumed long lost but apparently merely hibernating.

Gathering myself, I said, "I believe they are long gone. The roar was from no ordinary bear. That was the voice of Golden. Enough to spook anyone away. But we should stay put until the morning, just to be sure. Besides, we need rest before our journey out."

Matteo nodded in agreement and said quietly, "I'm so exhausted from today's tortures, I could sleep this very second."

"You lie down and nap while I stay up and keep my ears alert and my eyes wide open," I said while cradling the gun.

Matteo spread his sleeping bag and lay on his back and began gently snoring seconds later. I was envious of his ability to fall asleep since it was hard for me to fully relax due to my ghosts from the past. I looked around our special little shelter and tried to think as Matteo would with the significance of these surroundings. Here in this vast and seemingly endless forest lay a special grove of shrub trees. They did not appear natural, yet here they were, as our protectors, perhaps sent from the Heavens long ago with the sole purpose of being our saviors.

The willowy branches surrounding us were like an impenetrable fort, with the leaves as hardened shields repelling all spears and arrows of misfortune. Matteo would be proud of my quirky analysis.

As I stood guard, I looked back at him and scanned his entire being from his muddied shoes to the tips of his soiled fingers and stopped on his dirty handsome face which was still caked with dry blood, and I sighed in comfort. He appeared so vulnerable in his sleeping beauty. He was like a knight in shining armor, yet with a quick wink of my eye he reverted to the beautiful Matteo. I shook my head in disbelief that a great bear attack had blown me out of my endless rut, resurrecting my ability to possibly fly instead of crawl. And, inside this canopy, I had taken notice of this man in a different light.

As I continued to gaze at him, I reached out slowly and gently placed my hand on his chest. I listened to his steady breathing and felt the consistent beat of his heart. I felt my loins stirring. I felt slightly conflicted by the pleasurable sensation between my legs since it was clearly not the place or time for this reaction. But it would not stop. Amazed, I set the .44 down and began to touch myself instinctively with both hands. One caressed deeply my ample breasts, and they became swollen and stimulated. My other hand rubbed between my legs and an immediate explosion of ecstasy rocked me to the bone as I suppressed a scream.

Breathing as silently as I could, the orgasm calmed but I continued to grasp my expanded nipples and breasts wondering what it would be like to have someone of whom I approved touch them. I began to settle down and realized, with dismay, that I had peed some in my pants following the orgasm. Guess I lost control.

Wiping some sweat from my brow, I leaned against the trunk and thought, *What a strange, funny lady I must be! I just masturbated while watching the peaceful Matteo sleep.*

As delightful as this was, it confused me because how does one engage in sexual activity when surrounded by multiple death threats? Maybe it was a primal reaction to cope with the intense fear? Was I seeking pleasure to distract myself from immediate danger? It certainly wasn't premeditated. Well, it worked because now I no longer felt powerless, and I was comfortable and safe beneath the leaves and branches of our willow. I smiled while playfully blaming the whole episode on the peaceful Matteo. It had been a long time since I had experienced such pleasure. And the whole event took no more than thirty seconds!

I laughed silently again as I sat in wet pants with one hand on my chest, which reaffirmed the appropriateness of my original nicknames. It had taken some mental fortitude but suddenly I was proud, not ashamed of my lovely shape. For years, I had yearned for smaller boobs just to ward off so much attention, covering them up as often as possible. Shaking this off, I realized that life could be way worse, but my tragic event years ago had shattered all my self-confidence.

I felt progress brewing throughout my recent internal journey. I changed directions and returned to my appointed duty of guarding our little castle from the marauding hordes, enabling Matteo to rest while I came to the unrewarding realization that I had no other underwear or pants to replace my wet ones.

Matteo

I stirred suddenly as a fly landed on my nose, waking me. For a moment I had lost my bearings among all these flickering leaves in this swaying collage of foliage surrounding me. Looking to my left I smiled as my fearless guard, Gabriella, sat perched against the tree trunk fast asleep. I admired her innocent, youthful look knowing perfectly well a high level of resolute steel existed below her silky surface. And to top off her lovely current state a small amount of drool dripped from her lips. Checking her out further, I noticed she had peed in her pants. Poor girl had endured a bad day, as I had. Best to allow the sleeping beauty a rest.

I peeked out through our protecting branches and leaves to view the peaceful solitude of our neighborhood. This kind of scene had always been my happy place. My forest therapy I called it. The deep forest with all its supporting cast of greenery, flowing water, endless rocks and boulders, dirt, pine needle beds, and a vast array of living creatures. My intuitive source had thrived and expanded long ago in this type of setting, and I longed for its return. I sat, crossing my legs and resting my hands on my knees. I began the thoughtful process of allowing my strength to return while perched in this sanctuary of peaceful, fictitious safety. I started to sink into my space when suddenly I was interrupted by the affectionate voice of Gabriella.

"Hi. You're up and awake."

"I did nap quite well and thanks for guarding," I said, and after pausing I spoke while pointing at her crotch.

"I'm sorry you soiled yourself. That's so annoying but justified on this crazy day of ours. Do you have anything to change into?"

Blushing, Gabriella sighed and said, "I don't, so I'm just going to have to live with it, I guess."

"I have a pair of shorts you could use while drying out, if you wish."

"Well," she said hesitating, "that would be wonderful. I accept the offer."

I sifted through my backpack and handed her the shorts.

"We all pee in our pants from time to time. I've done it numerous times, usually when I laugh too hard," I smiled.

Gabriella took the cargo shorts and held them up inquisitively and remarked, "Looks like these may do the job."

I offered to step outside for her privacy, but Gabriella wouldn't let me.

"You don't need to leave but just look away and no peeking, Mister Dago!"

I sat facing away from her.

GABRIELLA

I slipped off my soiled pants and underwear and allowed myself to air out for a minute which felt exhilarating. Almost like doing an ice plunge in the Yukon wilderness. His shorts fit remarkably well. We had a similar fanny size with mine rounder and fuller. I fit in the pants with comfortable snugness.

"All done, Matteo. Thanks. How do I look?" I modeled

for him using all my professional moves such as hands on hips twirling around, creating a big laugh from Matteo.

***

MATTEO

"Don't make me laugh too hard. I might pee in my pants and would need to borrow back those shorts! Anyway, they look far better on you, Sweet Cheeks," I said with jest. "I am officially gifting them to you. Like an early Christmas present."

We both laughed and joked for a little.

Finally, I said, "You look like a woman who can get anything she wants, especially a man."

"Well, I guess I'll take that as a compliment. I know, I know, I'm just irresistible." She flipped her long hair back with flirtatious fancy, creating chuckles from us both.

"But I have to finish my unsolicited opinion about this person named Gabriella."

"I'm all ears." She sat on the ground with her hands on her lap.

"Even though you are gifted with just your being, you have not used your superior traits over the last few years for your immediate well-being. Remember beauty begets empathy, which leads to all sorts of advantages and can make your life easier. Although these characteristics were exploited years ago for your benefit, you now have selected another pathway to your current successful life, yes?"

"What makes you so sure my life is successful?"

"Good question and your answer?"

"I believe headway has been made, but I lack some

important finishing touches. I know I'm a bit confusing at times, so I think it might be wise for me to finish the story that I began in your tent. It's starting to get late, maybe eleven p.m., and even though it's still light out, we should eat a little and hunker down for a long day tomorrow. I believe we may have three to five hours of darkness."

I agreed and following an apple with cheese and crackers, we slipped into our bags side by side. We lay in lazy silence listening to the wild sounds as the fading light washed through our canopy.

"There is such beauty in this valley of trees. I'm surprised that more humans don't live right here. But I'm happy they don't."

"Maybe they are not welcomed by the forces of nature, just the gifted one with his strange, fly-fishing guide." Gabriella joked.

I laughed. "Why do you self-deprecate yourself? You seem quite normal compared to the freaks I know back home. You were very reserved when I first met you, but some of it does not make sense to me, probably due to the fact I only know your partial past? You are a beautiful soul, Gabriella. Embrace it as a gift. I mean, you could have a big, huge nose with a fat wart on it, stumbling around all hunched over."

She stared at me and then chuckled. "I could be a Wicked Witch of the North. Who farts, too!"

Laughing, I continued while shifting to another subject. "So, what does this epic, spiritual moment tucked away in the comfort of the willows symbolize for you, Gabriella?"

Looking pensively at me, she said, "Let me think about this for a second."

I watched Gabriella's dazzling eyes change colors with the dimming light.

Shifting around, she sat up in her sleeping bag and spoke.

"This endless willow grove is an escape for my simple mind, becoming a blanket of safety flowing over me in protection, relaxing me. As I absorb a connection with the fish in the breathing river, I have a deep connection with these willows and all that surrounds us, such as the shrubs and the glorious pines, the dense rocks and the delicate grasses. I feel so saved by it. I think it's one of the reasons I traveled to these parts, among other things. Does this make sense to you, Matteo?"

I nodded.

"The path that we follow through this wonderland acts as a boundary saying, 'Don't touch.' But I see it as an invitation to leap off the hamster wheel and engage with all that I see, the green life, and to touch the plants while smelling them, inhaling the fresh air and to misbehave to a certain extent, far away from human rule. And lastly, while all living things have a messaging system, the flowing river really has a voice which can be fiercely powerful but suddenly a whisper. It speaks to me all the time, inviting me to engage, to see everything while offering a sanctuary for many, especially my favorite fish, the beautiful trout. If I can get to this happy place for just a couple of moments or even hours, things feel brighter. My stress evaporates, creating some measure of success for me in various ways. My negative thoughts always come roaring back, but I'm making progress. This weird enough for you?"

I sat in silence as I experienced a sudden inability to speak due to Gabriella's thoughtfulness. Clearing my throat slightly, I said, "That was fabulous. I really liked it, and so inspirational. See, I knew it was hidden somewhere in your package."

She smiled. "I drew inspiration from your campfire analysis."

We settled back into our sleeping bags, and as I tried to sleep, Gabriella said, "Would you like me to finish up my storied past now? I feel ready."

"Sure, I mean we don't need sleep, right? We can all sleep someday when we are dead and buried."

"Well, that's a bit cryptic."

We laughed again, and Gabriella began.

GABRIELLA

"As I mentioned in your tent, the *Sports Illustrated* spreads catapulted me to another level. As the months progressed rapidly, my girlfriends Suzie and Franny and I became very close and attended most modeling functions together. This came at the demand of Miss Collins, who watched me like a hawk. It made everything seem safe and tolerable. But we could not always keep each other in sight, especially when my friends would head off with a man and wave me off.

"Often, I sat alone at a party or event which created an uncomfortable feeling in me. Men approached me, and while the interaction was pleasant, I refused their advances until one time. This man was very attractive and socially sound, and I did end up sleeping with him, and immediately I thought we were dating, but we weren't. I tried to address the issue, and he got angry and aggressive. He pushed me away when I refused to sleep with him again.

"I discussed this with Miss Collins, and she recommended that I take an escort when attending parties or events. And she recommended her uncle, Richard. He was older and acted as my surrogate father. Richard and I became inseparable, and I had to pay him, which was fine because he was pleasant and responsible, just like Miss Collins. Richard was tall, thin, and remarkably strong. His head supported a bunch of wild and curly hair that looked like a shag rug. At times he even looked mean, but I soon found out that he was extremely sensitive to the needs of others, and he always wanted to help me. He had spent time in a Vietnamese prison camp during the war but came out of it pretty well, I think.

"One life-changing night, I attended a party of an influential Hollywood person, whose name I did not recognize. Richard, as usual, came along with me and hung out across the room, having a drink while socializing.

"I met a pleasant man, and we chatted without stress for about an hour, and he invited me to see the house. Apparently, he was a close associate of the homeowner. The tour was fascinating, and we wandered through each astounding room, and eventually we came to the bedrooms. He showed me his room for his stayover. He gently closed the door, smiled, and kissed me confidently on my lips. I enjoyed it although it was a bit rough.

"He aggressively grabbed my chest, and I told him to stop. He got forceful, throwing me on his bed and pinning me down, then flipping me over. I let out a scream, but he clamped one hand over my mouth preventing me from breathing and started to run his other hand under my dress. I bit his hand, enraging him, and he slapped me hard.

"Stunned, I grew limp for a second, and he began to unzip his pants. Horrified, I screamed again as his hardness began to enter me. Suddenly the door burst open, and Richard grabbed the man, applying a chokehold on his neck. They struggled onto the floor for what seemed an eternity while I gathered my breath and wits. I noticed the man's eyeballs were rolling back into his head and told Richard to stop. Shaking, I tapped Richard's arm. But Richard kept pressing, and the man went limp. Once the man passed out, Richard asked if I was okay.

"I told him I was just shaken up. We both leaned down and turned him over, and with terror, I noticed that both his eyes were wide open. Was he dead? Richard instructed me to go to the bathroom and straighten myself out. He warned me not to touch anything while he attempted CPR, but it failed.

"Upon finishing up, I returned to the scene and watched as Richard dragged the body to the closet, stuffed him in there, and quietly shut the door. I asked if we should call the police, but Richard looked at me, placed his hands on my shoulders, and calmly told me that there was no way even though it was unintentional. They would still accuse us of murder. The owner of this house was a powerful Hollywood producer, and they would all come after us. We needed to calmly walk out of there as soon as possible.

"I agreed upon the realization of the tragedy and the potential ramifications. We hurriedly fixed up the room and wiped off all the surfaces to eliminate our fingerprints and headed out. I held Richard's hand and tried to act naturally.

"Over the next few days, trouble brewed as the man's death made the news, and the search was on for us. Unfortunately, there were cameras outside the front door, and we were spotted leaving the party early. It didn't take much time, and Richard was identified, and a warrant was issued. A day later, I too was pinpointed.

"Richard called me and told me he was in trouble and was planning to disappear. He said he couldn't go to jail for a mistake, and there was no way they could pin strangling a man that big on me. He told me to say that Richard had killed the man against my wishes. He even suggested that it was a crime of passion and that I was stuck in the middle. He said he would contact me when it was safe. My life had crumbled in a matter of minutes. I decided to turn myself in to avoid any further suspicion. My life took unfathomable twists, leaving me in emotional and financial ruin.

"I was accused of being an accessory to murder, lost all my modeling jobs, spent half my stored college savings on lawyers, and lost the respect of many people, but still managed support from my friends and parents, and especially Suzie and Franny, my modeling cohorts. They testified in court on my behalf, but no matter what we tried, I was found guilty of some sort of crime, which I never really understood. As I sat in court waiting for the judge to impose my sentence, I shook with fear. I did nothing but get raped by some violent, deranged idiot.

"The judge entered the courtroom and asked that I stand while she read my sentence. To sum it up in simple language, the judge was lenient and since the circumstances were convoluted and I had been assaulted and obviously did not kill the perpetrator, she sentenced me to two years jail time and one year of community service following jail time and restricted my daily activities to my parents' home, with trips allowed to buy necessities only. I sobbed following the sentencing while grappling with the enormity of it all and acknowledging the leniency of the sentence, which could have been crippling. My lawyer repeated how lucky I was to get a female judge who expressed some compassion. It could have been dramatically worse.

"The next year trudged along at a snail's pace, but I was forever grateful for the reduced sentence. During my second year, I received glorious news. I would be released early due to good behavior, and at the same time I received a phone call from Richard, which lifted my heart to hear his voice. We chatted for some time, and even though I begged him, he never revealed his whereabouts. I voiced my desire to leave L.A. forever with hope for his guidance to somewhere far away. Richard said he must go, but he would get a message to me with further information.

"Months went by, and one day I found a note slipped under my parents' front door addressed to me personally. I scurried into my room and quietly closed the door, sat on my bed and opened the envelope. Beads of sweat formed on my forehead as I took a deep breath in anticipation. It was a letter from Richard. In it, he suggested I reach out to man named Chuck and gave me his phone number. Chuck was an old friend to Richard, and he was ready to help me start a new life.

"Ok, so that's how you met Chuck," Matteo said. "How coincidental is that? But you never told me."

"Correct, and I had my reasons, foremost being I didn't know you, even remotely."

"Yes, makes sense. Please continue."

"Following six months of community service, and without the slightest contemplation, I called Chuck, and he planned for my trip to a place called Juneau with a room ready for my arrival. My parents were disappointed but fully understood my desire to escape and wished me well.

In less than a week my life in L.A. became nothing more than a distant memory of conflicting benevolence and terror, with the latter dominating my shattered soul. Jail time for merely existing as a young, harmless, dedicated female created far too much discourse within me. It was time for exfoliation.

"Flying to Juneau gave me ample time to reflect on all the positive aspects of my life, but concurrently festering sadness for the loss of my job, an entity that gave me purpose and self-confidence. But I was consumed by fear. My friend Jenny, a therapist, once told me that youth and play spurs growth, and growth spurs progress. While progress fosters maturity leading to hope, compassion, love and confidence, fears hinder them all. And she also reminded me that we all can be tainted by the corruption hiding in life. I knew my life had been interrupted by a fearful derailment, and my mind remained under constant repair. Perhaps I could return to that happy world at some future date. I was only thirty, but time must pass allowing the ill will in L.A. to fade away. Gone but not forgotten.

"The sheer vastness of Juneau's natural resources invigorated me with a foreign comfort I had never felt before and in direct contrast to the stress of the gargantuan asphalt highways of L.A.

"I smiled as I met Chuck exiting the plane. Here was this jolly man who embraced me with a bear hug and led me to his big red truck. He spoke about all the fabulous advantages of living in the region of Juneau. He constantly complimented me on my courage to journey all alone to this great wild. I told him that I had no real choice but to fly away as per Richard's advice. He reminded me that a friend of Richard's is a friend of his. He even cleaned up a room for me in his cabin.

"For the next couple of days Chuck hosted me and educated me about the history and quirks of Juneau. And as you know, Matteo, in the following four years I bought my own small home in Juneau, I became a ranger and a fly-fishing guide. Those two jobs gave me respite and an inkling of hope. So, there you have my updated life history. Impressed?"

"Yes, and quite devastating in many ways. So sorry, but you have done well in your journey. I now understand Gabriella," Matteo said.

We decided to get to sleep, and snuggled down in our bags side by side, and as usual, my mind began to overanalyze. I never discussed any intimate relationships with my girlfriends, so what gives?

I could not sleep although I was excruciatingly tired. I thought of our day and our flight from danger and our natural hideaway. I cringed when recalling my masturbation scene, which embarrassed me. I wish it didn't. At least no one knew.

I wondered what bizarre thoughts Matteo must have of me. I slapped my head trying to ignore my negative self-deprecating images. As I lay there, I hoped for further conversation with Matteo. He had awakened me from some locked cage, as proven by my sex with myself. I wished to hold him in my arms and thank him, but I remained in my sleeping bag. I sighed gently as I knew his day had been especially rough and he needed rest, as did I. Slowly my brain shut down, and I began to drift off when his voice stirred me.

MATTEO

"Gabriella, are you awake?"

She responded, "Yes, I can't sleep."

"I wanted to thank you, again, for supporting me today and helping me escape. I realize I'm repeating myself, but it is invigorating to know there still are good people in this hectic world!"

"You helped me too, Matteo. Like we said, we needed help, and we saved each other."

He rolled over and faced me.

"I have a personal question for you, and if you don't want to answer or feel threatened by it, then please just tell me."

"Okay, sure, go ahead."

"Well, I'm a little confused as to your persuasion. You know how rumors can flow in many directions. Are they true?"

GABRIELLA

I smiled at him and thought to myself that my plan had actually worked, and I was proud of myself. Everyone I knew in Juneau and Skagway assumed my preference was for women. I wanted all men to avoid me as I avoided them.

I smiled again at Matteo and gently replied, "I guess it all worked till now." Matteo gazed at me with confusion. "No, Matteo, I am not, and you are the first person I've told in many years. I did not want men to touch me in any way, and I thought…" I stopped while looking into his eyes with sadness.

MATTEO

"Well, that's a relief!" I leaned toward Gabriella and kissed her softly and pulled back. The kiss — it was a touch more than friendly, but far below erotic. She looked down and then back at me with hope, and I kissed her again with more passion, and we both pulled back. After a moment of discomfort, we both approached each other awkwardly and bumped our foreheads, and pulled back with a bit of a chuckle. Rubbing her forehead, Gabriella reached out and pulled me to her and we connected perfectly as our lips met, and our tongues flickered with emotional wetness.

GABRIELLA

We continued to kiss without hesitation almost as if we had hung in the balance of life and death. I abandoned all time and lost track of my relentless fears and tasted only his tongue as it was so gentle dashed with devilish intent. This moment was so new to me. I had kissed before, but this one melted my body and soul as I became one with him. My heart pounded as I desired him more than anything else in my life. Continuing to kiss we haphazardly peeled off one another's clothing. We kissed each other with purpose on our cheeks, and ears, mouths and breasts, all of which resulted in goosebumps rising over my body. His wet tongue on my breast sent me over the top. Oddly, I wondered if I smelled!

MATTEO

Even in her unbathed condition, she smelled exotic with skin as soft as silk and my hands caressed her chest, stomach, back and more. As our bodies entwined as one, I effortlessly entered her warm beautiful body, and our motions and emotions took center stage. We both raced quickly to ecstasy together as our bodies arched.

Gabriella experienced a sweet ache throughout her body, I hurt with love. Our pelvis push slowed to a crawl as we continued to caress and kiss each other, and we both teared up. Breathing steady, we remained as one. Staring at each other we both started to laugh and smile as this precious moment was unexpected by either of us.

"I think I was struck by you the first time you burst through those bushes to give me a fishing ticket. Not the most romantic moment, but it worked."

"I also felt something at that moment, but I discarded it, as usual, and continued this behavior every time we met. Do you think I'm odd?"

"No, quite the opposite actually, and I completely understand why now and am so grateful for your awakening." I whispered, "But when did you figure this out?"

"I became aware sprawled on the bottom of that hill after Golden had swatted me over the edge. I was saddened greatly at the thought of losing my friend Matteo. And I cried. It gave me an inkling of my love for you. But what happened later was the real clincher for me. But I hesitate to tell because you're going to think I'm extraordinarily strange, but I must get it off my chest."

"Sure, I'm listening."

She laughed and said, "I normally would never reveal something like this, because I feel it was somewhat perverted, and I'm slightly embarrassed. While I did pee in my pants, another event preceded that caused me to lose control, slightly."

"I don't understand. What was it? You spilled water on yourself?" I said perplexed.

"No, this is weird, but while you slept peacefully today, I masturbated right next to you while observing you." She blushed while watching my face intently.

"Oh!" I said with a pause. "That is so hip! Not sure what to say, but you must find me attractive after getting beat up, tied to a tree, scared shitless by the largest bear on earth, and shot at by random miners. And to top it off, I must stink to high heaven! When really thinking about it, it's quite a compliment, yes? My only regret was not witnessing the sultry event." Gabreilla sheepishly smiled. "Quite a day for you. Wow, you certainly made up for lost ground in just one day! Masturbate in my unknowing presence and then jump me as well. I'm impressed, Gabriella, and you are far from strange, just horny for the right guy."

"For sure, and it's like I ventured into uncharted territory. An awakening, of sorts."

"How did you enjoy the new landscape?" I quipped.

"It was exquisite." she said with a smile. "But maybe I was squatting on your land? A woman must do what a woman needs, right?"

"Well, yes, certainly, and I'm sure this is all my fault,

like my S'mores?" Laughing, we kissed and embraced again. It was timeless.

"I did not jump you, Matteo. We ravished each other," she laughed.

Pausing for a silent moment, I spoke, "I'm concerned Gabriella."

"About what?" she said sitting up.

"We must find our way out, and we both must make it. Not just one of us. I cannot afford to lose someone like you. I've lost too much already."

"Let me put it this way, Matteo. If you die, then I die. We need to make it. But the other option is we stay under the willow forever." She laughed.

"Good idea."

"Matteo, even though we are in extreme danger out here, I sense my body dumping some of my fear, and I have more hope now."

"Awesome. Your faith in hope is stronger than fear. I feel the same."

We zipped our sleeping bags together and while spooning, fell fast asleep swept up in nothing more than this tiny haven, our spiritual willow tree, lost in this endless wilderness.

I muttered to Gabriella, "I love you."

But she was long gone. I had not spoken those three ageless words in years, and it made me think of Judy again, and I smiled as I fell asleep because I knew Judy was smiling too.

Gabriella

I awoke briefly listening to his sexy snore and realized I had been allergic to the very idea of accepting someone into my pathetic life while ignoring the extent of my disease. A weight had been lifted. Both ball and chain were gone. I now trusted him to the point that exorcising the ghosts haunting me had become possible. His nakedness against mine was foreign but soothing, and I realized my soul had, in fact, never felt this way. It was a surge of power, positive and unrelenting. I must maintain its presence. But did he feel the same?

I told myself to stop my mental spin and embrace this singular moment while giving hope for a similar reaction from his body blended into me, right now, beneath our willow.

I slept soundly for the first time in years.

THIRTY-TWO
THE JOURNEY

Birds chirping woke me, and I briefly felt lost in my surroundings. Recognizing our au naturel tent, my senses returned. I rolled over to see the lovely Gabriella in full snore. I had to pinch myself of yesterday's realities and how happy I felt with Gabriella at my side. My perverted mind, which had returned with its recent awakening, thought that maybe this would be a good time to masturbate and get innocently even with Gabriella. But my practical senses prevailed.

I dreamed of returning to Juneau and back home in Santa Barbara but only with Gabriella as my escort. Otherwise, I would stay, if she would approve. I slipped outside to pee and noticed foreboding thunderheads covering the mountains above, even as peace and calm enveloped our willow grove. The area appeared clear of dangers, and I reentered our tree to find Gabriella fully naked gathering her clothes.

"Well, my pants and underwear are dry," she said with some devilish intent.

Scouring her beauty I said in jest, "But are you?"

"Very funny, Mister Dago. I might remain wet forever with you around."

We kissed passionately, arousing our flame, but we knew that we must move quickly on our journey. We were nervous about what lay ahead but reinforced each other with joking about our discoveries of each other.

After packing our bags, I thanked our friend the willow, stroking her long, delicate leaves and hugging her low-lying branches as they moved slightly in the subtle breeze. Gabriella exited, but I stayed for a few extra moments and held the willow branches with passion as I felt a surge of energy. But in short order it all dissipated, and I exited the willow to join my partner, Gabriella.

"Did you feel your instincts?"

"Yes, briefly but just for a second or two. I'm going to remain positive," I said with determination. Looking back at the willow, we both shed a brief tear knowing this willow held a special place in our hearts.

"I think we should give this special tree a nickname. Got any thoughts?" I asked.

Pondering for a few seconds, Gabriella chimed, "Willy! Yes, Willy the Willow!"

I laughed with approval and we both shouted, "Thanks Willy. Until another day."

Gabriella broke out her small camera, backed up, and asked me to stand next to Willy. I modeled with a poppy in my hand, and a forever picture was snapped. I did the same for Gabriella. We held hands and carefully proceeded on our journey. Our course led back to the river path as crossing the snowy mountains looked insurmountable. We walked through our old campsite and gathered a few more items such as power bars and two waterproof windbreakers. The downward chill in the weather continued as we approached more wintry days, a dangerous sign of Yukon's harshness to come. While walking Gabriella said, "It's rather strange, but even though we are in grave danger here, we somehow found the fortitude and gumption to make love? Seems almost like a dream. I've noticed that most of my fear has dissipated almost entirely. That hasn't happened in an eternity. How about you?"

"Now that you mention it, I notice the same."

"As my friend and therapist Jenny said before, fear destroys everything within our normal abilities, so how is it that it's suddenly gone?"

"Making love to the correct person, I think, may have something to do with it. I hear that sex decreases one's cortisol levels, which are directly connected to stress. You ever heard that?"

"No, but it sounds reasonable." She smiled. "I wonder how long that lasts?"

"Not long," I said without any proof. "We must jump each other all the time in order to be safe." I jested. Gabriella punched me again.

"Okay." She smirked.

Hastening back to our path, we traveled about a mile and came upon a disturbing sight. Three mangled bodies lay near the river. I drew the .44 and approached the carnage slowly. Mostly unrecognizable, we realized that they were probably the French-Canadian miners chasing us. Two automatic rifles lay at their sides. Whatever attacked did so with speed as neither rifle had been engaged.

Gabriella said, "Looks like the work of Golden again. Very similar to those dead poachers I found around Juneau."

I picked up one of the assault rifles and asked, "Have you ever shot one of these?"

"Yes, as part of my ranger training. These could be very helpful in our journey back, if we come across trouble. Let's hope not."

"I have never shot one of these, but you can train me," I said with a smile.

Gabriella flashed a thumbs up.

"Sure. These are AK47s, Russian automatic rifles used in warfare. They are very accurate and reliable."

Gabriella quickly popped out the clip and examined the quantity of bullets. She ran over to one of the dead miners and found a fully loaded clip and shoved it back in place in the rifle. In a few short moves, she prepared the rifle for firing and slipped on the safety latch.

"Did you catch all that?"

"Uhmm, sort of. Let me try my rifle." First, I immediately got stuck on releasing the clip, and Gabriella patiently guided me. Second, I found another clip on one of the bodies, and with her help determined it was full enough. Third, I struggled with setting the clip in place but eventually I shoved the clip into my AK47 until it clicked in. Smiling, I unwittingly swung the rifle toward Gabriella and said, "Well?"

Gabriella hastily pushed the rifle barrel away from her. "Don't ever aim this at anyone unless you mean to pull the trigger, okay?"

"Yes, of course, good point."

She rolled her eyes to the sky. "See that lever on the side? Pull that back to the rear and hold it there and visually check the chamber. Then ease the charging handle forward. Now you are ready. Put the safety on."

I was ready to go to war.

"Also, never put your finger on the trigger unless you are ready to fire. Rest it along the side of the trigger cavity or slightly above it. We will keep these on semi-automatic by pushing this lever to here," as she showed me. "If we run into big trouble, we can switch these to fully automatic, but the rifle is harder to manage and less accurate."

"What is the difference between those two options?"

"Good question since I assumed everyone knew what automatic means, but that was foolish. When on automatic, the rifle becomes a machine gun and you simply pull the trigger and hold it, and about ten bullets fire each second."

"Wow, that's crazy."

"Yes, it's a little wild."

"Got it."

Following my short lesson on the handling of an AK47, Gabriella and I gathered the two other clips full of bullets and continued. We left the bodies untouched knowing they now belonged to Golden.

As we prepared to continue, Gabriella hesitated and looked at me. "Does all the rifle talk make you reassess me at all? I don't want to scare you off!"

I thought for a second or two, realizing her concern.

"To be perfectly honest, I was impressed. I had no idea that the shy Gabriella possessed this military strength. I still want you!"

The rain came soon, and Gabriella said, "We need to find shelter. In about two miles there is a small hidden cabin inland where Dick and I would store supplies. It's boarded up to keep the animals out, but I know how to get in. We can wait out the storm there. I'm worried about Dick and the others. I hope they are okay."

I nodded and we hurried forward. I felt as if we were

being watched, but there were no signs, just my intuition. We approached the hidden cabin, which I could not see because the rain had increased.

"We are here. Help me move these branches." Gabriella started to shift away dead branches and as I helped, a small wooden door appeared. She loosened four screws with her knife, and we crawled through the opening, boarded it up, and stood up into a small room lined with box after box, piled high. It was only one room, and its overall construction was solid, giving the structure a greater chance of survival in the harsh weather. No windows at all, but there were a couple of pipes that led outside to allow some air flow. The cabin was extremely musty and smelled a bit, but it was the Taj Mahal compared to any other option. We lit some candles.

"Dick and his friends built this just for hunting and fishing and camping supplies in case we ever got stuck on our guide trips. I guess we are stuck."

I smiled and said, "I'm stoked! How lucky are we? Well done, Gabriella. You are my hero."

We dried off and that night we ate well, chatting for hours while spending intermittent time touching, holding, smelling, loving, and caressing each other.

Gabriella played with my chest and whispered, "I can hardly take my hands off your chest. I thought only mine was desirable, but I have discovered yours. I'm obsessed. Hope it's not too much. And by the way, I stink too."

"It's very arousing and please knock yourself out. But turnaround is fair play." I smiled while I stroked her chest. We continued for a while and then fell fast asleep. In the morning, we restocked our supplies and marched forward along the river path, waving goodbye to the secret cabin.

I followed Gabriella mostly because she knew the area

well, but also, I enjoyed the view of her sexy legs moving in rhythm. We chatted randomly about all the aspects of our lives, which lent validity to our aspiring relationship. We were in love, a grandeur neither of us expected, yet longed for subconsciously. In a few hours we found a safe, hidden area near the river where we rested and ate.

"I have one more important aspect of my life that I need to tell," she said.

I nodded in approval and listened.

"Dick is Richard, from my past."

I stopped chewing as I absorbed the comment.

"Yes, it's true," Gabriella said. "When Richard fled Los Angeles years ago, he came to Skagway with Chuck's help. It was there they agreed to call him Dick. His last name, Skidachy, is also false. All necessary to avoid any search for him. I never knew his proper last name. And he is missing and now you understand the true impact of his disappearance on me. He saved my life, but I could not save his." Gabriella began to cry.

I hugged her tightly and kissed and comforted her all that I could.

"But Dick would want me to forge on, so that's what we will do," she said wiping her tears as she stood and pulled me up.

"Just remember that you helped save me, and Dick would be proud," I said.

Gabriella smiled, kissed me gently and led the way. The storm had moved on, and blue skies returned, to our relief. After making good headway, we paused for a break and enjoyed the warm sun. We both agreed that a quick rinse in the river was more than necessary as we both were filthy and smelly. I kept guard while she bathed, and I was allowed to admire her in the water with the full appreciation of her earlier job in front of cameras. My dad had told me long ago, when I approached early manhood, that most folks look worse with their clothes off, but in this instance my dad had been wrong. To me, she looked perfect and apparently so did her previous employers. She was gifted, and it laid credence to all her nicknames that emboldened her. She looked like a statue of Venus, but more real, with beads of silky water flowing down her perfect skin. The sun reflected off her watery frame like sparkling diamonds. She finished up and exited the river where I dried her off enjoying my trance-like journey up and down her body.

She laughed and said, "Excuse me, sir, but I think my ass is plenty dry now!"

I stripped and ran out into the cold refreshing water.

***

GABRIELLA

I did a lousy job of keeping guard since all I could do was stare at Matteo and all his beauty. His shape dazzled me with his chest and fanny keeping my attention. Even though I had already seen him in the buff, this watery angle was especially gratifying. He reminded me of a sculpture I once saw in a museum, but this one was drenched in the glassy pure water of the river. I did love him so much, and I hoped he felt the same.

I did not have much to compare it with, but his cock looked big to me, and I suddenly lusted for him. I told myself to calm down with a giggle as I continued to admire him. How lucky am I to find such love in the wilderness? A gift from the heavens. Soon he emerged from the river, and I helped dry his back and grabbed him in the spirit of love. Soon we were dressed and on our way.

Matteo

The trail eventually became foreign to Gabriella since she had traveled this far into the wild only by boat.

"If we stay close to the river, it should lead us out. That's my guess, but I'm not sure how passible it will be."

"We will be fine," I said with fake confidence as I followed my guide and future. We continued our casual conversation about friends, Skagway, and even our infamous nicknames. I decided that her labels were more complimentary and accurate. She disagreed and loved mine, which was an about face from her initial opinion of Dago.

"Look, mine is a filthy degrading slur, while all of yours are sexual, indirect compliments."

"Nice effort spinning a negative into a positive, my Dago." She smiled. "No one used WOP on you?"

"Yes, but the preferred was Dago, so that was that," I said with a shrug. "I prefer the title when you preface it with Mister. Shows true affection!" and I grabbed her ass. She jumped.

"And what makes you think you can just do that on a whim, Mister?"

"Well, I am Italian, and in the old country, all the men grab ass any time they want. Part of their heritage," I joked as I suspected that would not be acceptable.

"Oh, really? You're lucky I didn't mind as much as

usual." She smiled, hugged me, and suddenly grabbed my ass with both her hands. I gave a little jump as she sang, "I'm Italian too, my dear!"

"How about you, Gabriella. Which nickname do you prefer?"

"None of them, honestly, but forced to choose, I guess I would take Sweet Cheeks since that part of me, as well as my chest, seems to draw the most photographic attention during my shoots. But Fanny is cute and unobtrusive and could be used in public," she said with confidence.

"Did you find any of your photo shoots demeaning?"

"At the time, no. It was flattering, but as time progressed, I longed for a return to the facial shots only — you know, eyes, hair, lips, and smile. But the full body photography earned the most money. I do miss it from time to time. Good memories, except for the ending, of course."

I started to speak further when Gabriella suddenly looked at me and gave the silence sign, one finger to her lips. Nearby, faint voices echoed.

Clutching each other, we hurried off the path into deep brush and prepared our weapons. Incoherent male and female voices interchanged and grew louder with their approach. Peering carefully through the bushes, we saw two men and several women working off the path about a hundred yards away.

"They seem to be picking something off the bushes," I whispered.

"There are a variety of berries in this area. Bears, moose, and deer eat them, I believe."

I nodded and said, "Looks like a family, possibly, gathering food. Maybe they can help us, point us in the right direction?"

"Miners live in these parts, and our guided trips stay clear of them. They know Dick and I accept them partially, but they are not to be approached. For some reason, they don't look like miners to me."

I gave a thumbs up.

Much to our dismay, we soon realized the men were equipped with rifles, and their speech was clearly French Canadian. The women said little while diligently collecting berries, remaining close to each other in a straight line. One of the men said something jumbled, and they all turned toward the river's edge and sat to eat and drink.

"Seems a bit odd," I said.

Gabriella agreed and we lay low, patiently allowing them to finish and to move on. As we watched and waited, I noticed something strange. All the women wore plain, nondescript clothing, nothing even remotely suited to the environment. One woman stood and stretched. Shockingly, I noticed that she was tethered to the next woman, ankle to ankle.

"You see that?" I whispered.

"Yes, so strange. Maybe they are part of a miners' cult," Gabriella said softly.

"Tied together? Like prisoners?"

"I don't know, but it stinks of danger."

Shortly, the group headed back along the path. We waited until they were long gone, then cautiously continued. Within seconds, a loud commotion broke loose. Screams, shouts and a roar shattered the silence along with a rifle shot. The confusion continued, then abruptly ended. We hid again in the bushes, and soon one of the women ran desperately in our direction. Gabriella jumped out, intercepted the woman and dragged her screaming into the bushes.

Putting her hand over her mouth, Gabriella spoke kindly, "Please be quiet. We won't hurt you. You speak English?"

The young woman nodded.

"Tell us what's happening."

The girl sobbed and tried to catch her breath. "One of us tried to escape, shot, a bear..." and she could not continue.

We hugged her and noticed she was not very old, maybe in her teens.

"Are you being held against your wishes? Like prisoners?" I asked.

"I don't know, maybe. Been here a long time." She collapsed again in tears.

The ranger in Gabriella stood up. "We need to help the others."

"Agree, but we have no idea what awaits us back there. We could all die."

Gabriella and I discussed the options and realized that if we did not help, it would haunt us forever.

"What's your name?"

"They call me Sofia."

"This is getting even more confusing, but anyway, you come show us the way. How old are you, Sofia?"

"Don't know, maybe eighteen?"

"Lead the way, sweetheart, but we must be quiet as mice," Gabriella instructed.

"You are the ultimate ranger!" I said.

We moved along the path. Up at the next corner, Sofia pointed ahead, motioning to the left. We took the lead with the young lady following behind with caution. Rifles drawn; we peeked around the corner. Three bodies lay scattered randomly, the two men and one of the women.

Near the river the remaining women huddled together comforting each other. Some cried. Venturing into the area of destruction, the four by the river became startled and began to make nervous noises, and I motioned them to be silent as Gabriella examined the bodies. The one woman had been shot dead, and the two men had been mauled, their faces beyond recognition.

"Had to be Golden, so we must be careful. He is close." My heart pounded as I carefully approached the girls, and Sofia followed me.

"It's okay you guys, they are nice and maybe they can be our friends," Sofia said.

I proceeded to gently untie their ankle restraints as the girls looked at me cautiously.

Gabriella came up and just stared at the young women and said deliberately, "This is nuts and we must take them with us, but they are not prepared for this. Any thoughts, Matteo?"

"I see the only option is to herd them back to your secret cabin and dress them appropriately and resupply."

Gabriella smiled and retorted, "You would make a great ranger." She led the group back a few miles as I headed up the rear. Once again, we left the bodies exactly as they lay. What confused me was that the remaining girls had not been killed or even touched.

Observing Gabriella confidently lead the group of confused girls sparked my thoughts, and what good luck it was to meet her. But, then again, maybe I created my own good luck, or as I have always suspected, I've been guided. But by what? Again, I tried to solve the question, but nothing came to mind, causing me to snap out of it and resume my responsibility of guarding the rear.

Once safely settled into the cabin, Gabriella and I opened

cans of peaches and Dinty Moore Beef Stew and joyfully watched the young ladies eat in peace. They were hungry and thirsty. I gathered some wood around the cabin for the fireplace while Gabriella rounded up coats and shoes for traveling, but could only find three extra sleeping bags, which would have to do. None of the women talked at all, but they did watch our movements intently. Even Sofia remained quiet. It was not long before they curled up together on the cabin rug and fell fast asleep. We laid blankets over them and sat back on the dilapidated couch in wonderment.

"Not sure about you, but this is a puzzle," I said with an air of discontent.

"Absolutely, and I'm thinking we should stay here for at least a night and let them recuperate. We can ask them questions in the morning."

Gabriella and I stripped to our underwear and snuggled on the couch. Caressing her created passion, but we thought better of it. Being so newly in love was difficult to ignore, but the circumstance with all these young women required our restraint. After a long kiss, we joined the others in slumber.

In the early morning, I slipped outside to pee, and the clear skies gave hope for easier travel. Gabriella and I made coffee in the fireplace and prepared food for the girls while also packing items for the trip. We hoped it would require only a day or two to reach the safety of a small town, maybe Atlin. Gabriella escorted the group out to relieve themselves and upon their return, they all sat quietly and ate.

Gabriella watched them intently and then spoke, "Would anyone like to talk?"

All the young girls looked at each other and Sofia

spoke, "We only speak if we are allowed." She spoke in broken English. We soon discovered that all of them spoke some French and English, and oddly enough, some very random Russian.

"Well, I'm going to allow you to speak, and I'll start with some questions. Sound good?" Gabriella slapped her hands together in jest. All the ladies nodded in approval. "First, this is Matteo, and I'm Gabriella. Now what are your names?"

Slowly each woman spoke.

"Anya."

"Mila."

"Tatiana."

"Sasha."

"Sofia."

"Anyone have a question for Matteo or me?"

Sofia stood, as she appeared to be the leader of this little group. "All of us are confused because we have never seen people other than our families and our kids back at our home. Are there others like you?"

Obviously, this was going to be difficult for these young ladies as it appeared they had been hidden from society.

I decided to speak, "You all have kids?"

"Yes," said Sofia. "But after a while they disappear, and we must make more. That's what they say."

"Who are 'they'?"

"Our family leaders, and we must do as they say or be fed to the bears."

"Do they say what your role or job is there?"

"Yes, we are workers."

Gabriella and I gasped.

Sofia said, "What is wrong? They say we are heroes back in our homeland."

Gabriella thought quickly and asked, "And where is homeland?"

All the girls looked at each other and shrugged.

"Okay, that's good to know. You all finish up while Matteo and I take a pee break."

Gabriella and I stepped outside, and I said, "We need to remain stoic and calm while they explain their lives. It's hard to remain straight-faced and supportive while listening to this horror."

"Geez, I almost barfed." After hugging, we headed back permitting Gabriella to take the reins.

"I'd like to go around and hear your ages and information about kids. Sasha, would you please start?"

Sasha nodded and stood up. "I'm about seventeen, I think, and I've had three kids." She sat quickly.

"Mila?"

"I think I'm eighteen, and I've had four," Mila said proudly.

"Tatiana?"

Tatiana jumped up. She had a baseball cap with all her hair tucked inside. "I'm about fifteen or sixteen, and I have one."

"Thanks Tatiana, and you Sofia?"

"Eighteen and three."

"Anja?"

"Sixteen and two." Anja clapped.

"Thanks! Well done, ladies," Gabriella said artfully. "And how far away is this place called home, Anja?"

"Oh, not too far. We can show you."

"Are all your kids at this compound?" Gabriella asked.

"No," said Sofia softly. "After a certain age, they are

sent somewhere else forever, but they say we can see them again someday."

"Have any of you seen your kids again?" They all looked at each other and then shook their heads from left to right.

As I sat in disbelief, Gabriella continued with precision and purpose. "Who was the father of your children?"

"Oh, that was different for each. We worked with each till pregnancy, and then they disappeared."

"Were you ever hurt during this process?"

They all answered with the same answer. None could remember much from their interaction with the various visiting men because they were asleep, they said.

Gabriella leaned toward me and whispered, "They were drugged." And she continued to the girls, "Do some of the women at this camp fail to make babies?"

"Yes, and they have to leave, but we don't know where, and it's sad for us," Sofia whispered looking down.

I stood and asked, "How many men stay at your home? And are there other women like you?'"

"About ten men," Sofia said. "And yes, probably another six or seven women. We all grew up together at this home, just not born there."

"Well, that's enough for now. Why don't all of you prepare yourselves for the journey. Matteo and I will speak about our plans."

We rushed outside again and just stared at each other sadly.

"I have no idea where to begin with this, but I do wonder if they wish to return to the only home they know, or to leave with us?" I frowned.

Gabriella rubbed her face and shook her head. "I don't know, and I have so many questions. However, we must not overwhelm them. A couple of them were proud of their production of kids."

We discussed strategy and while Gabriella was emphatically opposed to my suggestion, she capitulated, and it was agreed that I would have one of the women lead me to the location of the camp to report the site to the authorities upon our return to civilization. Gabriella would stay with the rest because all of them were comfortable around her. If any of the girls wished to remain at the camp, we would let them. Upon laying out our plan, we asked each woman if she wished to stay. They took a while and discussed it among themselves, and all of them agreed to escape with us. Tatiana quickly volunteered to reveal the whereabouts of the only home they had known. We had Tatiana change back into her original clothing to avoid suspicion if she were captured by the miners while on our little spy mission.

THIRTY-THREE
FLY AGAIN

With the rifle strapped to my back, the .44 in my belt, and Tatiana in the lead, I headed out. Gabriella was petrified at our separation as we understood embarking on this little secretive trek with the whole group was ill-advised. Too hard to conceal a large group or move quietly without detection.

"Remember, we can't lose each other. Be cautious, Mr. Dago."

I waved, blew a kiss, and disappeared down the path.

"Why did Gabriella call you Mr. Dago?" Tatiana asked.

"Oh, it's just my cute nickname, and we use those on occasion. Do you have one?"

"No, but I'd like one someday."

"It can be arranged by your friends," I said with laughter. "It's all just random fun."

Tatiana led me down the main trail adjacent to the river, but she suddenly veered off onto a smaller, uneven trail meandering through the forest.

I questioned the move. "You sure this is correct?"

"Oh, yes," Tatiana said with confidence. "Some nights Mila and I would escape to play in the woods and splash in the river. After a few hours, we would sneak back into our home, and no one ever knew. It was dangerous but exciting, and we knew that our lives might end, if we were discovered. We were crafty." Tatiana stood a bit taller than the other girls and exuded a certain level of higher intelligence.

"How did you learn to speak so well?"

"There was a small library in one room near our community kitchen, and I read everything I could get my hands on, including bizarre books that the men would bring. Just the script fascinated me. It allowed me to dream about the possibilities of something grander while helping my daughter despite the tragic knowledge of her eventual disappearance." Tatiana exited the trail and guided me through the thick brush to a small opening she called her 'secret spot' where we sat on log stumps previously arranged by her and Mila. We ate and drank in brief silence.

"You seem to know this area very well. Why don't you escape?"

For the first time Tatiana looked directly into my eyes. Her striking blue eyes revealed traces of lasting sadness as she spoke. "I'd love to, but I have no idea where to go, or how to behave or exist. Its dangerous outside our fort, and the other 'runners' have died. No one has ever made it, and the men bring their bodies back and hang them from trees to frighten us from trying the same." She paused, teared up, and continued. "I have another reason, but not now." Tatiana removed her hat, and long, light sandy brown hair fell past her shoulders. She was beautiful. She dried her tears and stuffed her hair back into her hat before we headed out.

We walked for a while and then I asked, "Do you remember your early life before coming to this compound?"

"No, I have vague memories, but they take no clear shape, nothing I can identify. I see figures without faces. Some of the other girls remember more, and it saddens me that I cannot. I really want to recall even bits of my childhood."

"Somewhere in Russia?"

"Yes, that's what they say."

"Keep dreaming all your good thoughts, and your lost memory may return," I said with hope. As we hiked carefully through the vast forest, a gentle wind moved the treetops as the sun filtered through to us.

Tatiana spoke. "Matteo, I would like a nickname now. Can you give me one?'

"Sure, let me think of something. But first, what are you known for among your girlfriends at the camp?"

"I know my way through the forest near our home."

"Aha! I will call you Trailblazer. Tatiana Trailblazer!"

She laughed and accepted her name with joy.

"We are close now, so we must be quiet." Our trail was covered in pine needles and cones, and Tatiana motioned for me to follow her on hands and knees through a maze of bushes leading to a rocky point where we gazed down upon the vast encampment.

I must admit it was impressive, remarkably developed with small cabins and larger meeting structures. Men were milling around the walls that surrounded the camp. Tatiana pointed out distinct areas surrounding the camp. These would be of utmost importance in guiding the authorities to find this craziness later. Lying there in observation, a sensation of my own past pulsed through my limbs. My intuition caught a breeze creating a jolt of premonition guiding something positive past my eyes in a flash of light. It took my breath away and then was gone.

"You okay, Matteo?" Tatiana asked and placed her hand on my shoulder. Her touch soothed me and calmed my racing heart.

"Yes, it's a long story but I had a flash of my lost clairvoyance, and it struck something wonderful in me."

"What is clairvoyance?"

"Great question, and one day I'll tell you in depth, I promise. But now we have to return and gather the others for our journey to freedom." I began to crawl back, but Tatiana remained and wept.

"What are you feeling, Tatiana? Do you want to return to your home here? It's fine if you feel that way."

"No, it's not that. I want to escape this prison, but I have one huge issue. Remember when we all said that our kids have been shipped away?"

I nodded.

"Well, I did not tell the truth. My child is still here! Her name is Claire. And I cannot leave her. She is about four or five, I know that her time to leave is coming soon and I must take her with me, which is virtually impossible because they guard the children carefully. But I would rather die trying than walk away from her."

"Wow, that's good to know. Yes, you should try. Anything I can do?"

"I need to gather myself, so let's return to my secret place where we can plan. It's too dangerous to stay right here in the sunlight. We could be spotted."

Back at the two stumps in her little hidden spot we sat

in thought. I examined her again and she reminded me of Judy with her determination and looks, making me smile. Tatiana spoke at length about how she could reenter the camp and secure her child as the guards slept. She knew that they were not concerned because no one had ever even attempted to steal away with a child. I continued to watch her. Questions randomly popped into my head.

"Since you and the other women interact regularly, then some must remember bits and pieces from their young past. Any mention of visions from the others?"

"Some say they remember a name or a mountain, and even a beach. One had a brother, and his name was Johnny. And Mila has a sister named Kirstie."

"Excellent! Maybe that spurs your memory?"

"Not so far."

Hearing those two names confused me. There was no relation to the women in our charge.

"Have you ever thought your original name may not be Tatiana?" I asked.

"Yes, because a few of the others feel that way and have a memory of another name. But not me," she said with frustration. "I am Tatiana."

Standing up, I walked back and forth in thought, and I realized that my senses were sharpening as my power was ebbing. This time it remained longer. I peered at the skies and wondered again about the identity of my guide. Somewhere way up there it existed, and I smiled. Looking back at Tatiana, I decided to engage her memory with a game.

"I'm going to try to help you identify a possible alternate name for you. See if any of these rattles your memory, okay?"

She nodded.

I began, "Emily." After thought, she said no…

"Mary." No…

"Lisa."

"That sounds familiar to me," she said and pondered. "But wait, I think that is Sasha's name," she said with disappointment.

Tatiana began to get frustrated, so we took a break and ate.

"What is the name they gave your child?"

"They called her Olga. But in secret, I called her Claire."

"Beautiful name. How did you come up with that?"

"Through all my reading. I liked the sound of it. Seemed civilized, unlike Olga, even though I'm not sure what civilized means," she said with a laugh.

"You are spot on, Trailblazer." We both smiled. "So, let's try more names, okay?"

Tatiana nodded.

"Stephanie." No…

Samantha." Thoughts and then no…

"Julie."

"That's Anja's name," she said smiling.

I wanted to continue with a certain direction in mind, but I became apprehensive about what could happen. I proceeded with my questions. "Just a couple more names."

Tatiana sighed and stared at me with her intellectual blue eyes.

My body shook slightly as my systems ebbed and flowed, and I said, "Judy."

Tatiana paused in thought, looked at me with hesitation, and said, "No."

"How about Rose?"

"No, but that's a pretty name."

Disappointed, I decided it was enough, but she sure

reminded me of Judy with her hair and her eyes. It gave me joy. We sat in silence, then Tatiana spoke with determination.

"I need to rescue Claire."

"Yes, you must. You be careful, and if things appear too dangerous, please wait till the following evening."

Tatiana gathered herself and ran off. It was agreed that I would wait in her secret place.

Turns out this was one of the longest waits in my life even though it was only two hours. It seemed like twenty. Looking back at my earlier life lessons, it became obvious that in many ways I was *stubbornly stupid*. Those two words made me smile since they were apropos. Should I use my intelligence as an overall gauge of my current level of stupidity? Sure, I did well in school and accurately predicted so many events. But now, without my skills, I've come crashing to earth where I slush through mud, bones, death, and chaos with reckless abandon, risking my life as well as those of others. All of this just to 'find' myself? Pretty self-centered and stupid. Lying flat on my back engulfed in a bed of pine needles, I stared at the pines and the sky. Looking around, I discovered Tatiana's sweater which she had dropped in her haste. I rubbed it on my forehead and clutched it to my chest while sitting. I plunged into my search with hopes of flying again.

Shortly, I stunned myself with the knowledge that I was not only flying but also soaring through the trees in my trance and further into the universe. My power had returned with unflappable energy. Ecstatically, I crossed my legs and focused on the immediate future. Multiple premonitions jumped in front of me, and one had rifle shots and bodies spread around while women and children were joyfully swallowed by the forest. My experience suddenly disappeared, and I snapped awake. Smiling, I viewed these visions as positive signs of my imminent survival while quickly discarding my 'stupidity' theory.

I longed for my helper in the skies to reveal itself. A meeting would justify everything. I absorbed the fading lights of the day and hoped for Tatiana's safe return.

As anticipated, she trampled through the bushes clutching blankets that housed the incredible Claire. We hugged each other, and Tatiana introduced Claire.

"Claire, this is my friend Matteo, and he is taking us to a better home."

The blonde Claire stared at me with her green-blue eyes and held out her arms to hug me tightly. I teared slightly as she reminded me of a young Rose.

She felt my tears and muttered "Happy!" And that we were.

"We must go quickly as they may discover that we're gone, but I hope not till dawn," Tatiana exclaimed.

Back at the cabin, Gabriella was first to jump into my arms while all the women joyfully grabbed Tatiana and Claire.

"I waited too long for you and Tatiana's return. Seemed like a lifetime. And who is this beautiful little girl?" she said.

"This is my daughter Claire." And she waved at Gabriella.

I laughed since I had felt as Gabriella did while waiting for Tatiana's return. "We must leave now and travel by night to get a jump on the miners," I said.

We all agreed that haste was of utmost importance, and everyone packed up and off we ventured into the wild darkness. Outside, Claire pointed to the forest and repeated the word "trees."

"Claire knows many words, but that's her favorite word which she repeats annoyingly."

We all laughed and hurried down the trail. Thankfully, the moon came up within the hour so finding our way became easier. Both Gabriella and I were petrified of a possible encounter with Golden, since we would be easy pickings for the wily bear, especially at night. Claire fell asleep in a makeshift sling we threw together for Tatiana. No one spoke a word for what seemed like hours, and we paused long past the miner's camp. And the weather cooperated. Finding a sheltered hiding area off the trail, our guests bundled up in close quarters to sleep. Gabriella and I stayed vigilantly awake.

Gabriella whispered to me, "Did you get a good bearing on that camp?"

"Yes, and I'm marking bushes along the trail to help when I return with the authorities. Hopefully, we can put a halt to this madness." I informed Gabriella of my interaction with Tatiana and my ridiculous hope.

"Sorry, but it is not foolish to think that. After all she does look like Judy, yes?"

"Remarkably so, but it's just me being silly. It would be like discovering the tiniest needle in the grandest haystack of the world," I sighed. "This fatalistic approach tortures me continually, resulting in identifying everyone with sandy brown hair and blue eyes as Rose."

"Maybe you can just adopt her as your new daughter. She has nowhere to go anyway!"

"Interesting thought," I smiled.

"Good to nurture hope, and besides, we discovered each other!" she said hugging me. She was correct. We kissed and embraced each other.

Gabriella

Running my hands all over Matteo made me realize the full extent of my years of abstention. But I had never felt this way with the others. It gave me such strength as I stopped at Matteo's chest and ravished him. I never knew how a male chest could be so inspiring! He moaned very quietly. I ground my hot crotch on his kneecap which sent shivers through my bones. He spun me over and lifted my shirt and massaged my breasts, and I hoped it would never end. Opening my eyes, the figure of Tatiana came into focus standing near us in curious observation.

"Oh, geez! Hi Tatiana. Sorry, did this frighten or confuse you?" Matteo rolled off and fixed his shirt and looked at Tatiana with embarrassment.

Our foolish actions were inappropriate considering the dangers that surrounded us, but we could not help ourselves.

"I've seen this between the men and all us women in our camp, but your actions were different. There must be something special between you two. I've never experienced that, and it was fun to watch and learn. How can I get this?"

"Someday you will, Tatiana. It comes naturally when you're with the right person. None of those awful people at your camp were correct. You have plenty of time to discover passion. I just discovered it."

Tatiana looked at both of us, and asked if she should leave us alone. We laughed and said no. We needed to rest anyway. Tatiana returned to Claire and the others.

"Guess we should calm down from here on out." Matteo sheepishly nodded with approval.

MATTEO

We achieved excellent time the next day since the clouds and rain were kind enough to stay away. Gabriella and I estimated one more day and night to reach the safety of somewhere civilized.

In an hour or so, we happened upon a fork in the trail, which caused us concern as none of us knew which trail to select. While everyone waited off the trail, I hiked down both trails but could see nothing to indicate the correct direction. And my intuition failed to pick one as well. As we all stood around and discussed it. Little Claire wandered over to the fork and blurted something incomprehensible. We all stopped and looked at her as she was pointing to the right fork and repeating her words.

"What is she saying, Tatiana?" I asked.

"I have no idea but apparently she wants the right fork."

We all smiled.

"Well, that decides it. We will go with Clarie's choice," I said, and off we marched to the right. I carried Claire to relieve Tatiana, which gave me great pleasure. She babbled things to me and rubbed my whiskers, and some words I could understand like 'rocks', 'bear', and 'trees'. She loved to say her own name while pointing at herself.

Then unexpectedly she said, "Dad." And hugged me.

I thought about correcting her, but figured it would be too confusing, so she carried on with it. Repeating 'dad',

'Claire', 'bushes', "rock," and assorted incomprehensible words, Claire sang to herself as we wandered down the path. At times, feelings of unease infiltrated my thoughts. I suspected we were being watched. Nothing materialized, but I swear I saw Golden in the distance more than once. He ran shivers down my spine.

Later in the day, we veered off our path in search of shelter for the night, and we stumbled upon a small, abandoned cave which provided comfort knowing we could not be blindsided at night. Plus, the foreboding skies threatened with ferocity. Gabriella and I gathered branches and foliage to create a blockage at the cave's entrance.

Shortly after, a fierce storm blew in with numerous loud cracks of thunder and streaks of bright lightning which penetrated our cave. Torrential rain pounded around our cave, and I had to reinforce the entrance with rocks and dirt to keep the water out. The wind howled like a thousand screeching animals. Having never experienced such a force of nature as this, it scared me, but not so much the young ladies. Living in these parts, they were used to it.

Gabriella snuggled up to me and said, "We are so lucky to find this cave. It would have been miserable to be trapped in the nightmare outside."

The storm continued, and after a light meal we chatted with the young ladies trying to unlock their true identities. Gabriella figured the horrors of their earlier life and the existence at the camp played a hand in their state of amnesia, some worse than others. Somewhere in their young minds this valuable information was locked in.

Claire spent much of the early evening perched on my lap, playing with my face while babbling random words. The storm subsided and Claire mentioned pee. With approval from Tatiana, I escorted Claire to the woods, as the storm took a brief break, and the sun began to drift beneath the cloud-covered mountains.

After relieving herself, we headed back to the cave. Claire pointed to the dense woods and said, "Bear."

I glanced in the direction of her point and noticed nothing.

She spoke again, "*Bear.*"

"Claire, I don't see a bear. Where?"

She pointed again at some thick bushes as they shifted peculiarly. Suddenly, the massive head of Golden appeared, and we stared at each other. I reached for the .44 but realized I had left it in the cave. We remained still as Golden examined us from a short distance with his ferocious eyes, but surprisingly he had no ill intent. And then he was gone. How did Claire notice the bear through such a crowded forest? Without further hesitation, we scrambled into the cave.

I recounted Claire's discovery of Golden, and Tatiana said, "Claire has impeccable hearing and vision within the forest, and I'm continually amazed by her command of ideas and words never mentioned by me. It's wild."

Upon darkness, Gabriella and I took turns sleeping and guarding. Tomorrow should be our final excursion to safety, barring any unforeseen circumstances.

Gabriella rose to take guard duties and whispered, "Something does not make sense to me. Why has Golden left us alone? He ignored the girls huddled at the river. He enjoyed your company as you were tied to a pine. And he refused to attack me at the bottom of the hill. What gives? This is the fiercest beast west of the Mississippi."

"Gabriella, I have no idea. Blows me away too. Lucky, I

guess. But I am thoroughly exhausted and need to sleep, so I'll see you in an hour." We kissed and fell asleep.

GABRIELLA

With contentment, I watched the sleeping group led by my handsome boyfriend snoring gently. I smiled at the ring of "boyfriend" since I never really had one, and the thought of existing with him forever sent thrills through me. I wondered if Matteo felt the same way, and if he would like to remain in Juneau or return to Santa Barbara?

I realized that he and I had not even mentioned dating, and I slapped myself for jumping the proverbial gun. My life had transformed radically in just a few days. I no longer was a fly-fishing, guiding ranger, but one with a man I loved accompanied by a gaggle of unidentifiable, precious young ladies along with one smart little girl.

Shaking my head, I thought it must be a dream, but it was not. Each of these young women was beautifully inno-cent even though all had suffered abuse. It would require patience and adoration to expel their demons and amnesia. Two could remember their names, which laid hope for the recovery of all. My time for sleep had arrived, but I allowed Matteo to rest longer before switching positions with him.

MATTEO

I sat with my rifle resting next to me as I watched all these females sleeping comfortably. No one back home would ever believe this. Claire sucked her thumb while snuggling with Tatiana, an image previously seared into my memory by the late Judy and Rose, but now creating a smile on my haggard face.

Drifting over to Gabriella, I examined her radiant beauty. Even with all her dirt and grime, I concluded that nothing living could match her. I dreamed she would desire me forever, but pressing her, in any manner, might send her back into her previous state of despair. Watching her made me horny, and while the thought of her classic masturbation event crossed my mind, I laughed it away whimsically. Tatiana shifted some as she dreamed and muttered something incoherent. I moved closer and listened as she slurred the words.

"Mom, Dad, please sing it again to me…" She faded back to deep sleep.

Old memories had floated subconsciously through Tatiana's mind invoking hope in me for her return to normalcy. I returned to my appointed position of defending the troops with a bold prediction and intuitive feeling of a successful tomorrow.

The following morning, we all crawled through our flimsy, dilapidated door into complete destruction. All of us stood still and gazed around in shock at a sight resembling the aftermath of a chaotic war scene. Trees had been felled, streams of muddy water raced on all sides of us, where just the day before there had been only dirt. Some of the trees were burned but fortunately the heavy rain had doused all the fires. A smaller wind still gusted directly up the canyon, splashing us with frigid air and dead leaves.

"Guess we were lucky to find the shelter of our cave," Gabriella said quietly.

We headed out early and even though the storm had made our passing treacherous, we had still made excellent headway by late morning. In the late afternoon we approached a town.

"Where are we?' I asked.

"Looks like the back side of Atlin. No one ever enters this way straight out of a rugged forest. But we did!"

"Best not to be noticed anyway."

Claire looked back and waved, and I asked, "What are you waving at, Claire?" as I gazed back.

"Bear." Upon looking again, I barely spotted a small dark figure on the ridge above us. Golden appeared briefly before wandering off.

"My Claire, you do have great vision!" She laughed and clapped.

"Looks like Golden kept the miners away." Gabriella said.

"Seems so impossible, but I'm really starting to believe it."

"Look, Matteo, you need to hunker down in the bushes here while I enter Atlin. We need to keep these girls out of the public eye until we return to Juneau. I'll find the hotel I have in mind and return to get you all when we're ready."

We all sat and rested in the forest and waited for Gabriella, who returned in about an hour. She brought apples with her. Most of the girls had never seen one. They all devoured them like hungry puppies and looked at Gabriella for more.

"More to come, ladies. Let's get to the hotel quietly."

Our exhausted troupe wandered into the small town of Atlin. Gabriella knew the owner of the Rustic Hotel and arranged a suite for us all, as the young ladies were nervous about seeing civilization and other people, and getting separate rooms could be problematic for this group. Gabriella and I decided not to reveal anything about the lost women. The possibility of miners roaming in this town loomed as a distinct likelihood. It was decided that I would be allowed to leave the room, for the young ladies and Gabriella could easily be recognized by the miners.

Venturing out to fetch food and water among surly characters proved unsettling, but it was a necessary chore. I walked slowly trying to remain calm. I found a small grocery store and loaded up.

"You have a big party somewhere?" the clerk asked.

"Heck no, just getting ready to wander back out to the wilderness with all my friends."

I strolled casually into the streets and called Chuck from a pay phone to relay the short version of our unbelievable escapade. He readily volunteered to grab his buddy, Hank, and drive their trucks to Atlin to escort us back to Skagway and Juneau in secrecy.

Later that evening Gabriella and I instigated various mind/word games to address the amnesia suffered by the young ladies. We started with Lisa (Sasha) and Julie (Anja) as they had a bit of a jump on the others by recalling their names. We threw out things like country names and pets and various cities and got a quick hit from Lisa.

"'San' comes to my mind," she said with enthusiasm.

"Like maybe a city somewhere? Like San Francisco? Or San Mateo, or San Diego," Gabriella said.

"Wait! It's San Diego!" Lisa jumped up. The rest of the gang all screamed in approval.

"So, your name is Lisa from San Diego?"

"Yes, I believe so." She started to cry with joy.

"Okay, this is excellent! Keep on thinking Lisa, and we've got you narrowed down to an area."

"How about you Julie? Stimulate any memories?" Gabriella said.

She shook her head, so we continued with other cities in California, and she put her hand up when we landed on Los Angeles.

"L.A. is a large area. Are there thoughts of trees or hills or large buildings or beaches?"

"What is a beach?"

"It's a huge expanse of water surrounded by white sand, like dirt but purer."

"Yes, I have a memory of that."

"Redondo, Newport, Manhattan, Malibu…"

"Malibu!" The girls screamed. Julie from Malibu.

We were on a roll, and Gabriella switched to pets, and it did not take long to discover Lisa lived with a dog named Nelli. All the ladies hugged each other but Mila, Tatiana, and Sofia were subdued as no progress material- ized for them.

We comforted them while reminding them of the lengthy process surrounding this grueling endeavor, and they all agreed to keep up their spirits.

Gabriella and I knew qualified experts would have to be involved at some point. We were just shooting from the hip, and performing quite well, we joked.

Landing on the two cities in California laid hope that the remaining three may have originally lived in California as well. Following dinner, Gabriella and I sang songs and discussed kid style foods and games to rattle their memories, but with little success. Everyone faded off to sleep.

In the morning, Chuck and his buddy arrived early, and they quickly loaded everyone into their trucks and left Atlin.

"Where in the world did you round up those two AK47s?" Chuck asked.

"Honestly, we took them off the mauled bodies of the criminal miners we found dead."

"How did they die?"

"Pretty sure it was Golden."

"It's nice to hear that great bear is still running wild," Chuck said with a smile.

Stuffed in the trucks and with time to spare, we continued our word games, further nailing the identifications of Lisa and Julie while Sasha kept repeating her dog's name, Bella, with no results. But she remained committed. Tatiana and Mila were still anguished in frustration even though Tatiana did, in fact, recall an unidentifiable song sung to her by someone lost in her memory. Claire, of course, interacted liberally with everyone throughout our long ride, never leaving my lap unless it was to hug Tatiana.

"Well, Claire, I've come up with a nickname for you!" I smiled.

She clapped her hands and stared at me. "What?"

"Since you and Golden seemed to have a connection, we will call you Claire Bear! Or just Bear for short."

She excitedly laughed and shouted, "Claire Bear!"

After a brief stopover in Skagway, we wearily arrived at Chuck's house in Juneau. Everyone settled into the warm enthusiasm of Chuck and his mountain lodge. Chuck cooked up some fresh trout for all the troops and served lemonade to the girls. They had never experienced such a drink and asked for more. Gabriella and I spent hours notifying authorities in San Diego and Malibu, with the judicious support of Uncle Tony. A joyous rapture erupted upon locating the families of Lisa and Julie, and arrangements were made to fly them home.

Both Lisa and Julie showed surges of emotional happiness and sadness, for leaving us was hard since we were considered family. We all committed to staying in touch and Gabriella and I promised to visit when time permitted.

Over the next few weeks, we made solid advancement on Sasha through discussing her dog, Friskee, and ultimately unearthed her name; Amy from San Francisco. Three down and two to go.

THIRTY-FOUR

MENDENHALL FOREVER

The next morning Gabriella and I headed out for a walk in the morning sun, and without invitation Tatiana and Claire Bear tagged along.

Gabriella laughed at me. "They are like our kids," she said.

"Yes, and selfishly I hope to fail at locating their families, so they can be ours," I said even though I knew that was impossible.

"I know, bittersweet. Hard to let them go. They certainly are attracted to us, especially Claire all over you!"

We hiked to the same boulder I had visited before and upon climbing to the top, I pointed at the Glacier. "Mendenhall."

Claire followed my lead and repeated the word with ease. Gabriella enlightened them regarding the history of glaciers and Mendenhall while I wrapped my left arm around Gabriella and my right arm around Tatiana with Claire Bear on my lap. We sat in silence adoring the picturesque landscape of forest grandeur meandering up to Mendenhall.

I spoke, "I think this is a good time for each of us to join me in closing your eyes and focusing our thoughts on our incredible journey from disaster to this magnificent rock with this beautiful vision of Mendenhall, a peaceful and safe sanctuary."

We all smiled, hugged, and drifted with eyes closed, into each of our own zones of wonder and dreams. I melted into my happy space filled with images of my past flying rapidly across my shuttered eyes, and I morphed into a zone I had not visited in years, a shining white sky filled with multicolored stars and clouds of soft white and gray.

The image cleared as my inner body tingled with new images of my mom, dad, a young Rose, followed by the effervescent Gabriella. The young ladies we rescued also flashed by, finalized with Tatiana and the precocious Claire. I smiled as my energy grew to previous levels, and I could sense the restoration of my intuitive strength. It made me think again of how wonderful it would be to adopt Tatiana and Claire, but would it be good for them? My adoption of these two would continue to devastate their biological families. These images floated away, replaced by two black spots, one slightly oblong and–the other round. This confused me, but they too faded and vanished. Through the last few years, images like the back dots would randomly reappear with no further explanation. Frustrating, to say the least. Shortly after, I emerged from my trance and my eyes opened upon the glacier.

GABRIELLA

With eyes closed, I laughed to myself while hugging everyone. I was amused by this sort of meditation which I had always dismissed in my younger years as something akin to the crazy hippies. Nevertheless, it was calming. I focused as Matteo had suggested on the journey that ended here at Mendenhall, and I meditated. Pride touched my heart knowing that I had helped so many escape to safety, followed by their emotional return to their long-lost families. My concentration shifted to Matteo and the unexplainable good luck of having met him and how my interest in him had grown slowly, understandably. Almost losing him had shocked me out of the doldrums into unprecedented love for him. How lucky was I? My deceased mom had always said hard work creates good luck for those sincere and honest about their passions. Once again, I realized that neither Matteo nor I had ever discussed our love. Did he feel the same about me? I must remain faithful to my emotional alignment with Matteo, something I always refused to do with anyone else since my trauma. It scared me a bit knowing I loved him. I opened my eyes to the sight of Mendenhall and sighed. Suddenly, a colorful butterfly landed on my hand. With wings of green, yellow and black, the mid-sized insect flapped its wings three times and fluttered off. I know Matteo would take this as some mystical sign. Thinking further, I decided that the butterfly, because of its metamorphosis from caterpillar to cocoon to butterfly might symbolize my own growth and change, and I smiled.

MATTEO

Gabriella, Tatiana, and I shared some of our meditative thoughts, and I gently reached over and kissed Gabriella, creating a grand smile on her face. I turned toward Claire and said, "Well, Claire Bear, what did you think about?"

"I didn't really think much, Papa Dago. I just watched the same image flow across my eyes time and time again."

"Fun, Claire! What was it?"

"Two black dots but each shaped differently."

"What? I saw those dots too." I said with amazement. "But they confused me. Wonder what they were? Do you know?"

"Gosh, I don't know, but they looked a little like skin. Dots are on human skin."

I thought for a second and asked, "Like moles?"

"Not sure what a mole is, Papa." Claire shook her head.

I rolled up my sleeves and found a small mole on my arm.

"Kinda like this, Claire."

She nodded.

"How interesting, Claire, that we both saw this strange image, and now I wonder..." But I did not finish my thought. My mind soared into a deeper revelation.

I turned to Tatiana and spoke with fear, then with exhilaration. "This will solve a nagging question that has dragged on me. Tatiana, do you have a mole on your lower left back side, and a smaller round one behind your right ear?" I held my breath.

She looked at me with welling eyes and without blinking she reached for me and hugged me tightly. "I don't know. I've never thought to look. It is impossible for me to see those areas."

Gabriella asked Tatiana to stand and slowly she pulled her pants down enough to see the most glorious, most beautiful, and most telling mole in the history of all moles planted firmly, in an oblong shape, on her lower left buttock. Gabriella nodded to me, and I stood and gently peered behind Rose's ear to find the smaller, round mole. The mystery of Tatiana was over, and Rose had resumed her rightful place.

"You must be my dad! Dad? But I cannot remember."

We both sobbed, and I said her name repeatedly. "Rose, Rose, ROSE!"

Everyone screamed with joy as Claire yelled, "Grandpapa Dago!"

"You are my daughter!"

"I wish I could remember."

I continued to hug Rose, as we all did, And I reassured her that eventually her memory would return. While we hugged and sobbed, a small ray of sunshine breached the top of Mendenhall toward our rock, inspiring my next action. And I sang *You Are My Sunshine*, an old song that my parents had sung to me when I was young, and I too had sung to Rose when she was young.

I sang it repeatedly, and shortly Claire joined in as did Gabriella. Rose looked at me, raised her hand to make us stop, and blurted out details of her old room at age five and some of her toys. I screamed with joy as the resurrection of Rose had begun.

Gabriella spoke, "How is this even possible? Its mindblowing."

"I'm being guided. There is no other explanation."

We all continued to grasp each other. Energy flowed between us dashing all negative thoughts from my mind. This unworldly spiritual moment was perfect in all ways, leaving me breathless and in a state of bliss. Tears flowed freely between us, and our happiness continued until halted by the one question I never imagined could or would arise this soon.

Rose turned toward me and asked, "Where's Mom?"

Continuing to hug Rose, I asked Gabriella to escort Claire back to the house while I remained with Rose. It was a tremendous amount for Rose to digest all at once, but I had no choice. I had to tell her about Judy's premature death. Clarifications of my intuitive skills could have left her in confusion, so I abandoned all talk concerning that until later. Clearly it was enough for one day, and my *daughter* and I headed back to Chuck's.

Over the next few weeks, we located Mila's family in San Luis Obispo, making our process final. Gabriella and I discussed and finalized our commitment to each other over tears of enjoyment, sprinkled with long kisses.

"I didn't know, especially after writing you a fishing violation, that I would actually fall in love with you?"

"I know, you can't make this stuff up! But I will admit I was smitten by you at our first encounter."

We sat quietly absorbing the reflective moments, and then with gentle conviction, while watching me intently, Gabriella added, "Oh, one more thing — I think I'm pregnant." Her statement was followed by a few moments of quiet shock as we looked at each other.

Disbelief and then joy ran through me. "So that willow was a magical tree," I said with joy.

Gabriella smiled and felt fulfilled while embracing the idea of unplanned motherhood. "So, you are happy?" she asked with hesitation.

"I can't think of anyone better to spend the rest of my crazy life with other than you and this surprise child."

"I believe I'm ready to write poetry again."

We grabbed one another and would not release each other as our tears flowed yet again. Following moments of happy silence, I asked, "Do you want to stay in Juneau or return to California?"

Without hesitation Gabriella said, "I think it's time for me to return, especially with all the recent dramatics in this region, and last but of course not least, there is *you*. Santa Barbara seems like a nice place where my future husband lives."

"What would you do since there is almost zero fresh-water fly-fishing in that area, and not many park rangers either?"

Hesitating a bit, Gabriella said, "I've never mentioned this to anyone because it felt silly at the time, and I was petrified of failure and what others would think of me. But I have more confidence now."

"Well, lay it on me. I'm excited to hear."

"I've had this crazy idea floating around in my head for years, and I would like to start my own clothing line, like a couture house. Make custom outfits." She paused, and I stared into her wide, inquisitive eyes.

"There is nothing crazy about that. It's a fabulous idea. The thought floated by my mind a few days ago. And you could compete with the likes of Chanel and Dior!"

"You think?"

"You would develop your individual style with your creative charm. Do you have a name for it yet?"

"I've been struggling with that, and I cannot use Valentina. I'm sure that has been taken."

"How about just *Gabriella* or even *Gabriella V.*? Do you know the best part?"

"What?"

"You could be your own fashion model. And you wouldn't need to hire anyone for that position, Miss Sweet Cheeks."

"Haha, yes true, and perhaps I could use you as well."

"I might shatter the lens. I'm no model."

"Not true, Mister Dago. I'll fix you right up."

The next day we informed Chuck of our return to California, and all three of us walked out to our favorite boulder to have a seat and to admire Mendenhall one last time.

"I want you two love birds to know how happy I am for you, even though I'm a bit sad about losing you, and I have some jealously that you have found each other," Chuck said sincerely. "Maybe someday I can find somebody too. Although I might have to clean up my act and lose a few pounds!" He laughed.

"You will not lose us. We promise to visit when we need a Chuck fix," I said.

"I will say, Gabriella, you had me fooled. I'm happy that I was wrong. It's hard to resist this Matteo guy, huh?"

"No doubt, and you must come visit us too. We would love that. But before all that you should finish your wonderful project, the gondola, and be proud of such an accomplishment."

Excitement flowed over us evenly with the realization that all the craziness had ended, our lives were settled, and incredibly my journey had concluded. Unbeknownst to me at the time, this was not the case.

THIRTY-FIVE
CHOICES

Over the next year, Gabriella and I immersed ourselves in our reunion with Rose, which went remarkably well. Her memory returned almost entirely while she readjusted to normal society, and she even located some of her old friends from when she was five years old. She continued to devour books, just as she did when she was three years old. She finally read *Moby Dick* and *Crime and Punishment*. Rose returned to school to finish up her primary and secondary education and smiled from ear to ear when she received her high school diploma. She entered Santa Barbara City College and began her path to becoming a psychotherapist.

We spent many hours trying to get Claire registered in America. Uncle Tony, my parents, and Judy's parents all helped immensely in this process, and all went well. Gabriella and I got married in a small ceremony.

Claire Bear continued her dazzling path of unmatched intelligence which no one could fathom. She remembered everything and learned words as if she already knew them. She was off the charts.

Finally, Gabriella delivered a bouncing baby boy, and we named him Pietro Anthony Ferrari.

I also spent endless hours working with Uncle Tony fruitlessly entreating the federal government to search for the criminal element we had encountered in the Yukon. They always refused since the event occurred in another country in a remote wilderness. The whole process was exasperating to say the least. We also approached the Canadian government as well, but after a long runaround, Uncle Tony came to me.

He said, "Matteo, the Canadians finally told me they have no time or resources to chase down heavily armed thugs in the middle of the wilderness at this time. They said that numerous unscrupulous miner groups exist in the backwoods, and the few attempts to arrest them have all gone badly. So, basically, they said no or get in a long line and wait even longer."

"I can't believe this. So, we must let them exist?"

"Yep. Nothing to do but get back to work and let it all go. And hope the governments eventually approach the problem. Be thankful for the few you rescued."

Slumping back to home, Gabriella repeated Uncle Tony's words, "Time to let it all go. We must be thankful for where we stand now, and the precious gifts of Rose, Claire, and Pietro."

Reluctantly, I nodded in approval and returned to our blessed life. I continued to help Uncle Tony solve bizarre crimes, and I soaked in the love of my family.

THIRTY-SIX
THE HOPE

A month later, I suddenly awoke in the dark of the night gasping for breath, hyperventilating.

"Matteo!" Gabriella grabbed my arm. "Are you okay?"

I calmed down and replied, "Yes, just a bizarre dream. Oddly, I can't remember it now." And I lay down and kissed Gabriella. She fell back to sleep, but I did not. The dream had not disappeared, but I decided I must think about it alone without discussing it with Gabriella. She would think it was insane, which it might have been.

After breakfast, I went for a walk alone in the woods, overanalyzing my crazy dream, and came to a unanimous decision between my skills, my soul, and my mind. I must pursue this vision.

Returning home, I sat down with Gabriella. "Honey, as we both know, my journey is not complete without my fulfilling the final chapter. While these filthy criminals still operate in the Yukon wilderness. I must attempt something."

Gabriella frowned at me, then smiled and said calmly, "You have tried numerous times to end their reign of terror without any support or understanding from the authorities. How can you let this go? I'll help."

"Before I can reveal the crazy plan, I must at least explore it on my own. I'll let you know in two days. Deal?"

"Sure, as long as the next two days do not involve something life-threatening, okay? I love you too much to lose you, Mr. Dago." She smiled.

I loved Gabriella endlessly for her unquestioning support, and I thanked her profusely. The next day, after kissing Rose and Gabriella as they slept, I packed a small bag and headed out. This was nuts, but it was worth a shot.

While traveling in my car, I thought about my past life and about what a strange but lively journey it had been. I smiled and cried over the ebbs and flows of my voyage, over all the incredible highs and disastrous lows dancing vividly before my watering eyes. Gabriella, Rose, and especially Claire had rescued me from my spiraling existence, from impending doom. I had achieved what I was looking for and lived to recount it all. Smiling to myself, I tried to tell my brain to relax, to forgive the sinful, and to enjoy my existence. A practiced acceptance. Try as I might, my stubborn mind refused to settle with my soul, not until I dealt with the evil existence of the corrupt Yukon criminals. My travels continued.

I reached my destination and checked into the hotel. I cleaned myself up, shaved, and dressed decently. I tried to justify my cleanliness, and eventually I could find no harm in this formality. After looking at my watch, I gathered myself up and headed to my appointment. Once in the elevator, I paced back and forth, attempting to talk myself out of this meeting, and the ridiculous absurdity of it all. The elevator stopped and the door slid open, and I stepped out.

After a few long seconds, the door slowly began to shut. I panicked, stuck my arm against the elevator door, and jumped in. I began the slow and excruciating journey back down to the bottom floor. When the door opened at the bottom, I froze and just stood there. Once again, the door shut slowly. It reminded me of my playful childhood years and how I would ride elevators up and down tirelessly, just for the joy of it. Taking a big breath, I deliberately pushed the button and headed back up. My intuition won out.

THIRTY-SEVEN
THE PLAN

Time barely moved as I sat uncomfortably in the waiting room, reassessing my situation. Sweating and shaking a bit, I got up and grabbed a magazine to help me readjust. It was a fly-fishing magazine, *Field and Stream*. It made me think of Gabriella, and I relaxed. Eventually the receptionist led me to a guest chair in front of the desk, and I stared at the back of the executive chair, which began to swing slowly around toward me.

The gentleman stood and held his arms straight out from his sides and said, "Hey! If it isn't da long-lost Dago! Good to see ya!"

I stood and said nervously, "Good to see you too, Bruno!"

We hugged each other firmly, although I'm sure I got the hurtful end of that hug.

Still holding my shoulders Bruno said, "How was your trip? Did you rediscover yourself to your heart's content?" He laughed.

"Yes! And it went well. Shall I give you a brief description of my adventure?"

"Speak," Bruno yelled. He always bellowed, and I had developed a certain resilience to his ferociousness. He walked over to his bar and poured each of us a bourbon.

"Since your return was inevitable, I saved a little Maker's Mark just for you."

I smiled and gave him the full detailed journey, all the way to arriving back home. It took a while and Bruno just listened and puffed his cigar and occasionally nodded. There was a brief uncomfortable silence as Bruno thought and then he said, "So, you did this gal Gabriella for da first time in a shrub? After failing to do her in da tent when she slinked in at night in her pajamas?"

Rubbing my forehead I groaned. "Can you be blunter? No, no Bruno. We made love under a sweeping willow tree, not a shrub, and it was quite romantic."

"Sheesh, what a Romeo you are, Matteo." He laughed again. "I think you shoulda done her in da tent, been betta, don't you tink? But then I think about it again, and no, you should not have done her in da tent because who wants to do a gal that just farted in da tent? Dats sloppy of her and disrespectful. But you know, since you two wild and crazy kids hadn't even bathed in days, well shit, I get it! Your both must have stunk!"

I gagged on my bourbon and laughed aloud with Bruno joining in. Why had I given him such details?

"You are one sick motherfucker, Bruno! But I already knew that. I never met a man so, let's say, forward with his opinions. Maybe that's why I've grown to like you, even though at times I feel like my life may end abruptly!" I laughed.

"You must have liked this gal, but I will have to meet

her to judge for myself, eh? With a name like that, she must be Italian."

"Yes, she is, and I believe her original family is from Northern Italy."

Bruno shook his head in disapproval.

"Dats a bit of a disappointment. My family is from da South, as you know. And da Northern Italians don't like da Southern Italians and vice versa."

"Oh, for Pete's sake, Bruno, she hasn't even been anywhere near Italy, so who cares? You would like her. Very smart, funny, and pretty to boot," I said.

"I don't care about da smart thing. Best if they are not too smart, you know?" he said puffing on the cigar, which was about to make me vomit. "And you mentioned dat Gabriella was a fly-fishing instructor? I've never heard of dat before. This chore is reserved for da men. She should just cook da fish you catch, yes? And she knows how to shoot a gun? I'm gonna have to meet this special gal."

"Yes, whatever you say, Bruno."

"Look, Matteo, people like me because I'm honest and it's a trait you oughta adopt. When I say I'm gonna cut your balls off and feed them to the alligators because you misbehaved, I'm being an upfront honest citizen, agree?"

"Yes, of course Bruno," I said shifting in my seat.

"So, I got another question for ya, Matteo."

I slipped down into my chair in morbid anticipation.

"Are you trying to tell me dat dis huge, ferocious bear decided not to rip you to shreds because he liked you?"

"Well, I'm not entirely sure why he did not, but for some bizarre reason, possibly connected to my intuitive gift, he shied away from destroying me. Kind of strange, I'll admit, but the bear reminds me of you, Bruno. Big, loveable, scary guy who decided against wasting me when we first met, remember?"

"I dink you caught me in one of my rare weak, sentimental moments. But looks like I made da wise choice, eh, my son?"

"Absolutely Bruno. I feel blessed."

"So, you got your power back, Superman?"

"Yes! I did and I'm thankful for the ability to shine again, maybe to assist the world even more than before."

"I bet you are here to get back to work for me full time, huh?" he said with a grin.

"Not exactly, sir. But I did commit to helping you from time to time. Do you remember when you walked me out allowing me to return to Judy and my life? And the last comment you made to me?"

"I remember da walk out, but not da rest. What did I say?" Bruno quizzed.

"If I ever needed help, please reach out."

"Okay, yes, I recall dat."

Bruno waved approval and I began. I enlightened the Boss with all my futile efforts to round up the criminals in the Yukon through both the Canadian and United States authorities. Even though most of my life had flourished with fabulous entertainment and personal rewards, the failure to prosecute these horrific brutes had left me unfulfilled. I explained my frustration with the legal systems in both countries and how I went as far as hiring a legal team to pursue it. All of it failed or was delayed indefinitely, languishing in a meandering line of red tape.

"So that is why I'm here, Bruno. I was hoping to get your help in capturing these criminals and turning them in for prosecution and sentencing in Canada." I stopped with a sigh and watched Bruno's face. The clock ticked very slowly.

"You want me to go up dere and snag these fellows and turn them in? Not so sure interfacing with da law is my best attribute, you know?"

"Bruno, but I have all the confidence in the world that this would be a snap for you," I said, kissing up.

"I will need ta speak with my Consigliere."

"What is that?" I asked.

"It's my legal counsel. I gotta say this has a remote chance of approval and would require your involvement to a certain extent. It's quite a large ask, Matteo. Go to da casino and gamble while I consult." He handed me a stack of bills. "Maybe you can snag some bad guys for me." He laughed. "Come back in a couple hours."

Back to my old and rewarding stomping grounds, the poker room. My euphoria grew, especially with the rebirth of my precognition. I expanded Bruno's one-thousand-dollar gift to approximately two thousand in less than an hour. While enjoying this, I reminded myself of its past antithesis and knew my ecstasy was temporary. So, I got a groove on.

An hour later I received a tap on my shoulder, and one of Bruno's men said, "Mr. Garbinelli will see you now, Mr. Ferrari."

I gathered my huge stacks and headed upstairs. At Bruno's desk, I meticulously stacked up my horde in perfect alignment and casually pushed it toward Bruno with a smile.

"Damn, Matteo, that's a little over five grand in less than two hours. Well done! If I was smart, I would sponsor you in tournaments. But my buddies in the industry wouldn't like it."

"It's all for you Bruno," I said gleefully.

"I know, you are trying to bribe me, but no need. Have a seat." He pointed to his side chair. Frank and Eddie were standing on each side of the Bruno. Bruno sighed, gazed at me, and began.

"When I was young, my father taught me to treat people with respect, but if they fucked with your family or business ventures, den all respect falls into the grey category, and all bets are off. Of course, I never committed any sin against anyone unless they gave me a good reason, right Eddie?"

"You bet, Boss, that's the truth," Eddie growled.

They all chuckled as I caressed my forehead again in disbelief.

"Anyways, Matteo, what you ask is impossible according to my Consigliere. He says you are not my family, so seeking revenge, or as you say justice, is not permissible. Our codes are strict and forbid it. I tried ta convince him dat you were exceptional and have helped my family with loyalty and dedication to our cause. But he said no, so I had to forget about it."

"Thanks for trying, Bruno. I knew it was a long shot," I said depressed.

"But after tinking for a while, I confronted my Consigliere again with how I thought of you as my *son* since I had lost my own. I developed a love for you like family. My consigliere changed his stubborn mind and gave me approval," Bruno said with a sly smile.

I sat stunned as it slowly registered, and I leaped up, ran around the desk, and hugged the big bear with all my might.

"You will help now?" I said eagerly.

"Yes, my son." With that Bruno handed me all my

winnings, less the one thousand, of course. He proceeded to escort me out with his considerable arm wrapped around my shoulders, with Frank and Eddie in tow. Outside his illustrious casino, Bruno stopped at a bench and invited me to sit with him.

"Matteo, did you know that all the people in this world are accomplished artists? Even the losers? Yeah, I learned dat from my father when I was very young. I watched him create a few fine masterpieces that were exquisite and thoughtfully arranged. I was impressed."

"Yes? What were his best ones? What medium? Canvas?" I said with curiosity.

"You know, it's just a little complicated to discuss right now. Not sure you would understand, so just take my word. I learned a lot, and I too, was able to paint a nice masterpiece a long time ago in my homeland. I'll tell you about it sometime. Anyways, everyone can create something unique. Some paint wid colors, some paint wid drinks, some wid food, and others paint wid sports, like soccer and you know what?"

"Um, what Bruno?" I said with a bit of confusion.

"I'm about to paint my second great masterpiece!" He smiled widely from ear to ear with infectious delight followed by a big draw on his cigar.

"That's fabulous, Bruno! I can't wait to see it. Possible hints of the subject matter?"

"I'll let you know when I've got it organized in my head," Bruno said with a nod.

"So back to the capture of these felons. What's the next step?" I asked.

"You head back to Gabriella, who I have yet ta meet, and I'll be in touch, capisce?"

"Capisco Bruno!" and off I drove, enthralled with the anticipation of my journey's end.

"Have you lost your mind? You asked Bruno, the mobster, to help you apprehend the Canadian gang?" Gabriella said in despair.

"Well, yes, I did. He rejected the idea at first, but he kind of thinks of me as his son, so he changed his mind. He will call us when he is organized, I hope! If he does not, then I promise to abandon any further search, okay?"

Gabriella looked at me with suspicion but smiled and calmly said, "Don't forget what you just said, Mr. Dago."

Within the week Bruno called and gave his final approval, and I screamed with joy. Gabriella fell out of her recliner. He instructed both of us to prepare for the journey and meet him at a predetermined location in Juneau.

"What? We must go?"

"We, especially you, must show him the location via boats. Maybe we can go visit our famous willow tree?" We both smiled and packed our bags. "Rose can watch the kids."

There was hope for closure now.

Three days later, and with my direction, everyone met at Chuck's Juneau house for the introductory lunch meeting before beginning our travels into the wild. Bruno showed up with ten capos. I was impressed. Albeit a bit scary, they were all quite professional in their overall demeanor and bowed to Bruno without question. All came heavily armed with automatic rifles, pistols, grenades, and even night vision military-grade goggles.

"How did you get all this heavy equipment into the country?" I asked.

"I have a cousin who has various operations in British Colombia and other places as well. He is well-connected." Bruno gave me an affectionate slap on the back. Upon meeting Gabriella, Bruno spoke again as I cringed in anticipation of his unfiltered mouth. "So, dis is da famous Gabriella."

"Yes, 'tis me! Hope you have heard decent things about me."

"Of course, and Matteo is correct. You are beautiful! We will hafta have a good talk someday, just you and me, okay?"

"Okay, Bruno, that sounds good." Gabriella glared at me.

Chuck was all in and excited about helping in any way he could.

Bruno took his time introducing his heavily armed support team, led by head capos Paolo, Augusto, Luigi and Gennaro. Apparently, the other fellas were not yet worthy of introduction. All spoke acceptable English. Gabreilla spoke about the boats and of engaging them outside of Atlin. She also reserved the same hotel in Atlin for everyone the day before heading into the wilderness.

That evening Gabriella and Bruno sat outside on the porch and got to know each other.

At first both sat quietly and admired the beautiful stars that glowed like illuminated diamonds in the dark.

Bruno broke out his cigar case and offered one to Gabriella.

"Thanks, Bruno. I've never had a cigar or a cigarette. I imagine it would make me cough. So I'll pass."

"Actually, you don't inhale da smoke. So, you should be fine."

Thinking carefully of the importance of the conversation, she reached out and took one.

"I'll give it a shot."

"My wife always avoided them, but you are not an ordinary woman, are you?"

"I would hope we *all* are extraordinary, yes?"

"Aha! Good response. Matteo told me some incredible tings about you. You are a Ranger and a fly-fishing expert. Would you be willing to teach me fishing some day?"

"Absolutely, but you would need to obey my every command." She said with a smirk.

"I tink I can adjust my approach just for you." And they both puffed for a few quiet seconds.

"I understand you like this Matteo and value his expertise. Why do you like him so?"

"As I told Matteo, I've grown to love him just like my own lost son, and I respect his opinions, to a certain extent."

"Why is it that everyone wants to take him on as their son? Both you and the guy, Chuck, want to adopt him. I mean, he already has parents."

"Yes, well, he is likeable, right? You like him. He is contagious."

Thinking quietly, Gabriella realized that Bruno was correct, as she adored Matteo as well, in her own, good way. The greatest, most handsome friend and husband ever.

"What will you do now that you're back in California again? No more wilds and bears and such."

"I have some ideas."

"You could come ta work for me in Vegas. With all your good looks and charm, you would be a great manager. My daughter, Camilla, is my Food and Beverage manager. She loves it. You would like her. She is about your age. And a beauty, just like you."

"Thanks for the compliment, but beauty is in the eye of the beholder, right?"

"Haha, true my dear, and my eye is always correct. I say what I mean, and I mean what I say." And he took a big draw on his cigar.

"That's quite thoughtful of you, Bruno. But what does that mean to you?"

"I got no idea. I just heard it once, and it's gotta nice ring to it."

"Very funny Bruno. Love it."

"So, if you don't wanna work for me, what great plans do you have for yourself?"

"My one big idea is I'm starting my own clothing line called Gabriella V. It's moving right along, and I'm excited about it."

"That's fabulous. I've been considering a massive overhaul of all our outfits currently worn throughout my casino. Maybe you could oversee their new design and production?"

"I would love to chat more about that. Its right up my alley."

Looking directly into Bruno's brown eyes, Gabriella decided to go out on a limb and asked, "Bruno, what is the nicest thing you have done over the years?"

"Kind of personal, ya know? Didn't Matteo tell ya not to ask too many questions? But it is a good one, so let me tink about." Bruno sat quietly and then his eyes lit up and he said, "A coupla years ago, I was in da local grocery store waiting to pay with this little old lady in front of me fumbling around in her purse trying to round up her cash. Turns out she was $4.50 short, and the cashier started to figure out what products ta take out. I told da old lady that I would cover what she didn't have in cash, and she gave me a big hug. Yeah, that was the best ting I've done in a while."

Gabriella just looked at him and started to laugh, thought better of it, and quickly backpedaled. "Well, that's great Bruno, but I bet you have done something grander than that!"

"It's the little tings that count da most, right?"

"Correct Bruno." Gabriella thought it best to stop pushing him.

"I don't tink there is much else I can remember right now, but let me tink about it, and I'll get back to you."

At that moment, I showed up and rescued Gabriella from further scrutiny.

"Gabriella is smoking a cigar? Bruno must have smitten you. I'm happy you two are best friends now, but shall we discuss plans?"

Breaking out a map, Gabriella showed the river journey that would take us close and then described the hike to the miner's camp.

"How will we transport the criminals out? Our boats can only hold all of us," Gabriella said.

"We brought along some inflatables and lots of rope ta accommodate doz thugs and anything else we need to take back, okay?" Bruno exclaimed.

"There are at least ten of these guys, not to mention the young ladies that we may encounter too."

"It will all work, trust me. I have a plan." Bruno grinned.

Gabriella had learned that at some point you don't question Bruno any further. Gabriella and I headed off to get some much needed rest before our final trek.

GABRIELLA

As I lay there listening to my sexy life partner and husband gently sleep, memories of all the events rattled my mind. I was experiencing a full circle back to Chuck's place.

The fact that I survived the entire journey and ended up with Matteo and our own child seemed a bit surreal, but it was real. And to punctuate this dreamlike trip with the discovery of Rose and Claire seemed impossible yet, that too, was real. Hard for me to grasp the significance of all of it. Just remain thankful, Gabriella!

All is good, but it did concern me that we were heading back into the lair of the lion. I was never much of a religious woman. I thought of it as a crutch for the weak, and the church only fulfilled the need for weddings and funerals. But all of this had some sort of spirituality to it and maybe there was a God or maybe Matteo is that? Or he is guided by God? Matteo wanted to pursue this avenue more than I did, but subconsciously I desired the same thing, and now I fully understood it.

I had lost a good friend in Richard, and gathering up these wilderness vermin was important. I could have let it all go, but Matteo constantly reminded me of the guilt we would have if a final effort were not attempted. It was a long shot, but these Italian guys certainly appeared prepared! Now, for the first time in my life I prayed, in earnest, for our well-being. I leaned over, smelled Matteo's hair and skin, placed my hand softly on his chest and joined him in rest.

THIRTY-EIGHT
THE MASTERPIECE

MATTEO

After days of travel, we all landed quietly in the same cove where Gabriella had taught me fly-fishing. All of Bruno's men had fishing poles to disguise their intent, just in case we were spotted. All the boats were dragged on shore and hidden in the bushes. Our hike began at once. It was decided by Gabriella and me that we would all hike to Rose's secret hideaway about a mile from the camp and silently set up there with no lights or fires that night. Bruno, Paolo, and I walked with stealth to the lookout boulder that peered down upon the compound of criminals. We all examined the map that Rose created, which matched what we saw. Soon we had a count of approximately eight miners and five women, some with young children. We returned to the hideaway and Bruno consulted his troops in Italian.

He turned to us and spoke seriously. "Tonight, we engage our plan."

"Outstanding, Bruno," said Gabriella. "We cannot wait any longer for this final assault."

Bruno sighed and said, "You two won't be going. It's not a safe place for greenhorns, and besides you might shoot one of us." Gabriella started to protest, and I grabbed her as Bruno began to glare.

"You two will stay here with Luigi as your guard, and we should return by sunrise or sooner. It depends on the resistance. Also, you may not go to the boulder to watch the activities below. Too dangerous, and besides, it is too dark to see anything."

We both slumped back on a tree and looked at Luigi, who saluted us. Methodically, Bruno and his boys attached silencers to their pistols and strapped on their night goggles and ARs. At 2:30 a.m. in the pitch dark they set out.

The next cold, dark three hours seemed endless as we hung out quietly in our tent, listening intently for any sound that might lend a hint of Bruno's success or failure. If Bruno failed, then our safety would be compromised. Luigi loyally kept guard, never resting. At the break of dawn, we paced the camp nervously while Luigi watched the trail. Without warning, two birdlike whistles broke the silence and Luigi returned the whistles. Gennaro appeared and spoke in Italian to Luigi.

"Bruno wants you to come now," said Luigi.

Gabriella looked at me with trepidation, and asked, "What happened?"

"It's over. Bruno wants you."

We smiled and hugged Luigi, who grinned shyly as Gennaro led the way.

Entering the compound, we encountered five young women, in their late teens it seemed, with three young children clinging to them. They all were relatively relaxed with two of the capos entertaining them with their indomitable Italian charm. The women became even more relaxed when they spotted another woman, Gabriella.

Gabriella ran to them and spoke English and French with them all. I followed Gennaro to the center of the compound where existed a shocking sight. Eight of the miners lay piled together, dead as doornails. Their weapons were stacked next to them.

Pietro greeted us and spoke, "There's two more we captured at the end of the compound with Bruno and Paolo."

"You killed them all? Capturing them was the plan, yes?"

Pietro just shrugged and Gennaro led us away to Bruno.

Gabriella caught up to me and yelled, "What the hell happened?"

"Maybe there was a fight? I don't know; let's wait for Bruno."

Finding Bruno, we discovered two miners were alive, a bit bloodied, and tied to chairs.

"Bruno! What the fuck?"

"Calm down," Bruno said. "They put up a litta resistance, so we had no choice but to dust those fellas back there, but we captured these two, and with a little persuasion, we identified that they are not Canadian miners, but top Russian bastards, and guess what? Dey are the ones buying the five-year-old girls from the miners! So, we got lucky and nabbed da two top dogs, ha! But they are like mice now." Bruno smiled proudly. "Happy now?"

Gabriella recognized Bruno's desire for encouragement,

so she said with remorse, "Well, yes, thank you, Bruno! Job well done!"

I looked at Gabriella in disbelief and asked, "But did all the others have to die?"

Bruno shrugged, which apparently is the Italian way of nebulously answering questions. "It is what it is. Dey never knew what hit 'em. No rifles fired or grenades lobbed. Just used our silenced pistols. Very effective. They had it coming, eh?" Bruno slapped my back with laughter. He continued, "But we also found another fella in bad shape back there in da barn." He led us to him. Gabriella screamed when she saw the man laying on a cot. He was beaten and bloodied, but he opened his eyes and smiled at Gabriella.

"Dick! You are alive!" She hugged him. Somehow, Dick had survived for months!

"Ouch, not too hard," he grimaced, but also chuckled. "It will take a little more than a good beating for me to give in! Remember, I spent time in a prison camp in Vietnam, and I was one of the few who escaped. I gave them no information." And he sat up. Holding him closely Gabriella said,

"I'm so glad you made it, Dick! I was so depressed about losing you! What happened?" Everyone started to clean him up while giving him small amounts of water and food.

"We were on a hunt for elk when suddenly five guys jumped us, and they overwhelmed us before we could resist. They took away our weapons and tied us up and began to interrogate us." Dick took a brief break to drink some water. "They walked away and upon returning, they proceeded to shoot my two clients point blank and knocked me out with the butt of a rifle. Next thing I know I ended up here with a splitting headache, and they continued to torture and interrogate me. I'm ecstatic you and Matteo showed up with your buddy. Who is he?"

"He is a good friend of mine from previous days," I said with wholesome ambiguity. "Bruno meet Dick."

Bruno gave him a light handshake. "Hope you feel betta, my friend. Okay, so what would you like ta do with these two other worthless, commie bastards?"

"It would be best to turn them into the authorities for prosecution," I said firmly.

Bruno sighed and led Gabriella and me to an old outdoor couch to chat alone.

We sat quietly for a few moments, and I spoke up. "Bruno, I'm going to make the assumption that you just painted your masterpiece, correct?"

"No shit, Sherlock. No matter what anyone says, you're no dummy, Matteo! Before making any snap decisions, let me advise you whether you want it or not. If we take these bums back to Atlin, den you will be on your own from that point on. As I mentioned before, I don't mix well with da police, especially from another country. You would need to turn dem in, and subsequently the authorities will want ta know who you are, and most likely, they won't believe you. The Russians will cry foul, and chaos might evolve. If it even made it to court, your daughter, Rose, and the other girls would be dragged back up here to testify, causing all these young gals much stress and trauma, especially reliving their nightmare. Capisce?"

"What else should we do with them, Bruno?" Gabriella asked.

Bruno shrugged and extended his arms out and said, "You two lovebirds talk it over. It's your call."

Bruno strolled away back to the Russians to continue

his interrogation, while I held Gabriella's hand and sank into flux about our dilemma. Damned if we do, damned if we don't.

Gabriella spoke. "Obviously, this is a no-win scenario, but let's sidetrack for a second here and play one of your groovy, spiritual, uber analytical games with our current situation. Okay, Mr. Dago? Would you like to start?"

Looking at Gabriella, I reminded myself of how much I loved her and replied, "You start, Sweet Cheeks."

She pushed me with loving intent. As we watched Bruno's capos methodically attach small explosives devices to the walls of the rickety compound, I said, "Looks like they plan on leveling this shithole, firmly eliminating its existence."

Gabriella went into deep thought while rocking back and forth, a trait of hers I enjoyed more than anything, and she began, "I am not religious, as you know, but this feels like Heaven colliding with Hell, God confronting the Devil, and good battling evil. These structures, in this compound, are the Devil's post piles, and the eight dead miners are nothing more than the Devil's disciples. These surviving females were captive angels, now free to spread their wings and soar again. If we had failed in their liberation, the pure flowing river would turn to violent molten lava laying waste to everything in its path."

Staring at her, I mumbled, "You are too good at this now, Gabriella. I cannot match your vigor. You win!" I smiled. "But one question. How do you and I and Bruno fit into your analysis?"

Gabriella thought for a moment and said, "We are the saviors guided by your invisible god, Matteo. Are you any closer to meeting this force?"

"No, I still can't find what I'm looking for. Everything

else has fallen into place except that. Maybe this piece of the puzzle was not meant to be."

We sat in silence and Gabriella eventually broke the stillness. "We cannot allow any part of Hell to escape and breed, can we?"

"Of course not, but we must do what's morally right and turn them in. It would be an injustice to do otherwise, right?"

Gabriella turned to me. "What the authorities did to me in Los Angeles was an injustice. Sometimes life isn't fair."

We sat quietly for a few long seconds, and I turned to Gabriella. We stared at each other and without any further words, we nodded in agreement. I walked alone to Bruno while Gabriella returned to the young ladies.

"Bruno, do you remember when we first met, and I was tied to your side chair?"

"Of course, I tink you peed in your pants!"

"Almost, Bruno, almost." I smiled. "And do you remember what Frankie and Eddie wished to do with me?"

"Is dis some sort of a trick question, Matteo? Yeah, I remember. Remove your fingernails, break your kneecaps, strangle you, stuff you in a barrel, chuck ya in Meade." Bruno suddenly smiled realizing what had just happened. "Aha! You are no dummy, just like my son."

"You now have Gabriella's and my choice, except for the Meade part. I'm sure some other body of water will suffice." I shrugged, held my arms out and said, "Capisce?"

"Yeah, capisco." And Bruno bowed.

I turned and walked away to join Gabriella and the girls. We made them block their ears since in the distance we could hear various shrieks, screams, horrific yells, forlorn begging, and sobs; then sudden silence.

On our lovely boat ride back to Atlin, I couldn't help myself and asked, "Bruno, did you bring lots of barrels with you?"

"No, but the trout, wolves and even that crazy Golden bear will all eat well tonight!" and he laughed, slapping my back yet again, almost causing me to fall overboard.

"And Gabriella, you asked me a few days ago what the nicest ting I've done in da last few years, remember?"

Gabriella nodded.

"Nabbing these bad guys and making your lives happy and complete, capisce?"

"Capisco!" Gabriella smiled.

Our journey was complete.

THIRTY-NINE

WALK AMONG GODS

Over the next two years, Gabriella delivered a bouncing baby girl, who we named Grace, and life was good. I resumed my job with Uncle Tony and had quite a good kill rate on the unsolved crimes. My clairvoyance had returned completely. Gabriella continued the research and development of her Gabriella V. clothing line. She even landed a few small clients. It didn't take long before Bruno reached out to her and asked her to handle all his casino outfits. Gabriella was on her way.

Rose continued her recovery, which she realized would be a lifelong endeavor that would never be entirely complete. She began studying psychotherapy and was determined to earn her license. I was proud of her for her gallant journey toward something peaceful while helping others.

Claire, between nine and ten, excelled in just about every category of school and sports. Her popularity was over the top, and she found school studies too easy, but we refrained from moving her to a higher grade. She loved all her friends and was quite the leader of her large group. She seemed too intelligent but blended well with all groups.

One day Gabriella came to me and commented on Claire. "You think it's possible that Claire has inherited your innate powers?"

"I have not thought in that way, but you may be right. Wouldn't that be astounding? What about Rose?"

"I don't see that in her. Do you?"

"No, just wondering. If it's true, it appears to have skipped a generation, huh?"

Gabriella nodded in agreement.

"At an appropriate time, I'll broach the subject with her," I said.

Rationalizing to myself, I thought that if Claire did not possess my intuition, it might confuse her to speak of it. After all, she was only nine or ten years old. But then again, that was my age when I became aware of my peculiarity. I concluded, brilliantly I might add, to test Claire by arranging a flag football game in our backyard with Claire and all her sports-minded friends. Within fifteen minutes of play I had a secure answer, and I sat on the front porch steps holding my head in disbelief. How did I miss the signs? I must be getting old!

Claire Bear dominated the game, defense and offense. She predicted plays and player movements. She was always on the winning team regardless of her teammates. Thinking back to when we met, things began to come into focus. She repeated anything she had heard and listened to everything around her, as if she were absorbing the energy from her surroundings. Hyper-aware, I would call it. She selected the correct fork in our path as we escaped from the miners. She was aware of

Golden's presence when all the others were not, including myself.

Oddly, she felt comfortable near him. Apparently, she knew he would not harm us. Claire sat in my lap more than in anyone else's. While I thought of it as endearing, possibly she sensed the importance of my connection to Rose when I had few clues? Others remarked that Claire was just highly intelligent, a little ahead of her age group with a photographic memory. Nothing too extraordinary. But that is what people also said of me at an early age. It did raise my eyebrows when realizing that Claire seemed far more advanced than I had been.

"Gabriella, you may very well be correct in your assessment of Claire Bear."

Following the game and after all the girls had returned home, I approached my incredible granddaughter. "Shall we go for a stroll, Claire Bear?"

"Sure, Papa Dago! Let's go to the forest."

Holding Claire's hand, I looked back at Gabriella smiling as she gave me a thumbs up followed by the peace sign. God, I loved that woman! As we left, Gabriella ran to us, threw her arms around my shoulders and slipped a folded piece of paper into my hand.

"What's this?"

"I finally wrote some poetry! You can read it later." And off she ran.

Claire and I walked for a while chatting freely about how much fun she had with all her friends today. She never mentioned her superiority during the flag football games.

"Claire, do you realize how much you dominated today's games?"

"Oh, sure, but I'm careful not to gloat. I don't want to hurt my friends' feelings."

"Smart girl! Don't want to alienate all your classmates. Claire, do you ever get the feeling that you are exceptional in any particular way, other than the obvious like your performance on the field today?"

Claire thought briefly and spoke up. "I do Papa, and I know I'm gifted, just like you."

"You think I'm gifted? In what way?" I said with surprise. How would she know this? Did Gabriella tell her or maybe it was my parents?

"I can just tell, Papa, that you can predict, you can see things that others can't, you have a great sense of what's right and wrong. You help others, and you are more than aware of the troubles surrounding everyone else. I'm not sure what the correct words are to describe this. Do you know?"

I stopped dead in my tracks and looked with amazement at Claire. "Intuition, clairvoyance, premonition, subconscious, visceral to name a few. Maybe ESP. And telepathy too."

"Isn't that interesting that my name is part of that one word, clairvoyance?" she said with a smile.

I could barely speak, realizing this young girl of about ten was far ahead of me! She had my skills, but she was even more advanced.

"Well, isn't that fun, Claire?" We hugged and laughed. "When did you first realize your advanced skills?"

"I think I was about four or five, right before you were guided to us and rescued us. I realized I had something special because my mom didn't see or predict the things I did. It was me who led us out of the thick forest back to the city of Atlin, without even a scratch on any of us."

"Did you ever wish to question me about it?"

"Sure did, but I was worried that you would not accept me or my words. I was scared. I was concerned about being labeled crazy because I'm always thinking and predicting and guessing and accurately too, you know?"

"All too well, Claire Bear," I said with enthusiasm as the excitement of squaring off with another soothsayer gave me cause for celebration, and now I did not feel so alone. "When I was younger, only my parents, Judy and Uncle Tony were aware, and later Bruno and Gabriella... and now you!"

"I'm so happy, Papa Dago! I don't feel so weird, and I wish to write about it and tell everyone we know. Would you be fine with that? The world should know us!"

"Sure, Claire Bear, it's about time for me to embrace it all and share it."

"Isn't it great that there are three of us, and maybe five, and maybe more?"

I became speechless once again, but slowly gathered myself. I said, "There are more? Who are they?"

"You don't know?"

"No."

"Golden for sure!"

I could not walk any further while absorbing all of Claire's revelations. I perched on a log at the edge of the path and Claire sat holding my arm.

"Did I do something wrong, Papa?"

"No, no, not at all. I'm just overwhelmed by your smarts and a bit disappointed that I didn't pick out Golden sooner. Of course he is similar. It is so simple and clear now. It explains why he only attacked poachers around Juneau. It explains why he didn't kill me or Gabriella when we first met him. He also did not kill the five young ladies at the river, but he did waste all the miners when he was presented with the opportunity. It explains why no one could ever catch or kill him. He was always warned! What else?"

"He escorted us out of the wilderness without any trouble from the miners. He probably attacked them when they got close. He liked me, and I liked him. We both saw him in the distance, and then he would vanish, like a ghost."

"Yes, you were comfortable with his presence while the rest of us, even me, were hesitant, to say the least. He guarded Gabriella and me while we hid in the willow grove. So do you think there are two more of us?"

"Yes, I'm not totally sure, but I believe one is the bald eagle you saw in the boat, and possibly the raven you met years ago. My senses keep repeating those birds."

"Wow, okay, Claire, they absolutely could be. What else could justify their coming so close to me? And now that I think about it, the eagle did appear while I was tied to the tree with Golden so close by. They must know each other and are guided as well. Maybe there are far more throughout the world."

"I think so, and maybe we can run into them someday. And, Papa, isn't it great how we are randomly guided?"

"Yes, but wait a minute! Do you know how we are guided? And by who?"

"Of course, but don't you?"

"Claire, I've been searching my whole life for the answer to this riddle. What or who is it?"

Claire laughed, realizing my lack of understanding, and said, "Well, I always notice you looking up frequently, so I thought you knew. Look up and tell me what you see, Papa Dago."

I looked up for the millionth time in my life and said, "Okay, Claire Bear. I see the spacious sky, I see the warm sun peeking through the huge trees, I see mystical clouds floating by, I see many birds flying in and out of the trees, I see fluttering butterflies, I see the universe is all its grandeur, I see a plane in the sky, and I see..."

Claire stopped me. "Papa, what is moving other than the birds that is noticeable to our eyes?"

Looking up again, I gazed around. "The plane?"

"No, what else?"

"Some insects flying around, and the tree tops swaying ever so slightly in the wind," I said, still confused.

"Papa," Claire said with hesitation. "There is no wind today."

I looked up again, and the trees stopped swaying, and then started and then stopped. I took a large gasp of air, held, and released it.

"The trees? It's the *TREES!*"

"Yes, Papa. And they have all the power and emit things that can guide us. Especially the grand old trees. They all communicate with each other. It's like they are one big underground web of roots, I guess, not noticed by most. And they can put out signs and simple signals. And it is sent to all living things in the world, but you and I and Golden were simply born with the ability to accept their guidance, that's all. The trees want us to do what's right, and help the world survive so they can survive. This is my best guess to explain the way we feel. I'm sure there are more of us, and we should try our hardest to find and play with them."

I began to tear up with astonishment over Claire's character and her ability to analyze all this with ease. She was far ahead of me. I hugged her and laughed with joy and relief. I looked up one last time to see the entire forest sway not more than a few inches from left to right.

Claire and I rose up, I cleared my wet eyes, and on we walked.

In a few moments, Claire spoke up again, "You know what, Papa Dago?"

"What now, Claire Bear?" I prepared myself for something more startling.

"I've decided to change my nickname. I will no longer be Bear."

"Okay, so what will it be, smarty pants?"

"Call me Yukon."

Smiling down on Claire I said, "Give me your special hand, Yukon."

We held hands and walked the meandering trail fading away into our special place, the kingdom of our heavenly forest, home of the majestic trees.

There is wilderness not only in nature
but also in every human, making
everything inseparable.

The Wonder
By Gabriella Valentina

In my hectic, scattered younger years,
I lived among many memories of fear.
But still appeared in front of lenses and light,
Until one day a nightmare came to me with fright.
Scattering my life and locking me in my cage,
Not allowing me to retake center stage.

Yesterday, when life was not so fine,
I drowned it out with abundant wine.
What can I say?
Is there a softer way?
Finding it hard to fancy anyone,
I give little hope to no one.
Better for me, you know, they say.

Over the years, I morphed toward intolerable,
While he suffered into adorable.
With his approach, I became reasonable.
Are there grounds for inseparable?

But today the rain washes me clean,
Giving me the fresh look of a beauty queen.
Let's do this another day,
Then it will be another place and time
And maybe I will be almost fine.

Long leaves drift from my Willow.
Will my friend come to my pillow?
I sprinkle love dust over his chest,

Allowing me to give my caress.

As sun seeps with fog feet through the leaves,
Shining down upon my natural bed.
Will he fly to my honeycomb like bees?
Or will he dance softly in my head?

Giving me hope for salvation,
While forging a path to resurrection,
You ignited my desire,
And set my body on fire.

Time has come today,
As he moves without stray,
And with surprise he comes my way,
Never alone again, I say.

Wherever my brain abruptly flew,
Would it go with or without you?
I rationalize, hypnotize, and moralize.
If only I could socialize.

While in the dark, I walked alone,
Calming as it may be, it shocked my zone,
As being just one, I wanted two,
Then it came to me, it may be you.

There was a time not long ago,
As I grew faster than a river flow,
When everyone saw me for my behind,
There was one who scanned my mind,
And that one was you,
Who came to me with a different view.

He is not just a boy, as I first surmise,
But a wonderful boy, one of thought and surprise.
Stumbling through forests of wood, bush, and bling,
Searching for a long, lost something,
But not just random anything.
I shuck and shake with my erratic play,
Ignoring all the signs that drift my way.
Then, under the magical willow we melt with wonder,
And surprisingly my cage lifted, enter my lover.
I suddenly wake to the spirit of you.
No longer alone as before, we stand together, the two.

He is not just a boy, but a wonderful boy.
My friends call him my toy
But he is so much more than that.
He is a package of joy.
He is not just a boy, but *my* wonderful boy.

At the same time in space,
I, too, am *his* wonderful girl.
Full of mischief and grace.
Shining for attention like a perfect pearl.
White as white without flaws,
Flapping my wings with much applause.
I am his wonderful girl,
Shining forever as *his* pearl.

ACKNOWLEDGMENTS

I am indebted to the following legendary people for their solicited contributions and opinions to this book:

The fantabulous team at Acorn Publishing.

My Beta Readers: Mark Madden, Joel Maloney, Anne Flett, John Herman, Anthony Angellotti, and Randolph Stern.

My Champion Readers: my wife, Jenny Burnell, my daughter, Carly Burnell, and my son, James Burnell, for always being there for me in times of need.

My Book Club Boyz: Michael Main, Jacques Thiebaud, Tracy Burnell, Dean Pratt, Robert Nolan, and Kenny Derscheid for unknowingly inspiring me to continue writing.

George Backmann, author/actor/editor.

My dog, Nelli, for her never-ending love and dedication to me, and her constant positive attitude as long as I carry treats!

When in doubt, just sit down and write.

ABOUT THE AUTHOR

A graduate of UCSC and UCSB, Navy brat Bryan Burnell majored in creative writing and English literature. After selling his successful office furniture business, which he ran for three decades, he started paying more attention to the story ideas that had accumulated in his mind over the years. Free time allowed him to finally bring life to his first book, *Saving Yukon*. This long-time Santa Barbara resident loves the meditative aspects of swimming, gardening, golf (despite his high handicap), and an occasional shot of good bourbon. He is married with two grown children and a spoiled Labradoodle named Nelli.